To SARAH, YOU ARE AWESOME! ♥

DEATH IS THE MOTHER OF BEAUTY.
ONLY THE PERISHABLE CAN BE BEAUTIFUL,
WHICH IS WHY WE ARE UNMOVED BY ARTIFICIAL FLOWERS.

-WALLACE STEVENS

NYCC 2018!

xxx

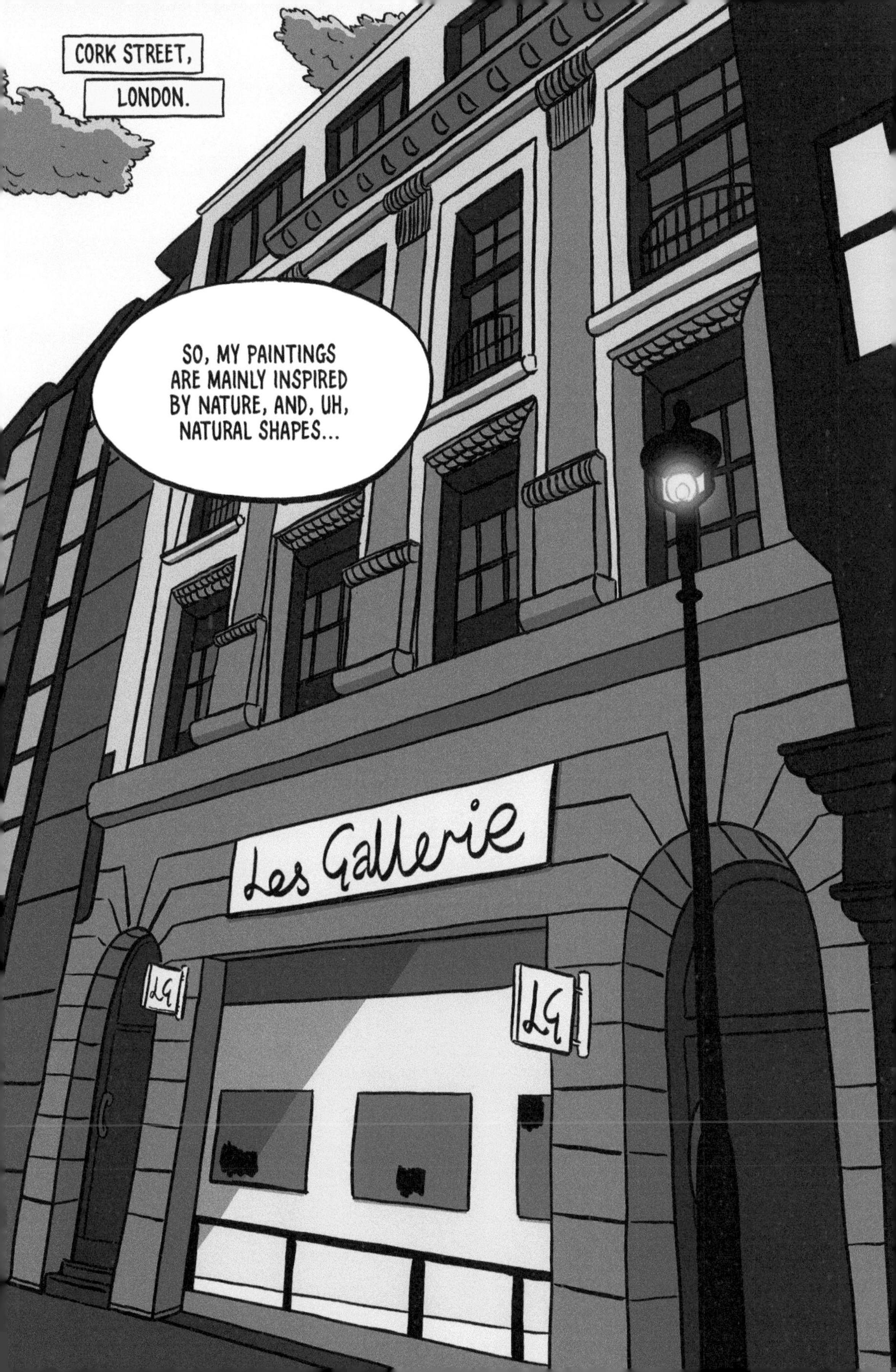
CORK STREET,
LONDON.
SO, MY PAINTINGS ARE MAINLY INSPIRED BY NATURE, AND, UH, NATURAL SHAPES...
Les Gallerie
LG
LG

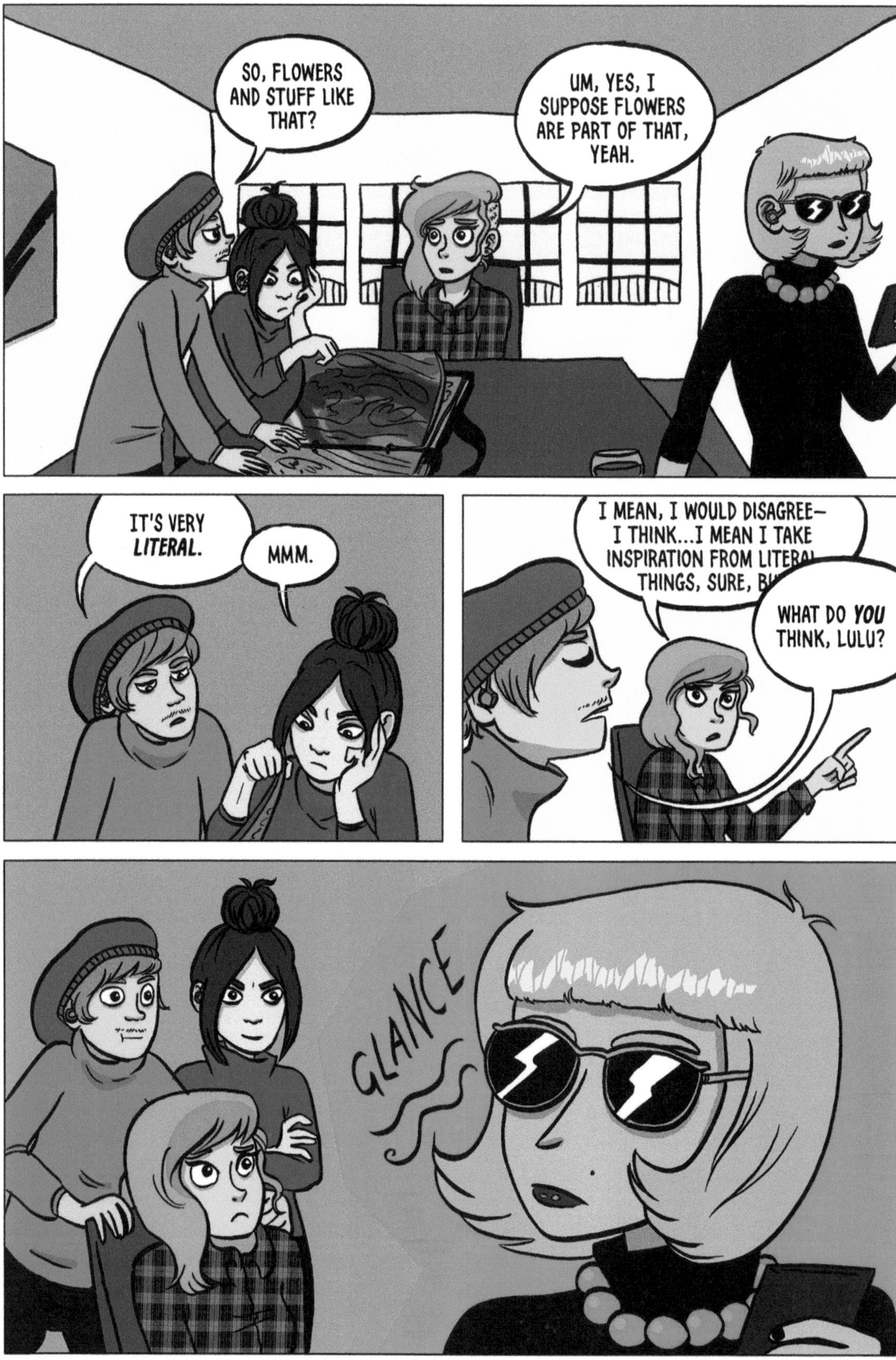
SO, FLOWERS AND STUFF LIKE THAT?
UM, YES, I SUPPOSE FLOWERS ARE PART OF THAT, YEAH.
IT'S VERY *LITERAL*.
MMM.
I MEAN, I WOULD DISAGREE— I THINK...I MEAN I TAKE INSPIRATION FROM LITERAL THINGS, SURE, BU
WHAT DO *YOU* THINK, LULU?
GLANCE

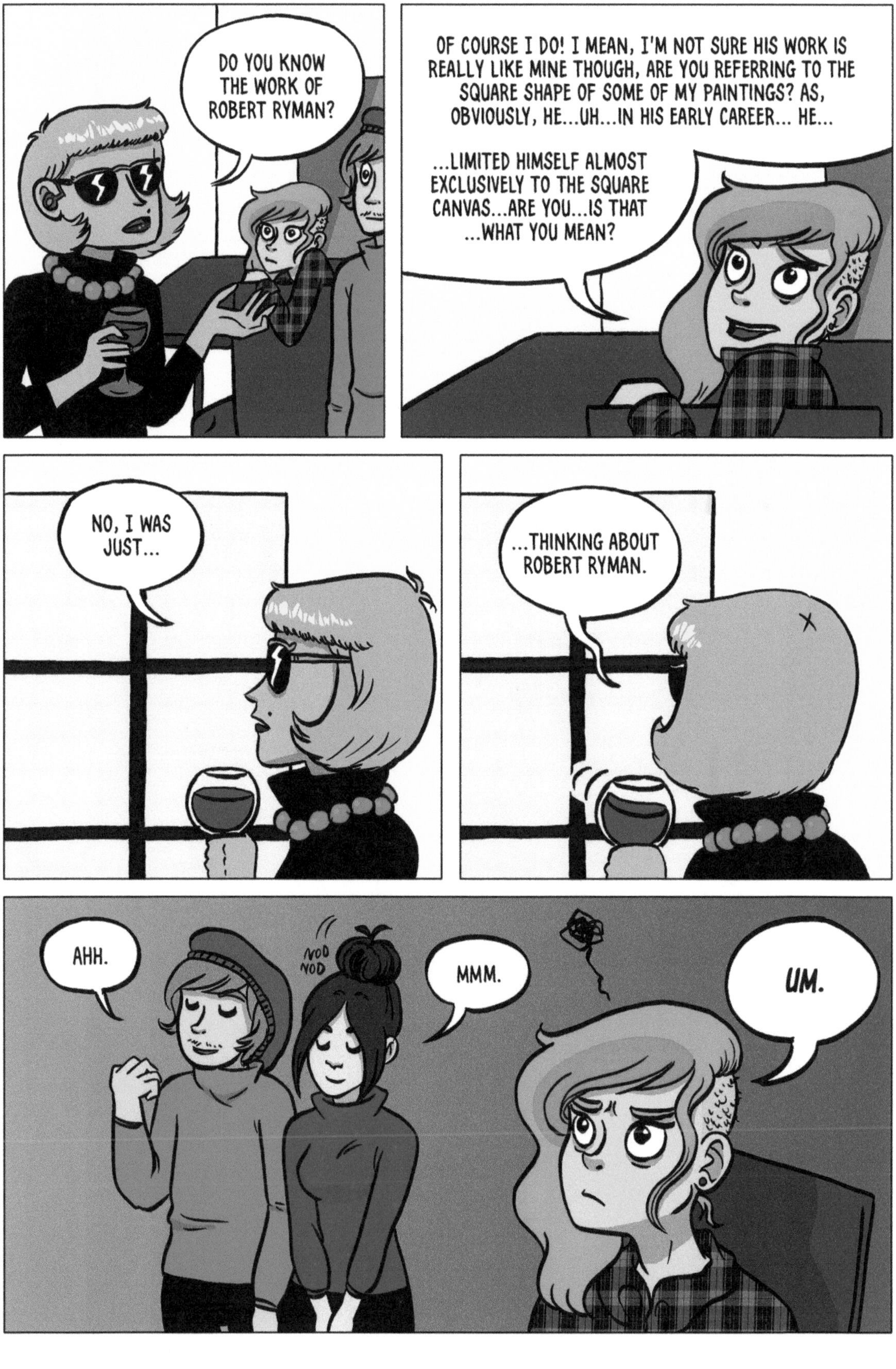
DO YOU KNOW THE WORK OF ROBERT RYMAN?
OF COURSE I DO! I MEAN, I'M NOT SURE HIS WORK IS REALLY LIKE MINE THOUGH, ARE YOU REFERRING TO THE SQUARE SHAPE OF SOME OF MY PAINTINGS? AS, OBVIOUSLY, HE...UH...IN HIS EARLY CAREER... HE...
...LIMITED HIMSELF ALMOST EXCLUSIVELY TO THE SQUARE CANVAS...ARE YOU...IS THAT ...WHAT YOU MEAN?
NO, I WAS JUST...
...THINKING ABOUT ROBERT RYMAN.
AHH.
NOD NOD
MMM.
UM.

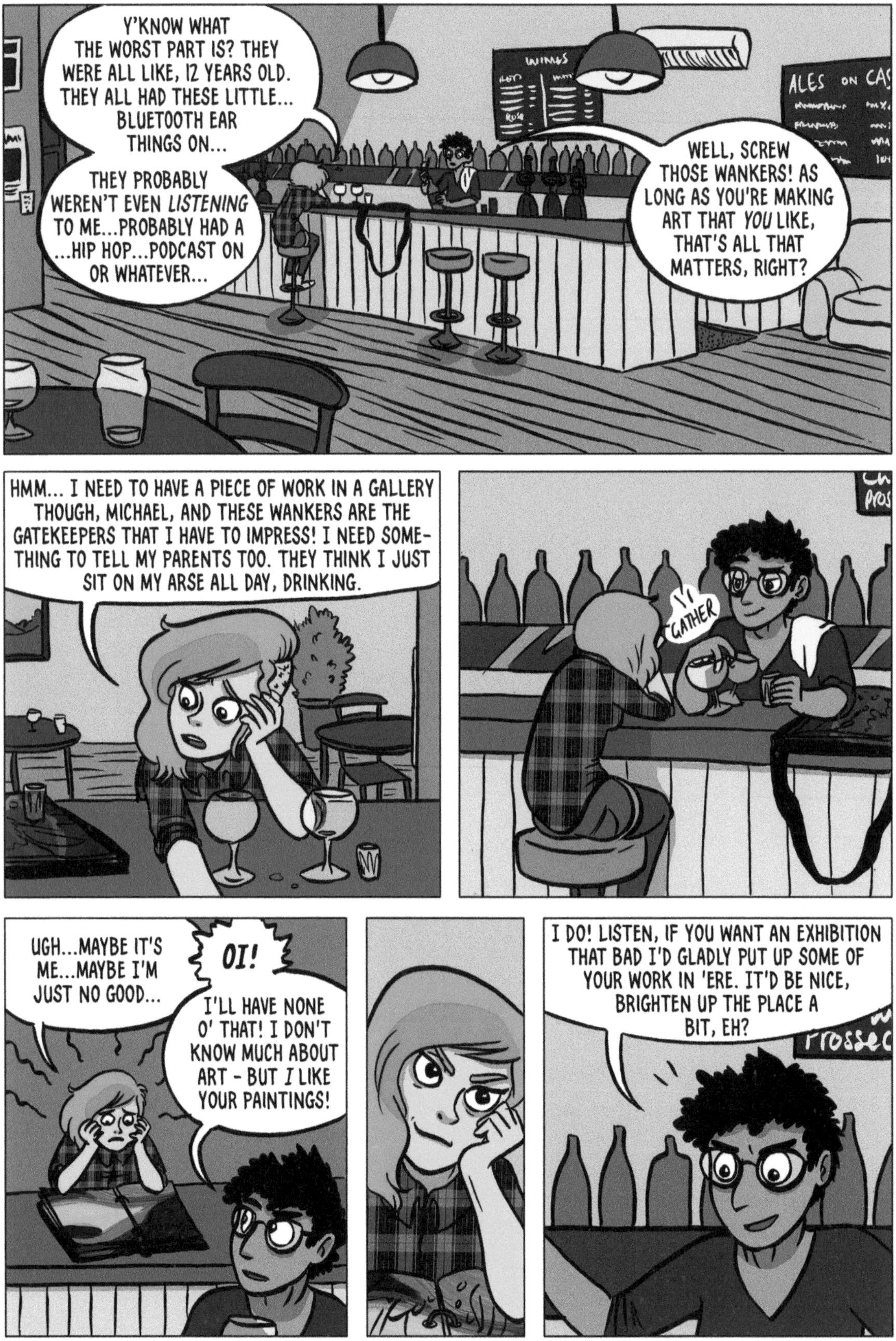
Y'KNOW WHAT THE WORST PART IS? THEY WERE ALL LIKE, 12 YEARS OLD. THEY ALL HAD THESE LITTLE... BLUETOOTH EAR THINGS ON...
THEY PROBABLY WEREN'T EVEN *LISTENING* TO ME...PROBABLY HAD A ...HIP HOP...PODCAST ON OR WHATEVER...
WELL, SCREW THOSE WANKERS! AS LONG AS YOU'RE MAKING ART THAT *YOU* LIKE, THAT'S ALL THAT MATTERS, RIGHT?
HMM... I NEED TO HAVE A PIECE OF WORK IN A GALLERY THOUGH, MICHAEL, AND THESE WANKERS ARE THE GATEKEEPERS THAT I HAVE TO IMPRESS! I NEED SOMETHING TO TELL MY PARENTS TOO. THEY THINK I JUST SIT ON MY ARSE ALL DAY, DRINKING.
GATHER
UGH...MAYBE IT'S ME...MAYBE I'M JUST NO GOOD...
OI!
I'LL HAVE NONE O' THAT! I DON'T KNOW MUCH ABOUT ART - BUT *I* LIKE YOUR PAINTINGS!
I DO! LISTEN, IF YOU WANT AN EXHIBITION THAT BAD I'D GLADLY PUT UP SOME OF YOUR WORK IN 'ERE. IT'D BE NICE, BRIGHTEN UP THE PLACE A BIT, EH?

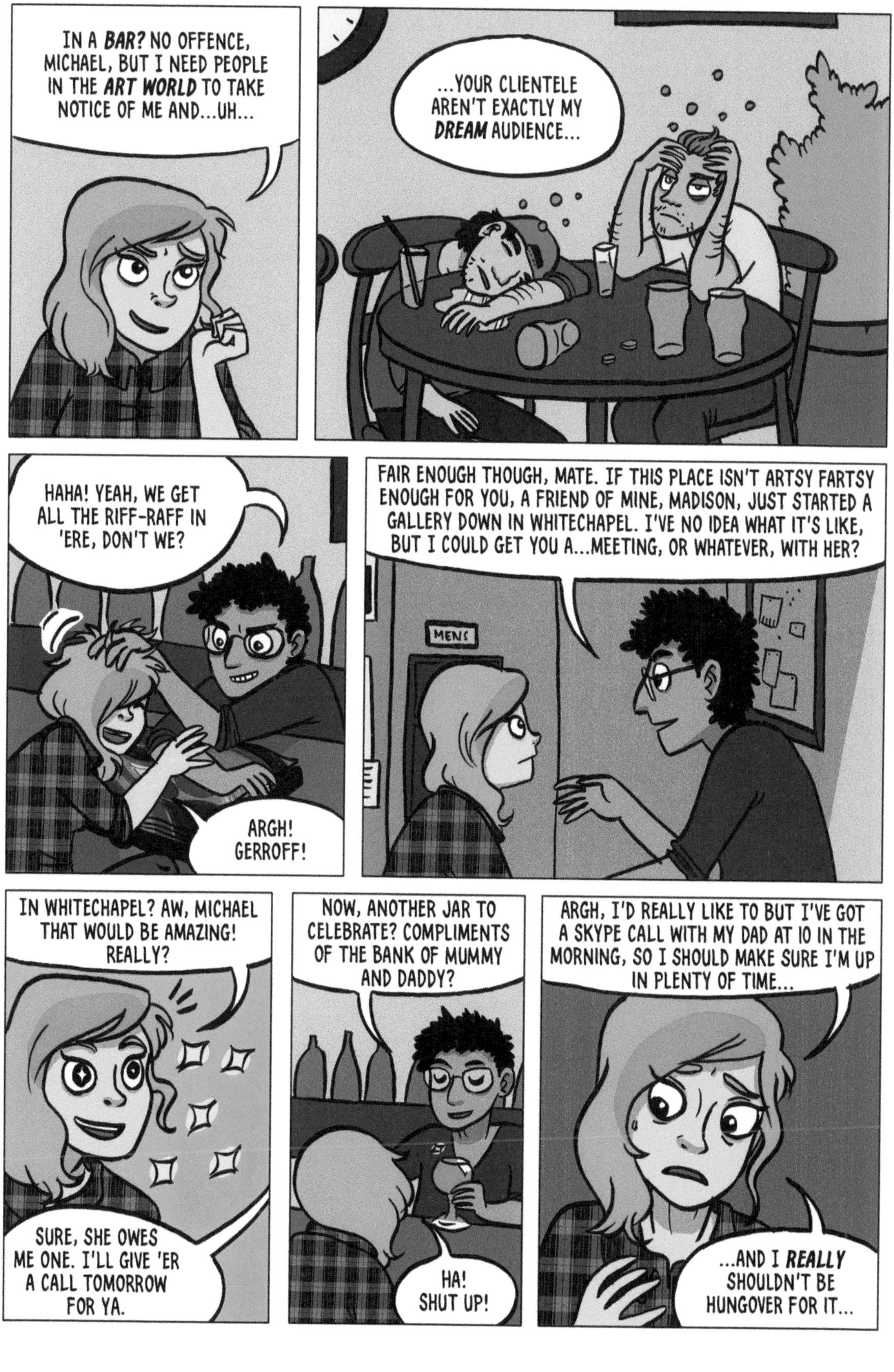
IN A *BAR?* NO OFFENCE, MICHAEL, BUT I NEED PEOPLE IN THE *ART WORLD* TO TAKE NOTICE OF ME AND...UH...
...YOUR CLIENTELE AREN'T EXACTLY MY *DREAM* AUDIENCE...
HAHA! YEAH, WE GET ALL THE RIFF-RAFF IN 'ERE, DON'T WE?
ARGH! GERROFF!
FAIR ENOUGH THOUGH, MATE. IF THIS PLACE ISN'T ARTSY FARTSY ENOUGH FOR YOU, A FRIEND OF MINE, MADISON, JUST STARTED A GALLERY DOWN IN WHITECHAPEL. I'VE NO IDEA WHAT IT'S LIKE, BUT I COULD GET YOU A...MEETING, OR WHATEVER, WITH HER?
MENS
IN WHITECHAPEL? AW, MICHAEL THAT WOULD BE AMAZING! REALLY?
SURE, SHE OWES ME ONE. I'LL GIVE 'ER A CALL TOMORROW FOR YA.
NOW, ANOTHER JAR TO CELEBRATE? COMPLIMENTS OF THE BANK OF MUMMY AND DADDY?
HA! SHUT UP!
ARGH, I'D REALLY LIKE TO BUT I'VE GOT A SKYPE CALL WITH MY DAD AT 10 IN THE MORNING, SO I SHOULD MAKE SURE I'M UP IN PLENTY OF TIME...
...AND I *REALLY* SHOULDN'T BE HUNGOVER FOR IT...

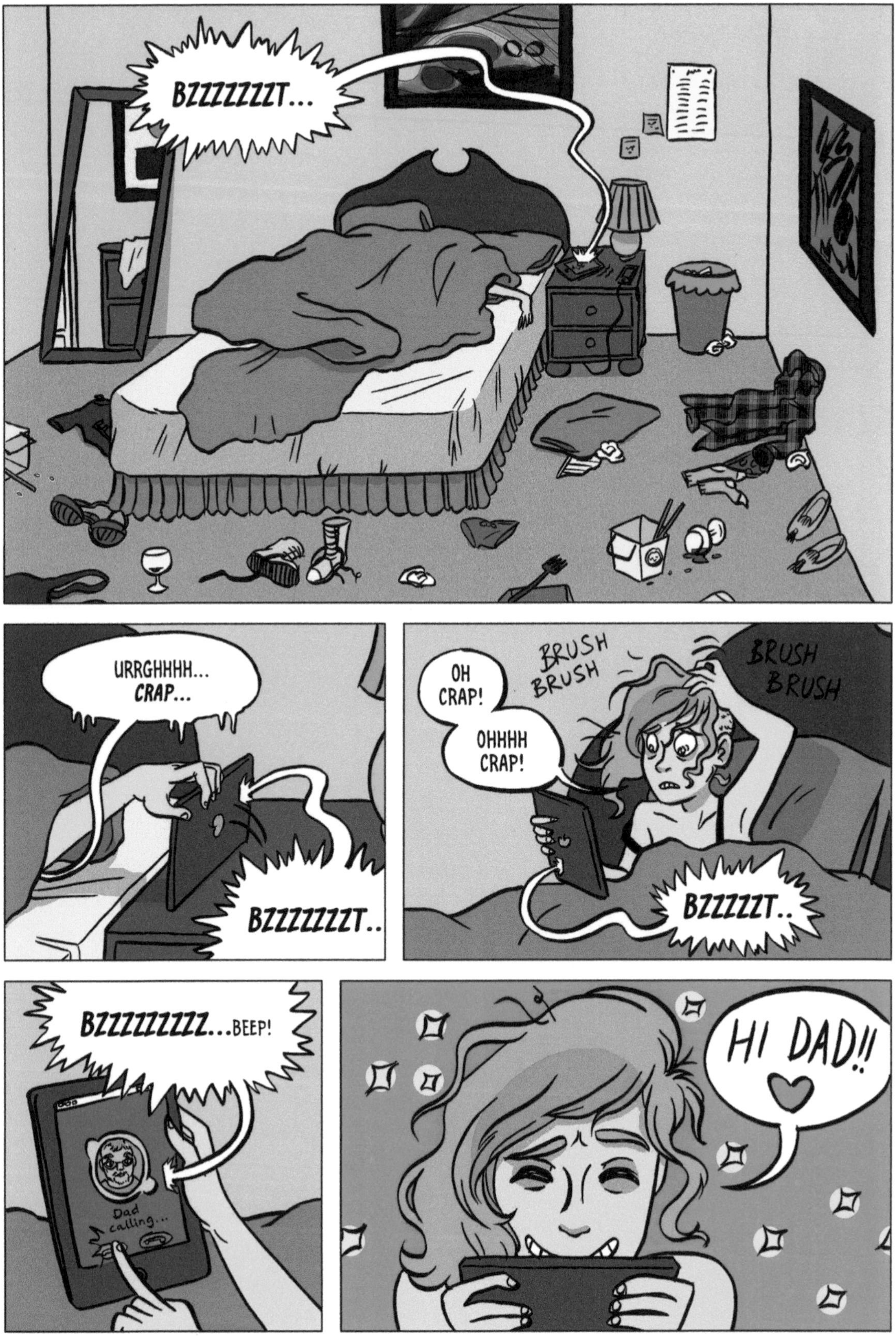

BZZZZZZZT...
URRGHHHH...
CRAP...
BZZZZZZZT..
OH
CRAP!
OHHHH
CRAP!
BRUSH
BRUSH
BRUSH
BRUSH
BZZZZZT..
BZZZZZZZZZ...BEEP!
Dad
calling...
HI DAD!!

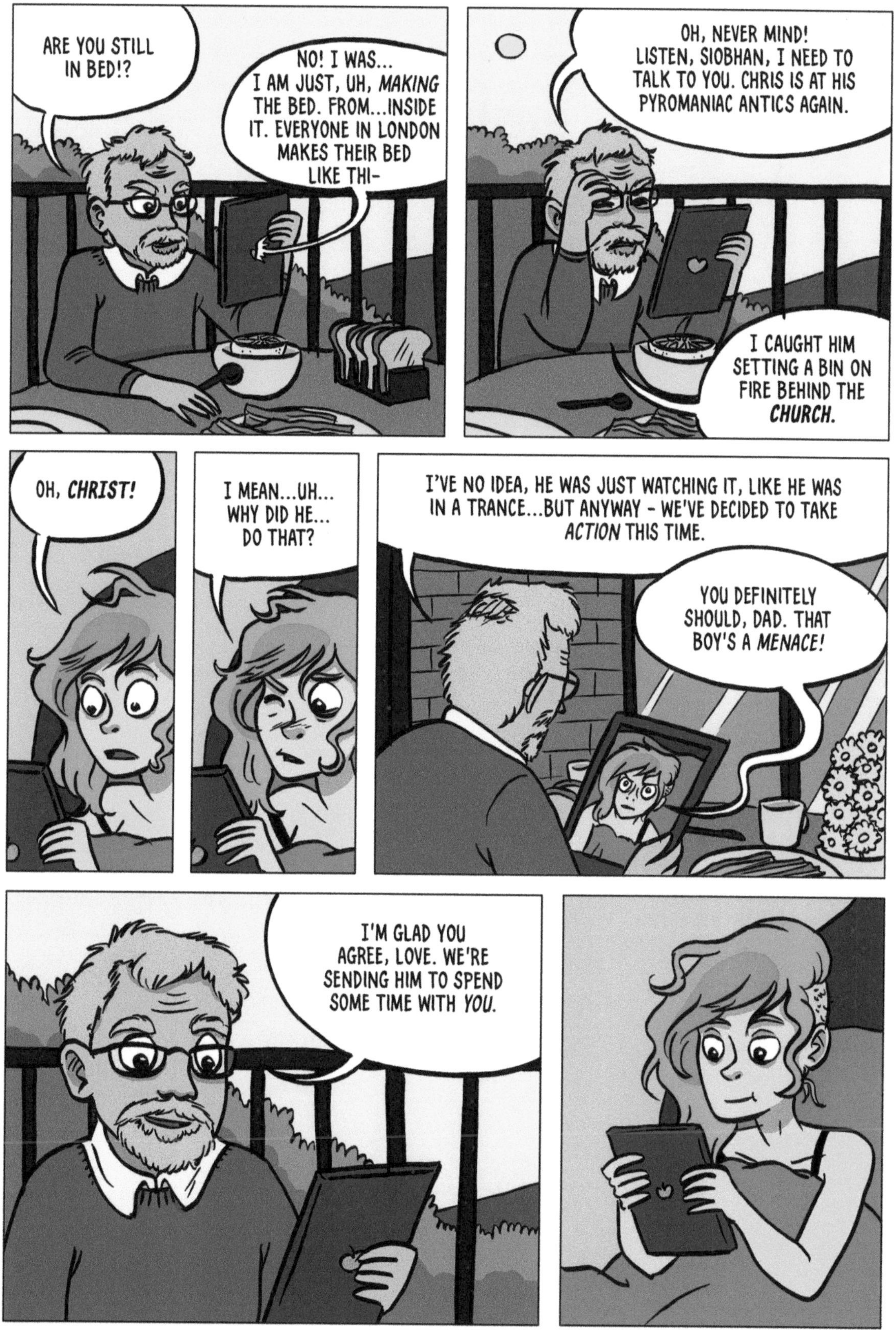
ARE YOU STILL IN BED!?
NO! I WAS... I AM JUST, UH, *MAKING* THE BED. FROM...INSIDE IT. EVERYONE IN LONDON MAKES THEIR BED LIKE THI-
OH, NEVER MIND! LISTEN, SIOBHAN, I NEED TO TALK TO YOU. CHRIS IS AT HIS PYROMANIAC ANTICS AGAIN.
I CAUGHT HIM SETTING A BIN ON FIRE BEHIND THE ***CHURCH.***
OH, ***CHRIST!***
I MEAN...UH... WHY DID HE... DO THAT?
I'VE NO IDEA, HE WAS JUST WATCHING IT, LIKE HE WAS IN A TRANCE...BUT ANYWAY - WE'VE DECIDED TO TAKE *ACTION* THIS TIME.
YOU DEFINITELY SHOULD, DAD. THAT BOY'S A *MENACE!*
I'M GLAD YOU AGREE, LOVE. WE'RE SENDING HIM TO SPEND SOME TIME WITH *YOU*.

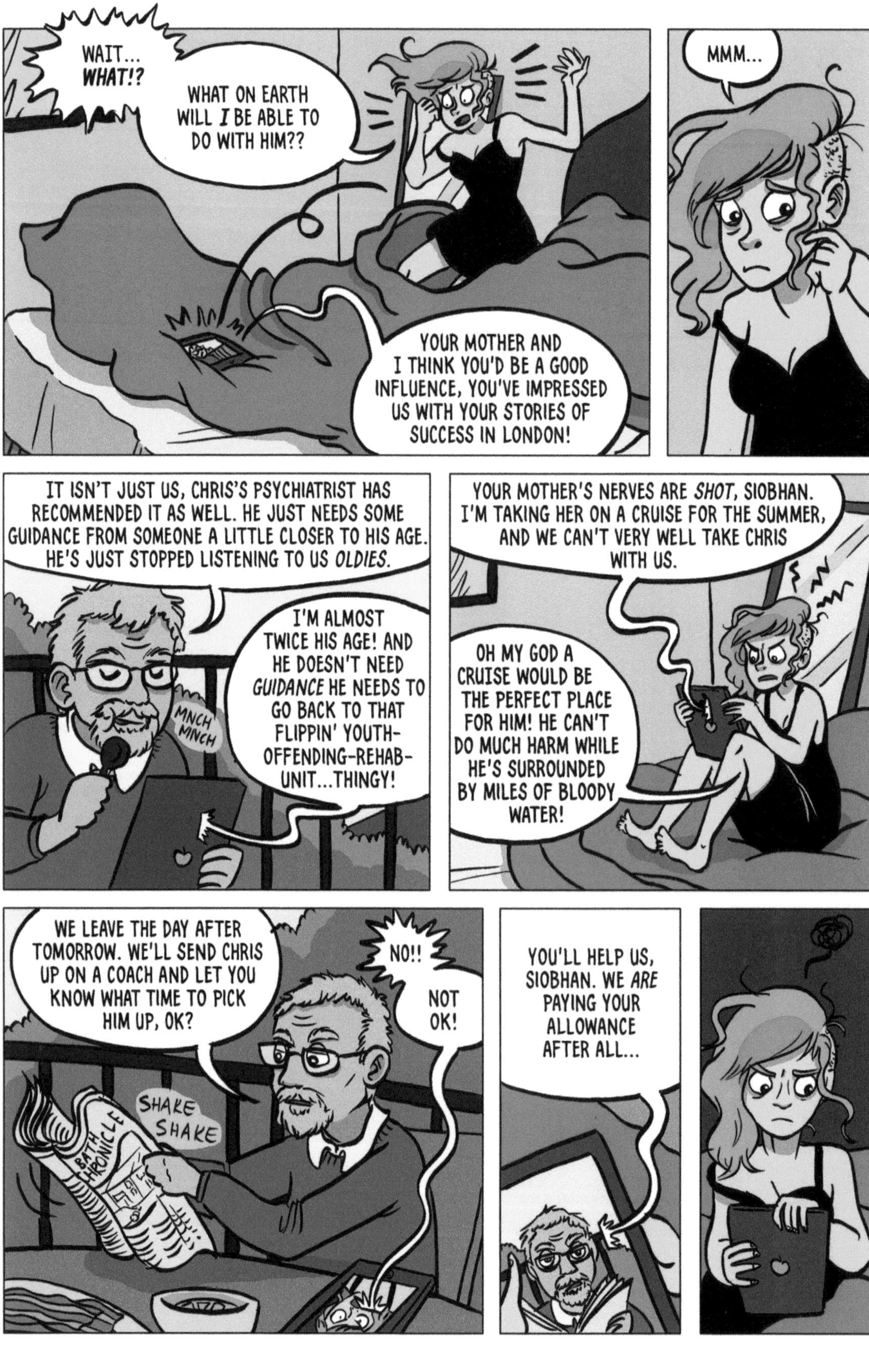
WAIT... *WHAT!?*
WHAT ON EARTH WILL *I* BE ABLE TO DO WITH HIM??
YOUR MOTHER AND I THINK YOU'D BE A GOOD INFLUENCE, YOU'VE IMPRESSED US WITH YOUR STORIES OF SUCCESS IN LONDON!
MMM...
IT ISN'T JUST US, CHRIS'S PSYCHIATRIST HAS RECOMMENDED IT AS WELL. HE JUST NEEDS SOME GUIDANCE FROM SOMEONE A LITTLE CLOSER TO HIS AGE. HE'S JUST STOPPED LISTENING TO US *OLDIES*.
MNCH MNCH
I'M ALMOST TWICE HIS AGE! AND HE DOESN'T NEED *GUIDANCE* HE NEEDS TO GO BACK TO THAT FLIPPIN' YOUTH-OFFENDING-REHAB-UNIT...THINGY!
YOUR MOTHER'S NERVES ARE *SHOT*, SIOBHAN. I'M TAKING HER ON A CRUISE FOR THE SUMMER, AND WE CAN'T VERY WELL TAKE CHRIS WITH US.
OH MY GOD A CRUISE WOULD BE THE PERFECT PLACE FOR HIM! HE CAN'T DO MUCH HARM WHILE HE'S SURROUNDED BY MILES OF BLOODY WATER!
WE LEAVE THE DAY AFTER TOMORROW. WE'LL SEND CHRIS UP ON A COACH AND LET YOU KNOW WHAT TIME TO PICK HIM UP, OK?
NO!!
NOT OK!
SHAKE SHAKE
BATH CHRONICLE
YOU'LL HELP US, SIOBHAN. WE *ARE* PAYING YOUR ALLOWANCE AFTER ALL...

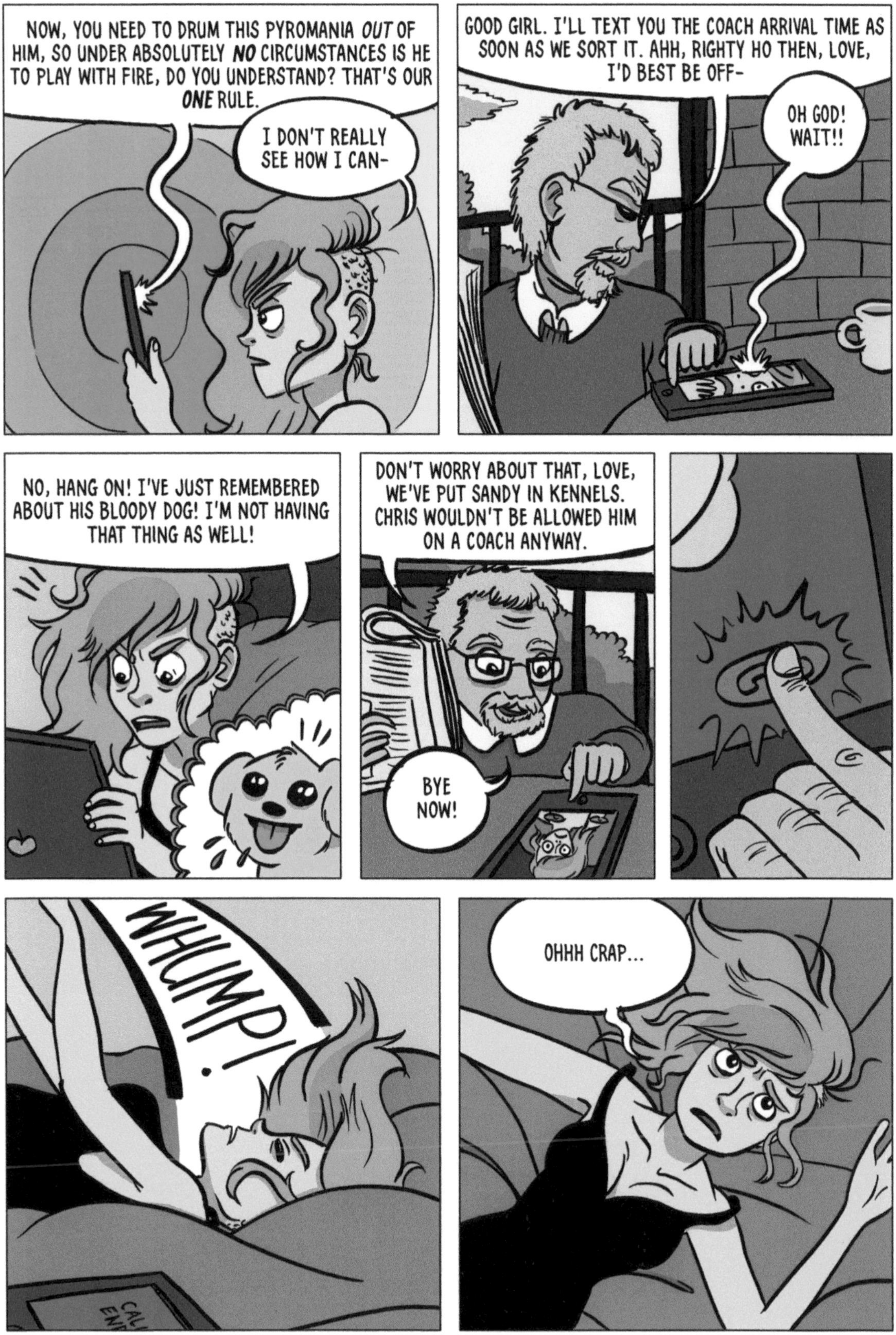
NOW, YOU NEED TO DRUM THIS PYROMANIA OUT OF HIM, SO UNDER ABSOLUTELY NO CIRCUMSTANCES IS HE TO PLAY WITH FIRE, DO YOU UNDERSTAND? THAT'S OUR ONE RULE.
I DON'T REALLY SEE HOW I CAN-
GOOD GIRL. I'LL TEXT YOU THE COACH ARRIVAL TIME AS SOON AS WE SORT IT. AHH, RIGHTY HO THEN, LOVE, I'D BEST BE OFF-
OH GOD! WAIT!!
NO, HANG ON! I'VE JUST REMEMBERED ABOUT HIS BLOODY DOG! I'M NOT HAVING THAT THING AS WELL!
DON'T WORRY ABOUT THAT, LOVE, WE'VE PUT SANDY IN KENNELS. CHRIS WOULDN'T BE ALLOWED HIM ON A COACH ANYWAY.
BYE NOW!
WHUMP!
OHHH CRAP...

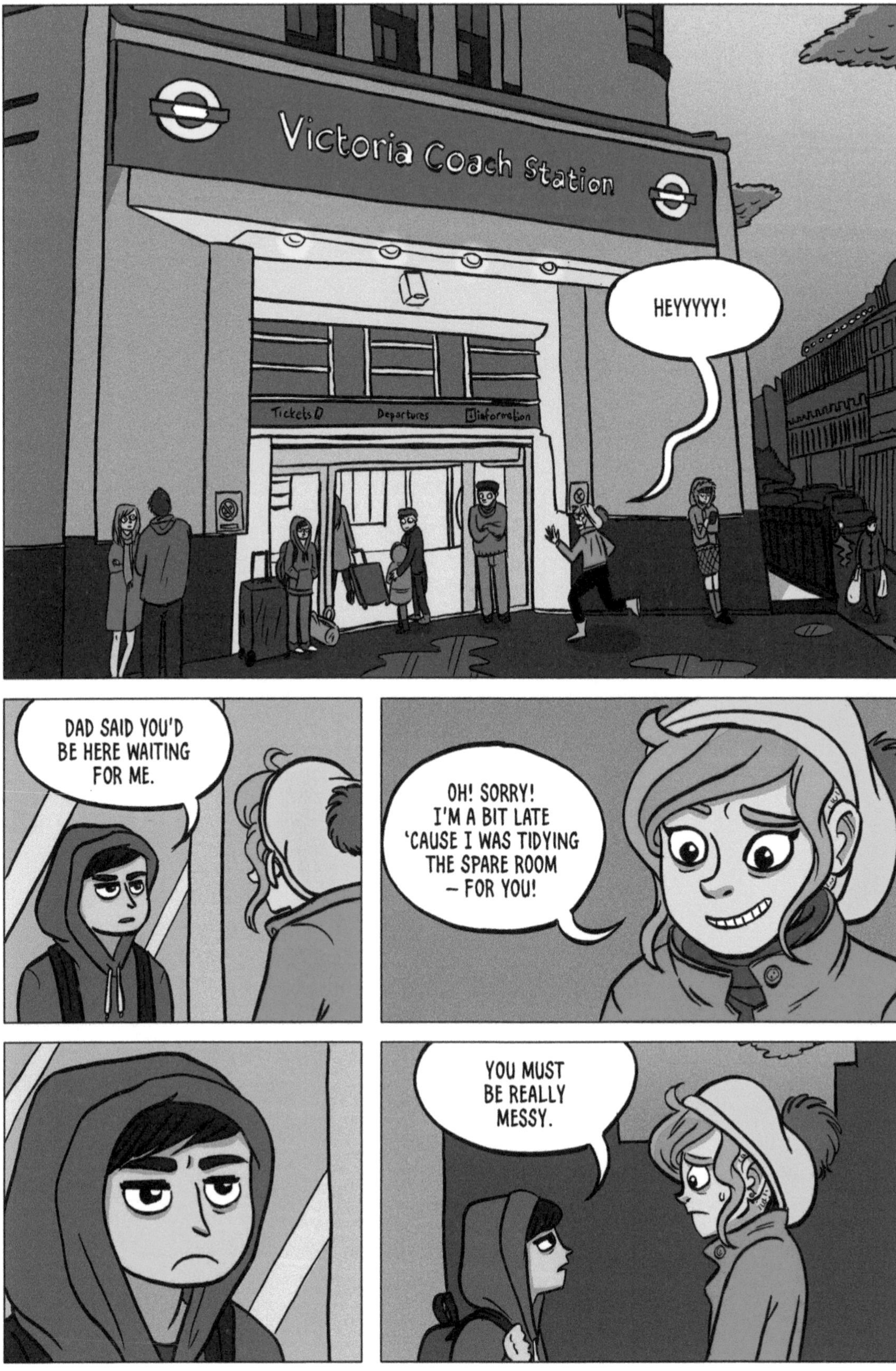
Victoria Coach Station
Tickets
Departures
information
HEYYYYY!
DAD SAID YOU'D BE HERE WAITING FOR ME.
OH! SORRY! I'M A BIT LATE 'CAUSE I WAS TIDYING THE SPARE ROOM – FOR YOU!
YOU MUST BE REALLY MESSY.

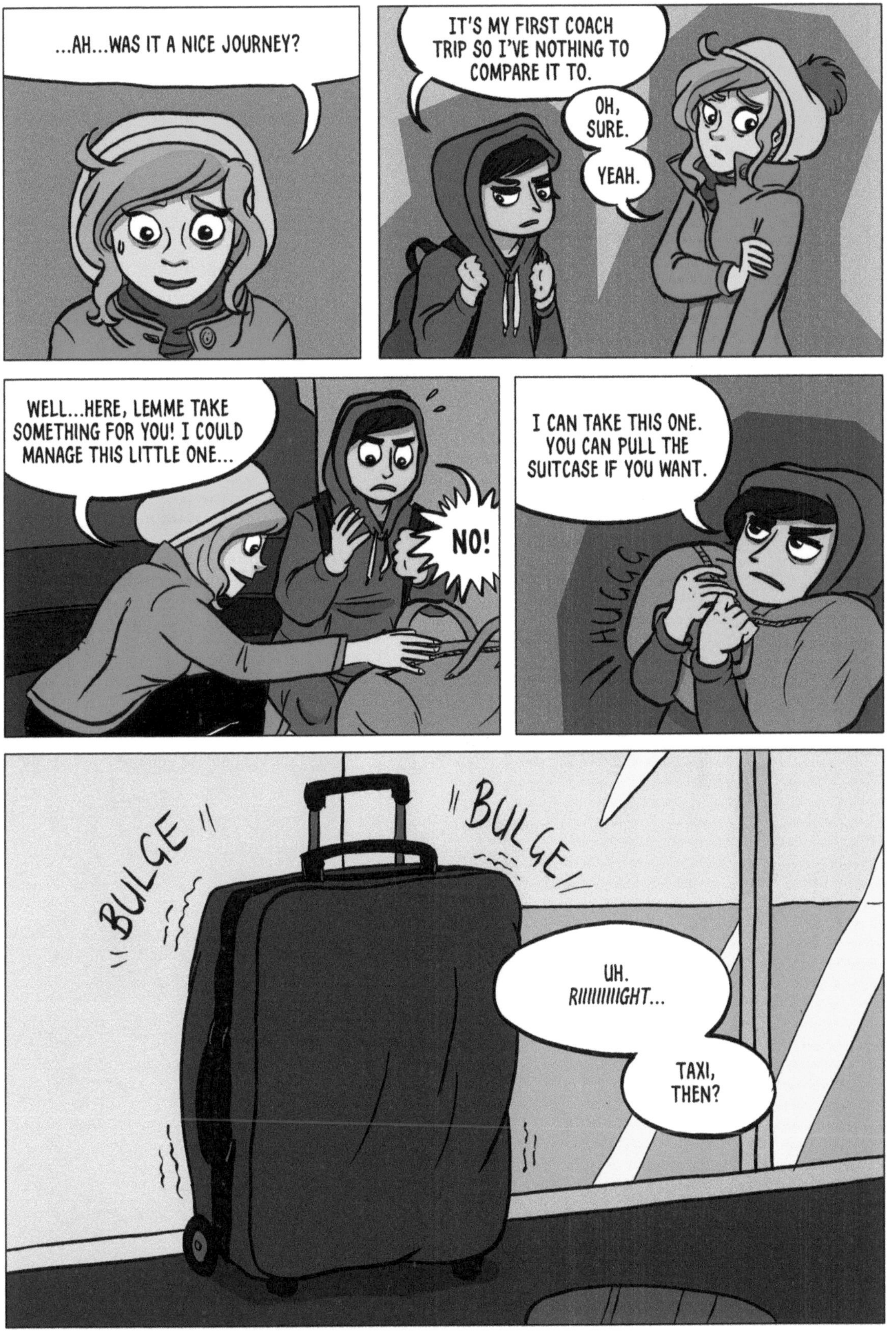
...AH...WAS IT A NICE JOURNEY?
IT'S MY FIRST COACH TRIP SO I'VE NOTHING TO COMPARE IT TO.
OH, SURE.
YEAH.
WELL...HERE, LEMME TAKE SOMETHING FOR YOU! I COULD MANAGE THIS LITTLE ONE...
NO!
I CAN TAKE THIS ONE. YOU CAN PULL THE SUITCASE IF YOU WANT.
HUGGG
BULGE
BULGE
UH. RIIIIIIIIGHT...
TAXI, THEN?

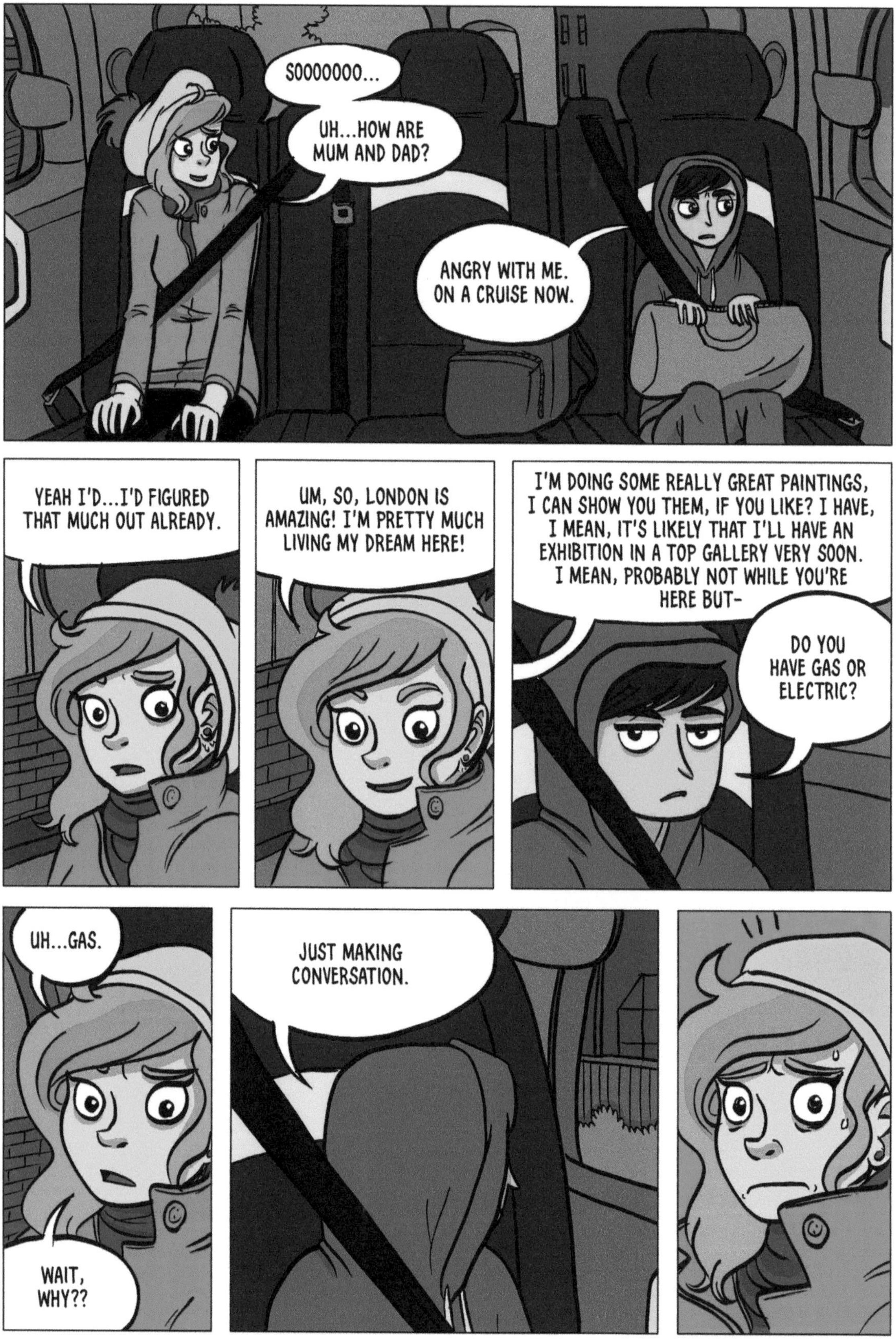
SOOOOOOO...
UH...HOW ARE MUM AND DAD?
ANGRY WITH ME. ON A CRUISE NOW.
YEAH I'D...I'D FIGURED THAT MUCH OUT ALREADY.
UM, SO, LONDON IS AMAZING! I'M PRETTY MUCH LIVING MY DREAM HERE!
I'M DOING SOME REALLY GREAT PAINTINGS, I CAN SHOW YOU THEM, IF YOU LIKE? I HAVE, I MEAN, IT'S LIKELY THAT I'LL HAVE AN EXHIBITION IN A TOP GALLERY VERY SOON. I MEAN, PROBABLY NOT WHILE YOU'RE HERE BUT-
DO YOU HAVE GAS OR ELECTRIC?
UH...GAS.
WAIT, WHY??
JUST MAKING CONVERSATION.

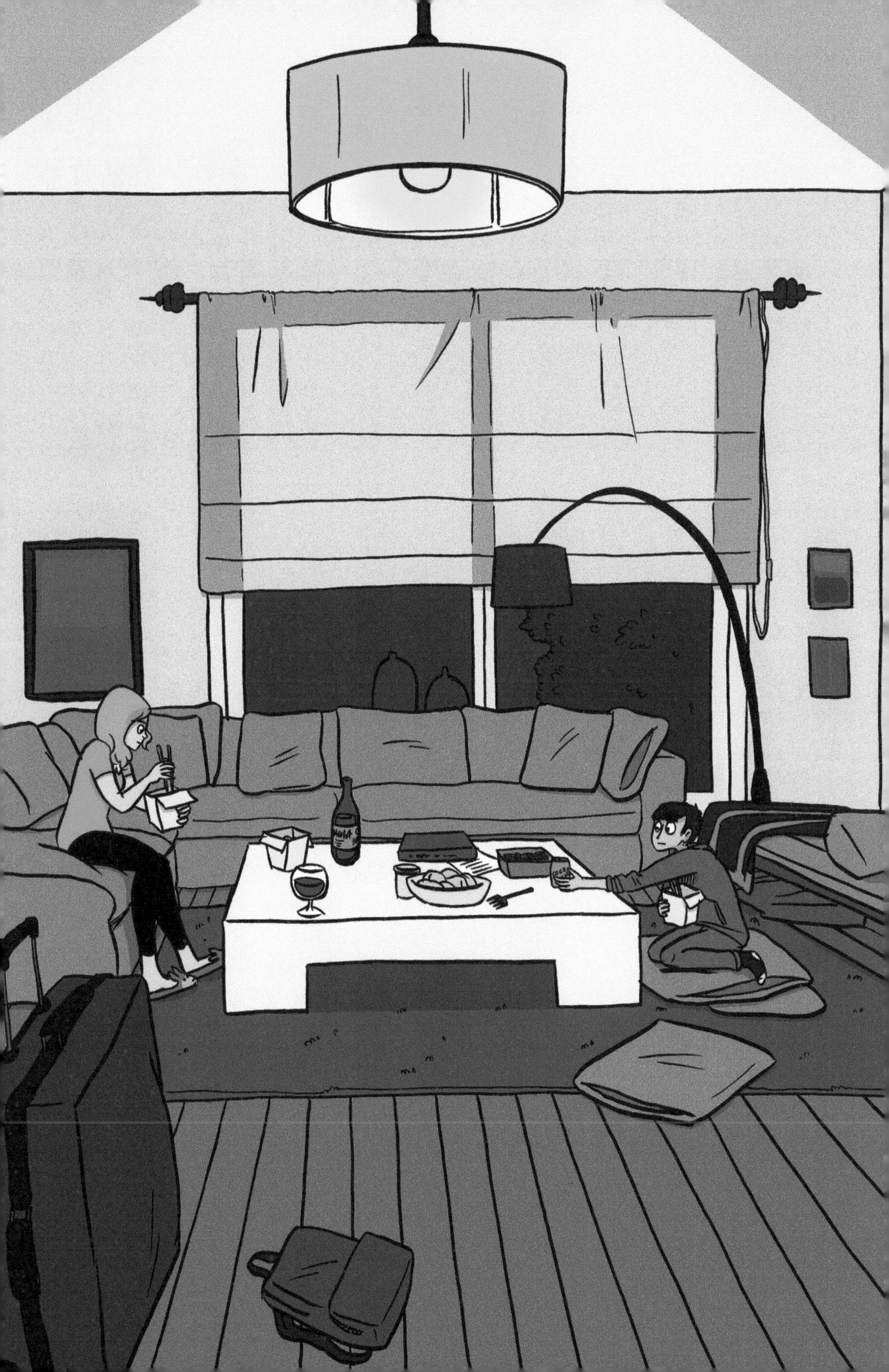

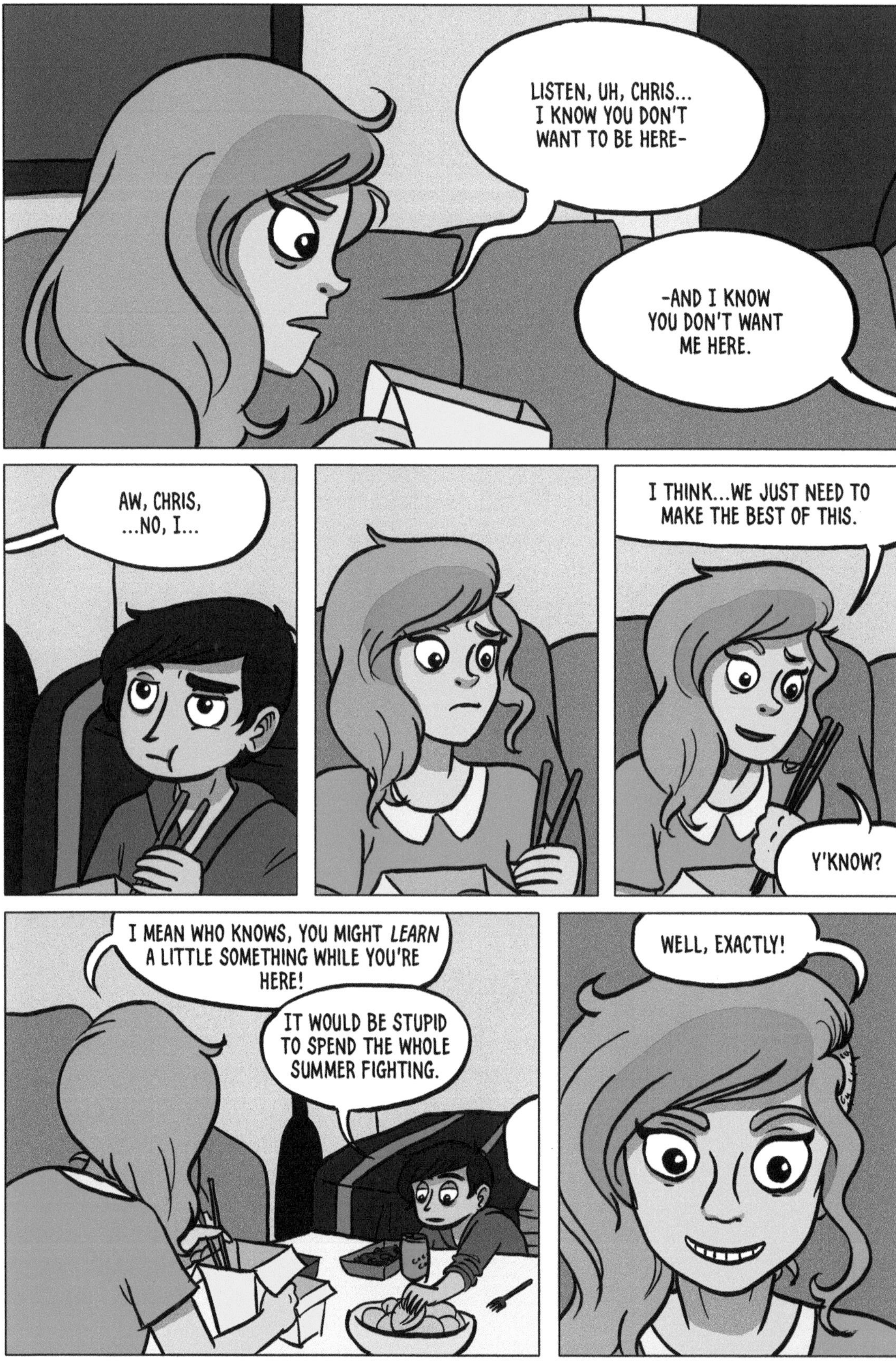
LISTEN, UH, CHRIS...
I KNOW YOU DON'T
WANT TO BE HERE-
-AND I KNOW
YOU DON'T WANT
ME HERE.
AW, CHRIS,
...NO, I...
I THINK...WE JUST NEED TO
MAKE THE BEST OF THIS.
Y'KNOW?
I MEAN WHO KNOWS, YOU MIGHT *LEARN*
A LITTLE SOMETHING WHILE YOU'RE
HERE!
IT WOULD BE STUPID
TO SPEND THE WHOLE
SUMMER FIGHTING.
WELL, EXACTLY!

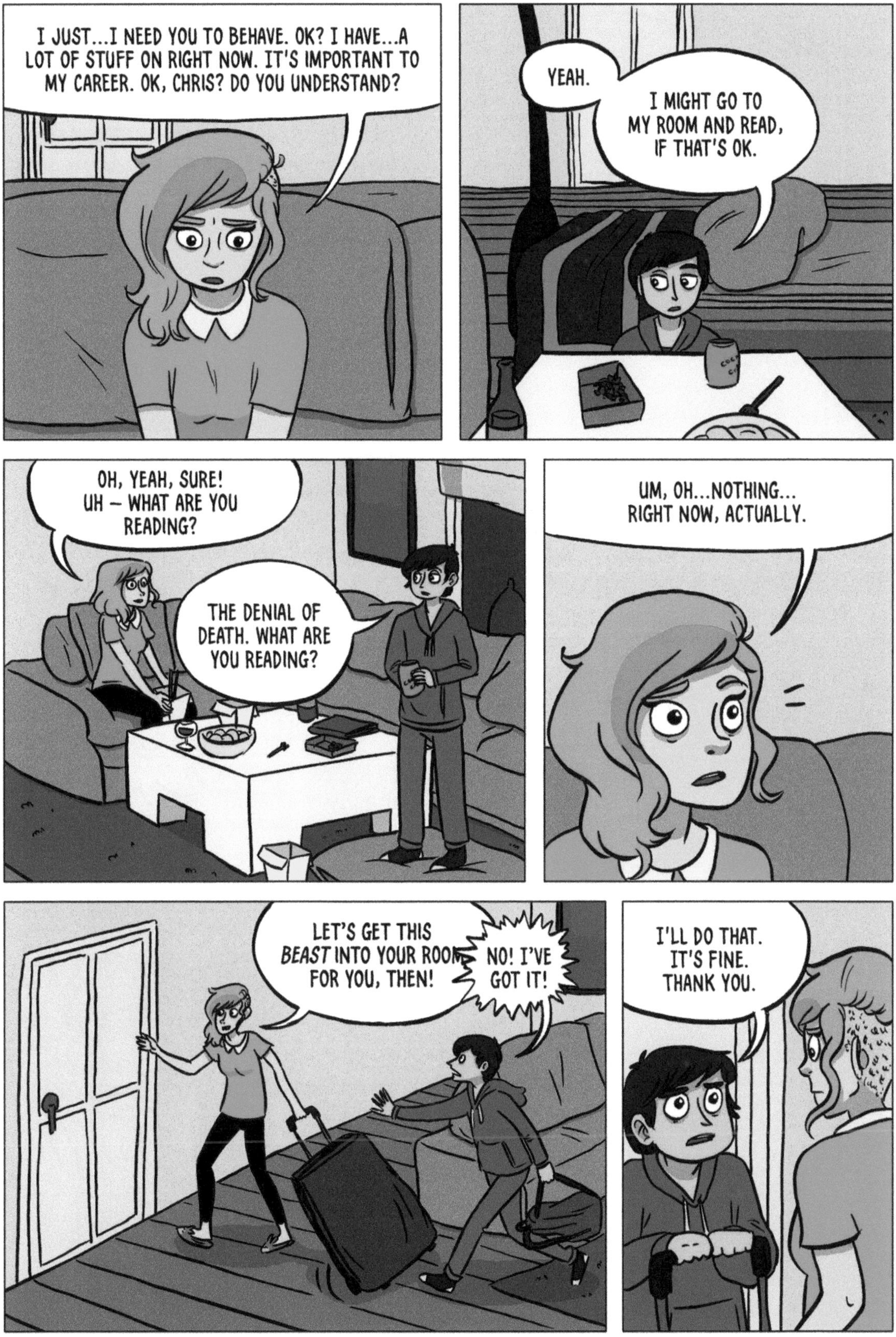
I JUST...I NEED YOU TO BEHAVE. OK? I HAVE...A LOT OF STUFF ON RIGHT NOW. IT'S IMPORTANT TO MY CAREER. OK, CHRIS? DO YOU UNDERSTAND?
YEAH.
I MIGHT GO TO MY ROOM AND READ, IF THAT'S OK.
OH, YEAH, SURE! UH – WHAT ARE YOU READING?
THE DENIAL OF DEATH. WHAT ARE YOU READING?
UM, OH...NOTHING... RIGHT NOW, ACTUALLY.
LET'S GET THIS *BEAST* INTO YOUR ROOM FOR YOU, THEN!
NO! I'VE GOT IT!
I'LL DO THAT. IT'S FINE. THANK YOU.

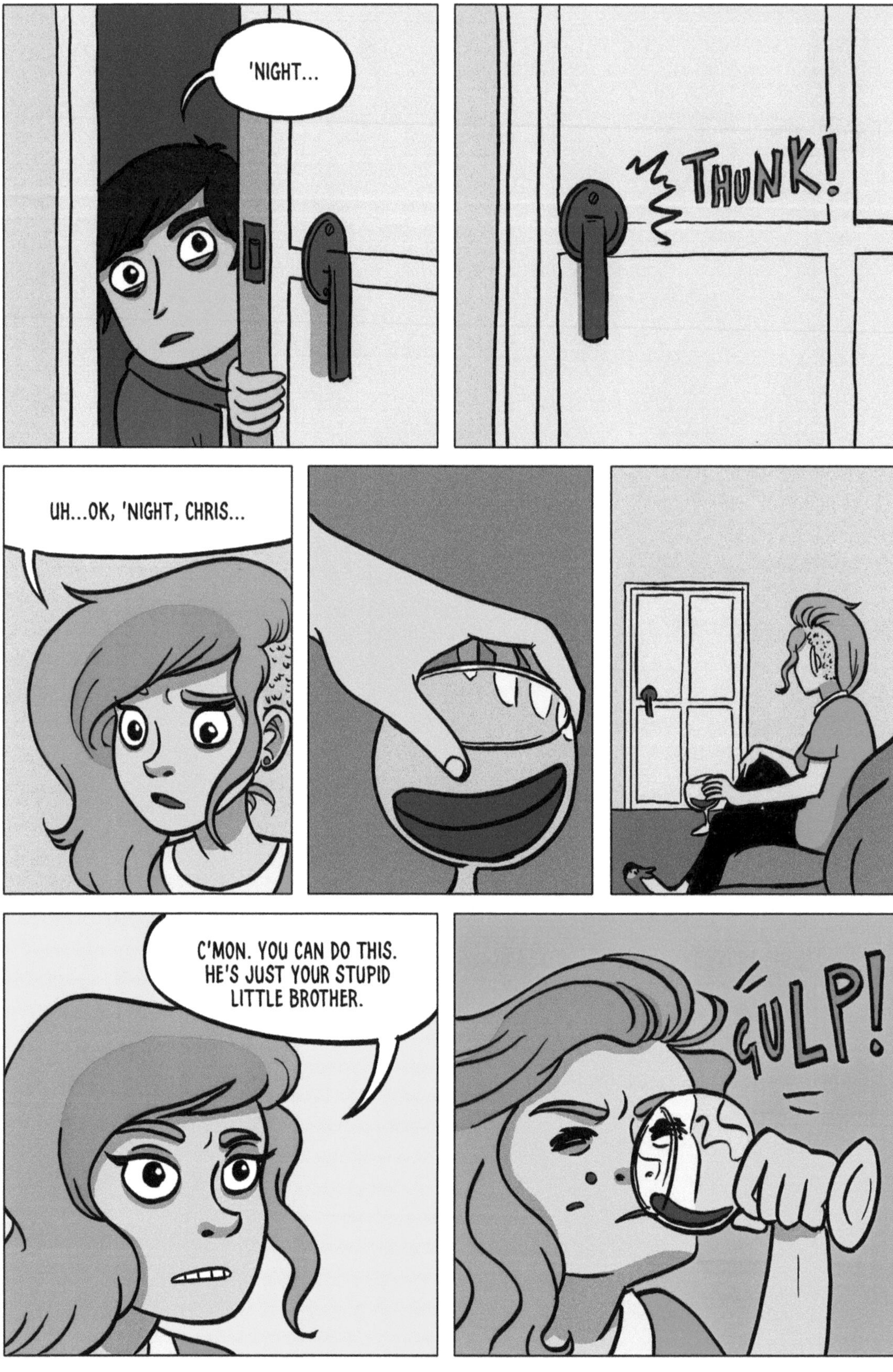
'NIGHT...
THUNK!
UH...OK, 'NIGHT, CHRIS...
C'MON. YOU CAN DO THIS. HE'S JUST YOUR STUPID LITTLE BROTHER.
GULP!

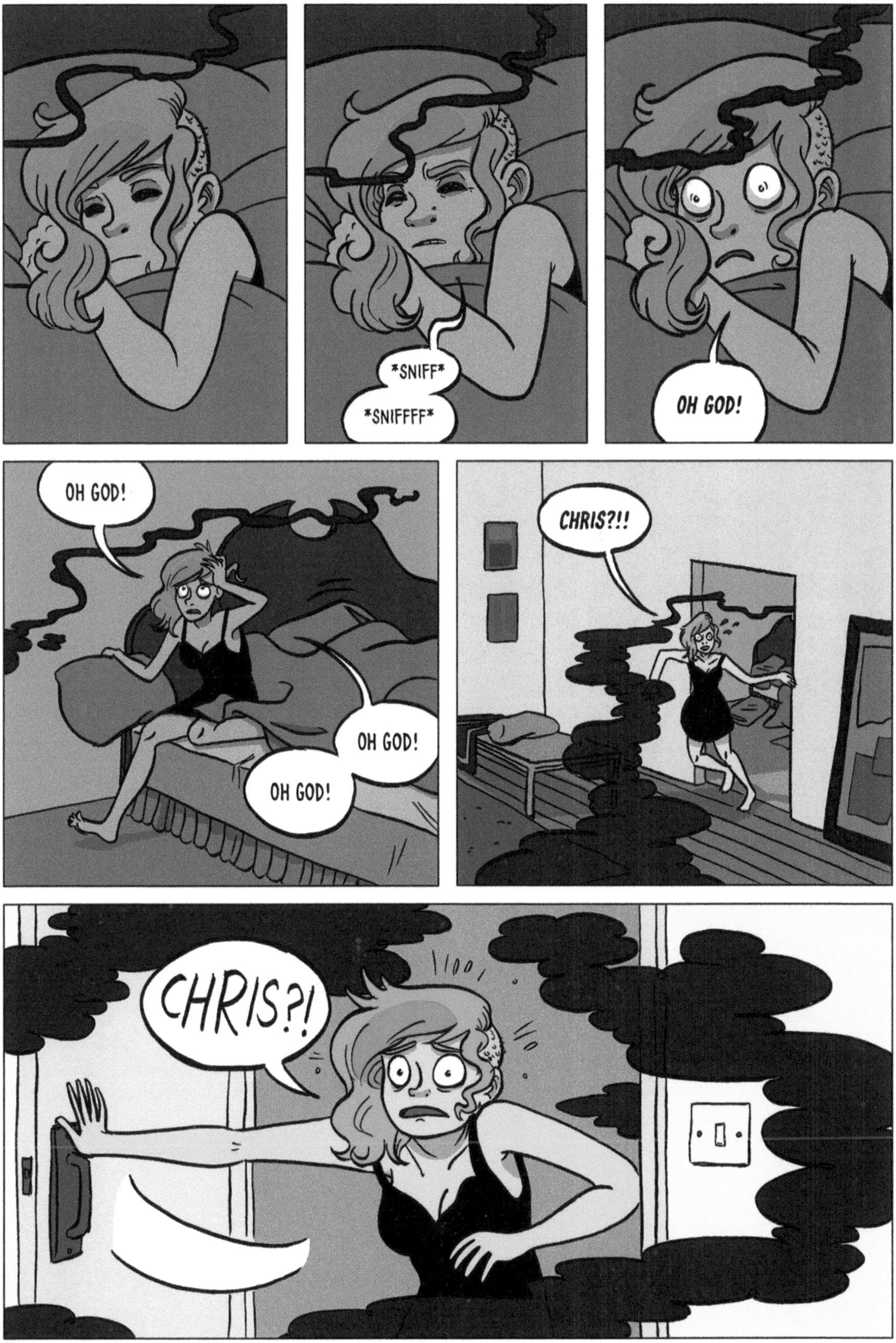
SNIFF
SNIFFFF
OH GOD!
OH GOD!
OH GOD!
OH GOD!
CHRIS?!!
CHRIS?!

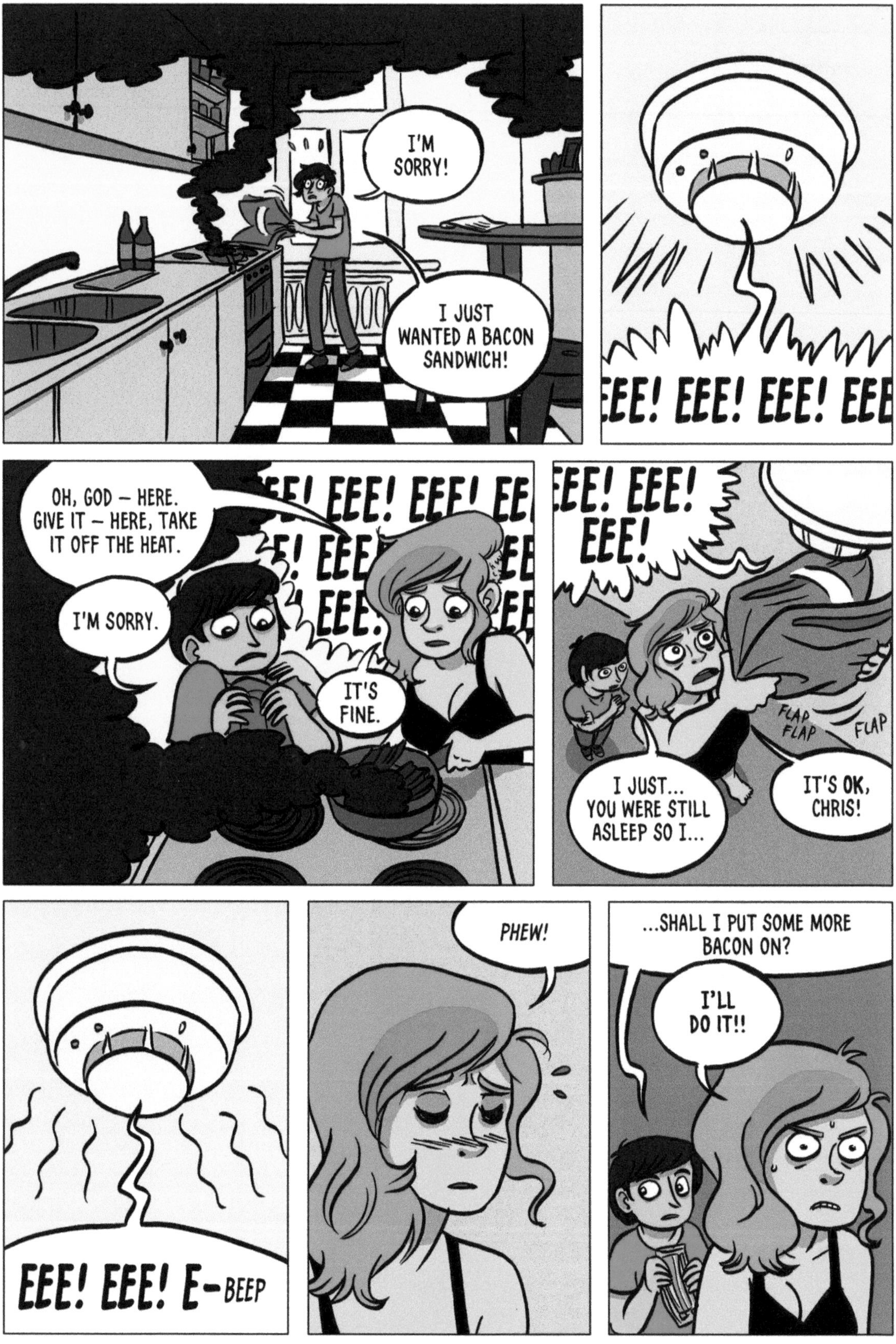
I'M SORRY!
I JUST WANTED A BACON SANDWICH!
EEE! EEE! EEE! EEE
OH, GOD – HERE. GIVE IT – HERE, TAKE IT OFF THE HEAT.
EEE! EEE! EEE!
I'M SORRY.
IT'S FINE.
EEE! EEE! EEE!
I JUST... YOU WERE STILL ASLEEP SO I...
FLAP FLAP FLAP
IT'S OK, CHRIS!
EEE! EEE! E–BEEP
PHEW!
...SHALL I PUT SOME MORE BACON ON?
I'LL DO IT!!

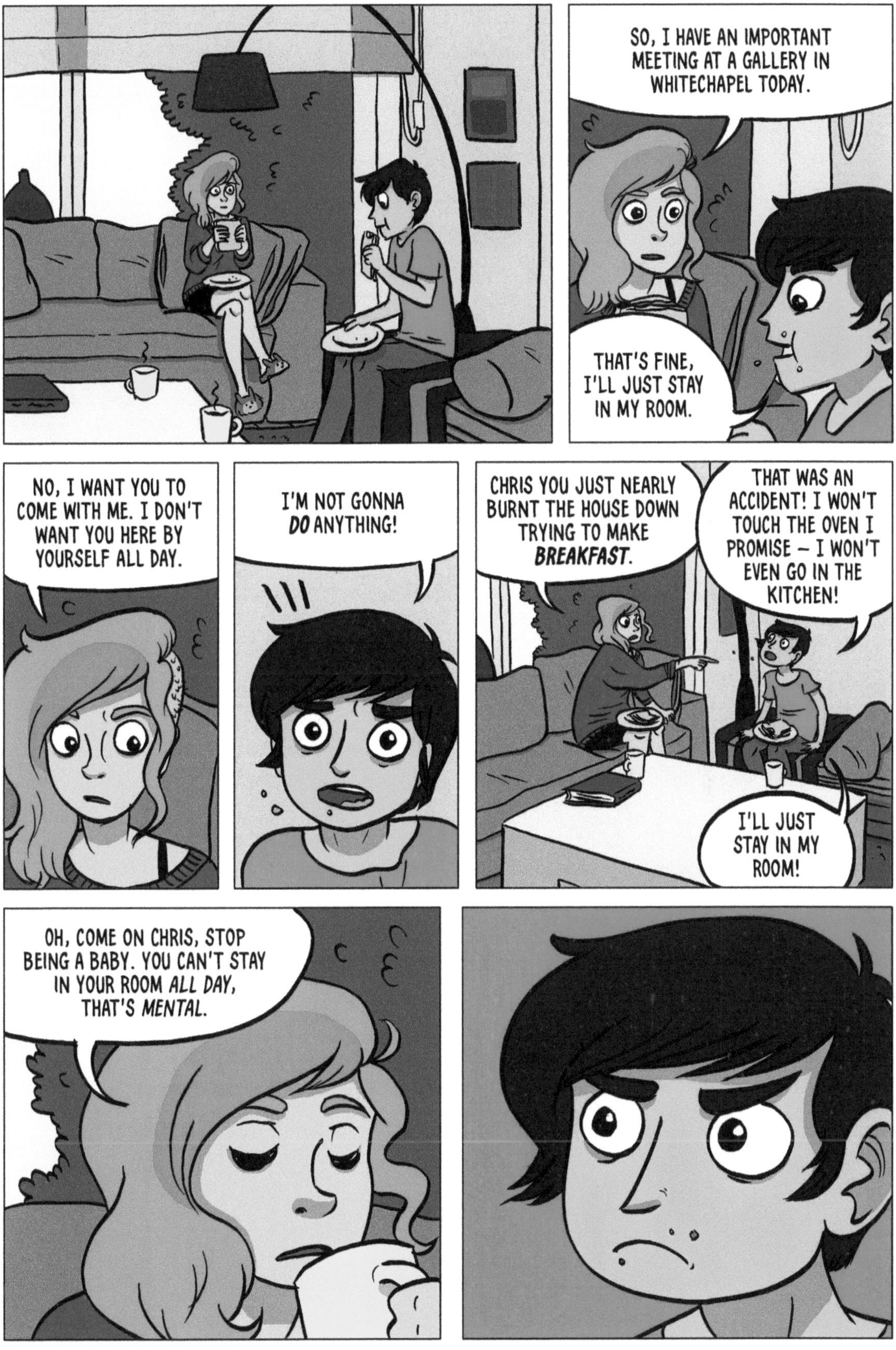
SO, I HAVE AN IMPORTANT MEETING AT A GALLERY IN WHITECHAPEL TODAY.
THAT'S FINE, I'LL JUST STAY IN MY ROOM.
NO, I WANT YOU TO COME WITH ME. I DON'T WANT YOU HERE BY YOURSELF ALL DAY.
I'M NOT GONNA *DO* ANYTHING!
CHRIS YOU JUST NEARLY BURNT THE HOUSE DOWN TRYING TO MAKE ***BREAKFAST***.
THAT WAS AN ACCIDENT! I WON'T TOUCH THE OVEN I PROMISE – I WON'T EVEN GO IN THE KITCHEN!
I'LL JUST STAY IN MY ROOM!
OH, COME ON CHRIS, STOP BEING A BABY. YOU CAN'T STAY IN YOUR ROOM *ALL DAY*, THAT'S *MENTAL*.

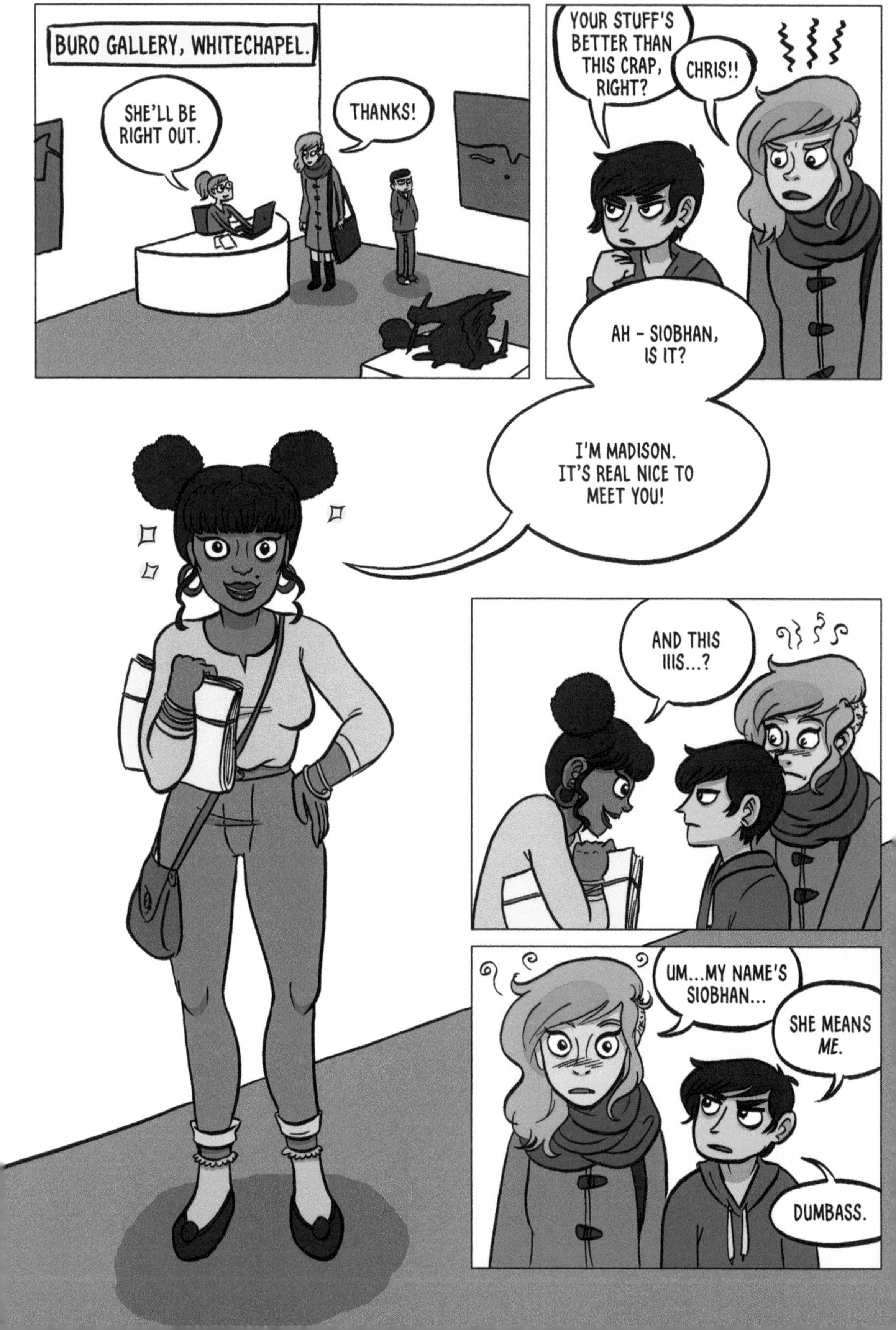
BURO GALLERY, WHITECHAPEL.
SHE'LL BE RIGHT OUT.
THANKS!
YOUR STUFF'S BETTER THAN THIS CRAP, RIGHT?
CHRIS!!
AH - SIOBHAN, IS IT?
I'M MADISON. IT'S REAL NICE TO MEET YOU!
AND THIS IIIS...?
UM...MY NAME'S SIOBHAN...
SHE MEANS *ME.*
DUMBASS.

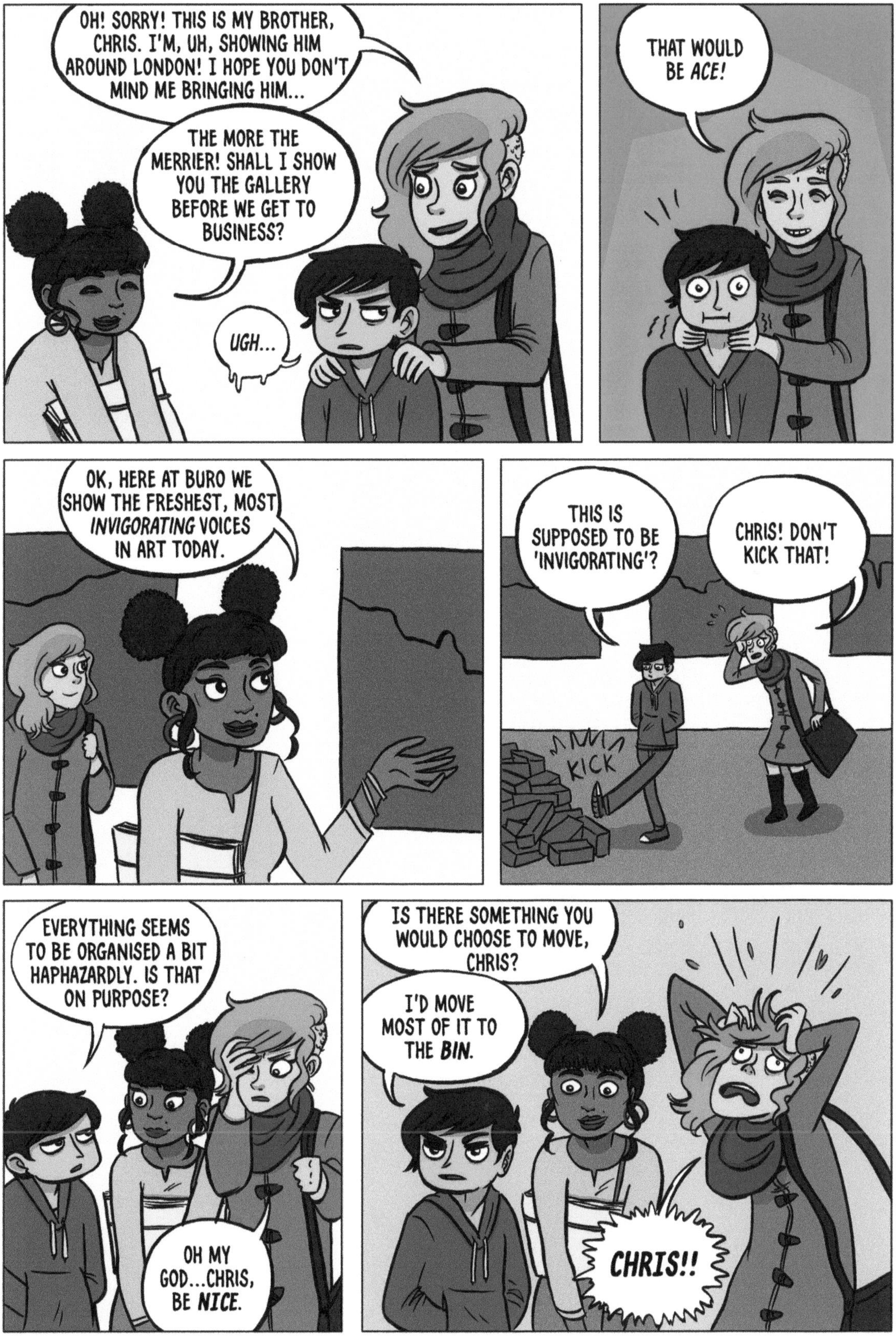
OH! SORRY! THIS IS MY BROTHER, CHRIS. I'M, UH, SHOWING HIM AROUND LONDON! I HOPE YOU DON'T MIND ME BRINGING HIM...
THE MORE THE MERRIER! SHALL I SHOW YOU THE GALLERY BEFORE WE GET TO BUSINESS?
UGH...
THAT WOULD BE *ACE!*
OK, HERE AT BURO WE SHOW THE FRESHEST, MOST *INVIGORATING* VOICES IN ART TODAY.
THIS IS SUPPOSED TO BE 'INVIGORATING'?
CHRIS! DON'T KICK THAT!
KICK
EVERYTHING SEEMS TO BE ORGANISED A BIT HAPHAZARDLY. IS THAT ON PURPOSE?
OH MY GOD...CHRIS, BE **NICE**.
IS THERE SOMETHING YOU WOULD CHOOSE TO MOVE, CHRIS?
I'D MOVE MOST OF IT TO THE **BIN**.
CHRIS!!

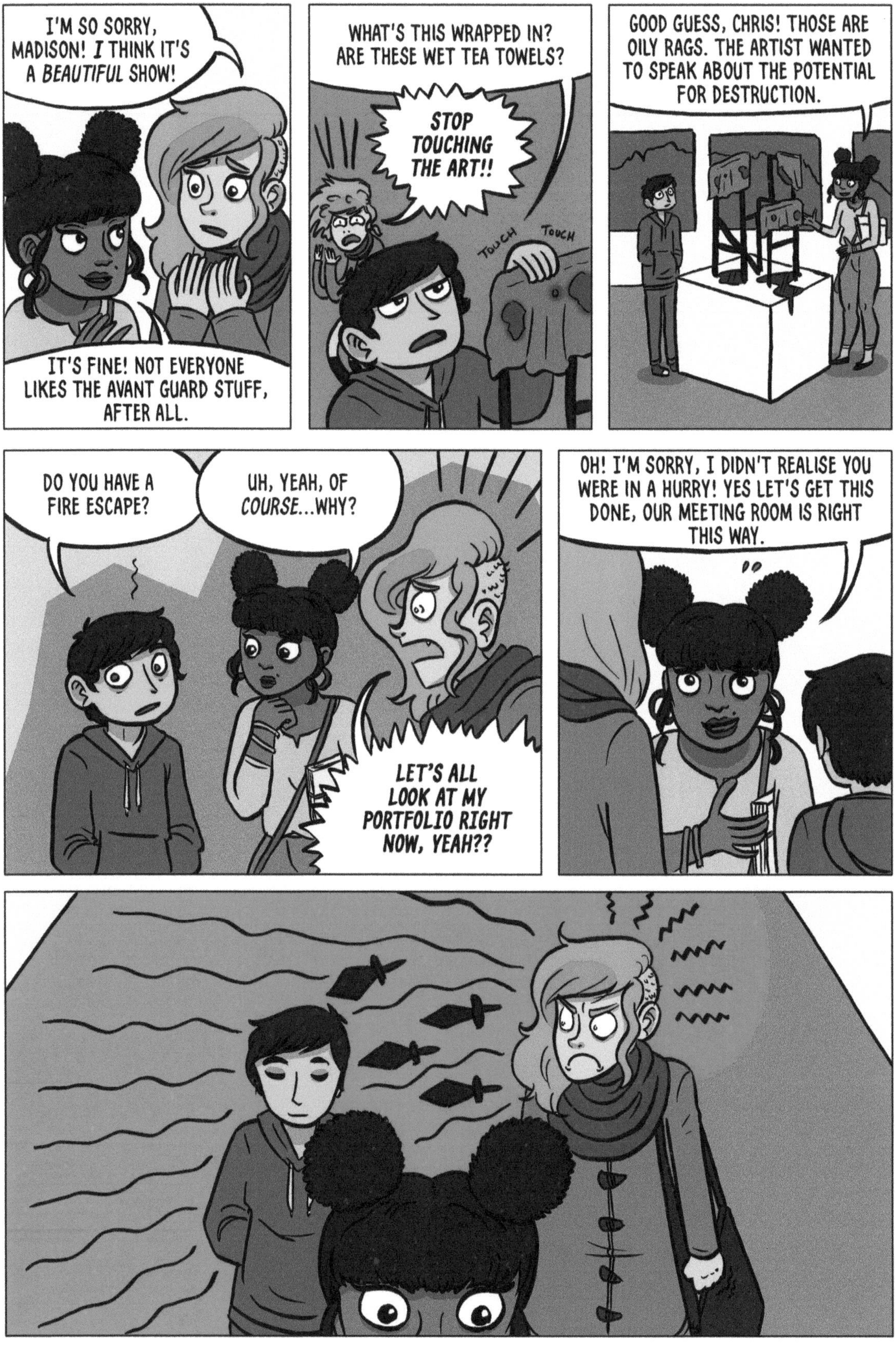
I'M SO SORRY, MADISON! I THINK IT'S A BEAUTIFUL SHOW!
IT'S FINE! NOT EVERYONE LIKES THE AVANT GUARD STUFF, AFTER ALL.
WHAT'S THIS WRAPPED IN? ARE THESE WET TEA TOWELS?
STOP TOUCHING THE ART!!
TOUCH
TOUCH
GOOD GUESS, CHRIS! THOSE ARE OILY RAGS. THE ARTIST WANTED TO SPEAK ABOUT THE POTENTIAL FOR DESTRUCTION.
DO YOU HAVE A FIRE ESCAPE?
UH, YEAH, OF COURSE...WHY?
LET'S ALL LOOK AT MY PORTFOLIO RIGHT NOW, YEAH??
OH! I'M SORRY, I DIDN'T REALISE YOU WERE IN A HURRY! YES LET'S GET THIS DONE, OUR MEETING ROOM IS RIGHT THIS WAY.

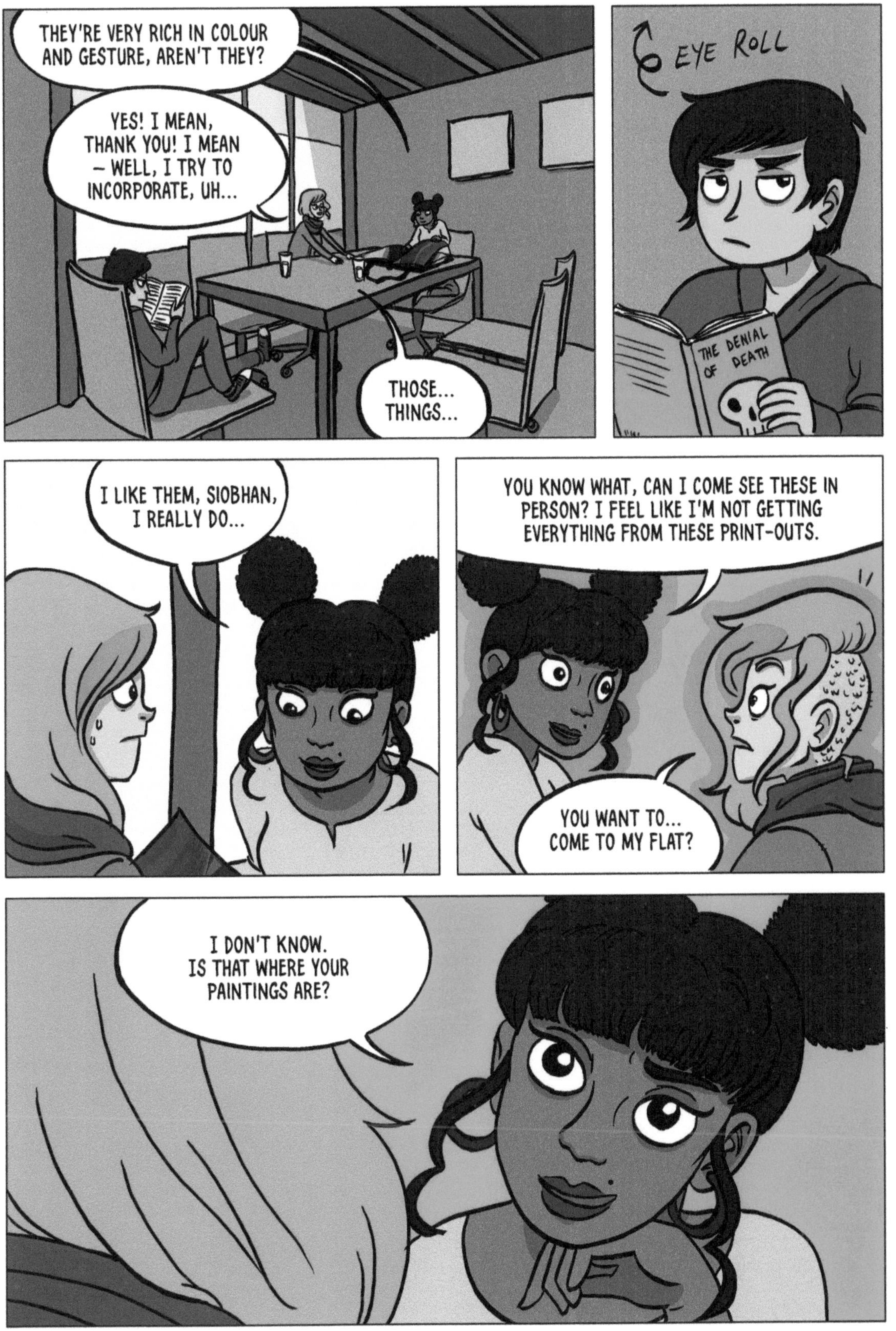
THEY'RE VERY RICH IN COLOUR AND GESTURE, AREN'T THEY?
YES! I MEAN, THANK YOU! I MEAN – WELL, I TRY TO INCORPORATE, UH...
THOSE... THINGS...
EYE ROLL
THE DENIAL OF DEATH
I LIKE THEM, SIOBHAN, I REALLY DO...
YOU KNOW WHAT, CAN I COME SEE THESE IN PERSON? I FEEL LIKE I'M NOT GETTING EVERYTHING FROM THESE PRINT-OUTS.
YOU WANT TO... COME TO MY FLAT?
I DON'T KNOW. IS THAT WHERE YOUR PAINTINGS ARE?

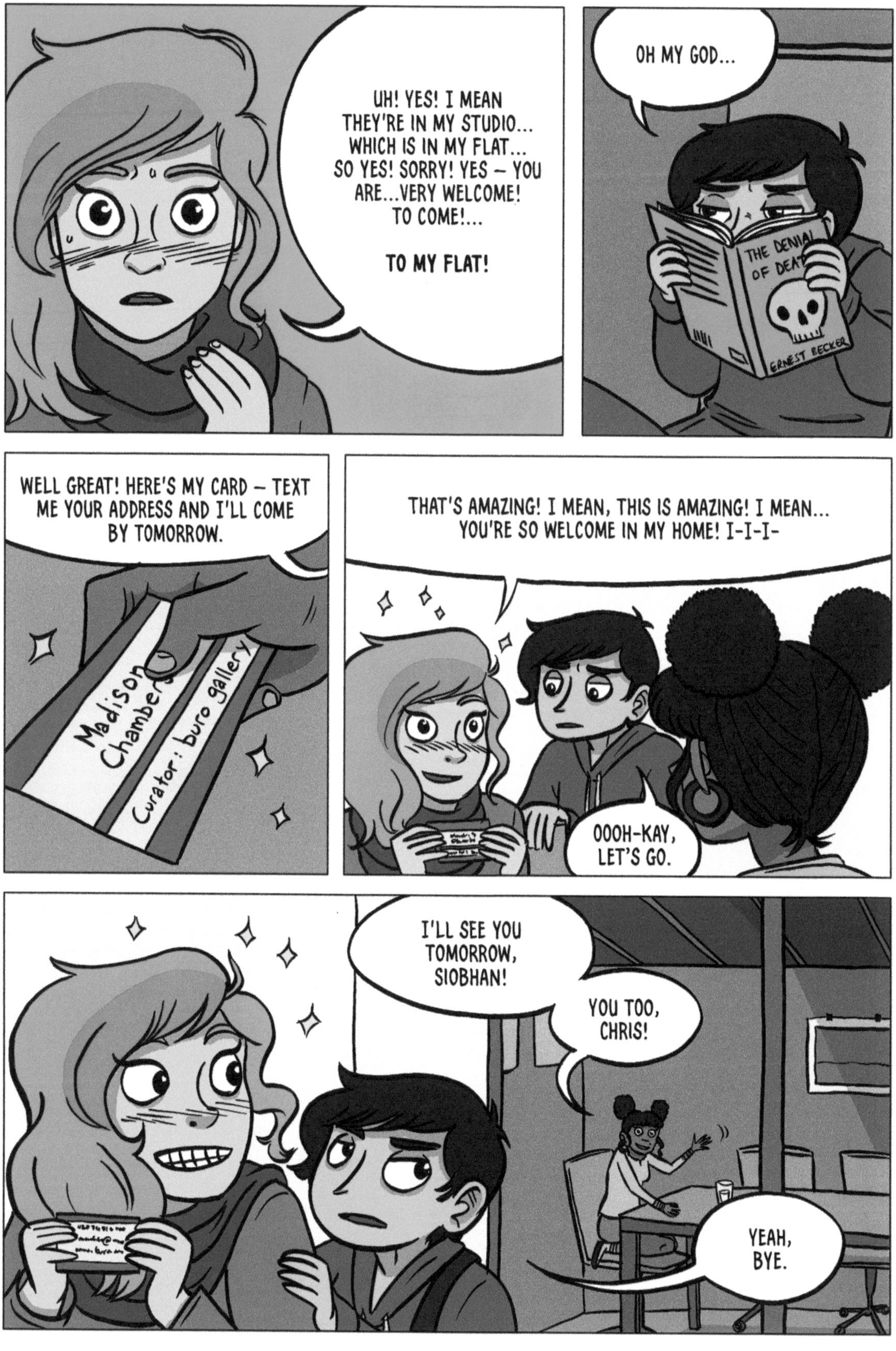
UH! YES! I MEAN THEY'RE IN MY STUDIO... WHICH IS IN MY FLAT... SO YES! SORRY! YES – YOU ARE...VERY WELCOME! TO COME!...
TO MY FLAT!
OH MY GOD...
THE DENIAL OF DEAT
ERNEST BECKER
WELL GREAT! HERE'S MY CARD – TEXT ME YOUR ADDRESS AND I'LL COME BY TOMORROW.
Madison Chambers
Curator: buro gallery
THAT'S AMAZING! I MEAN, THIS IS AMAZING! I MEAN... YOU'RE SO WELCOME IN MY HOME! I-I-I-
OOOH-KAY, LET'S GO.
I'LL SEE YOU TOMORROW, SIOBHAN!
YOU TOO, CHRIS!
YEAH, BYE.

Madison
Chambers

Curator: buro gallery

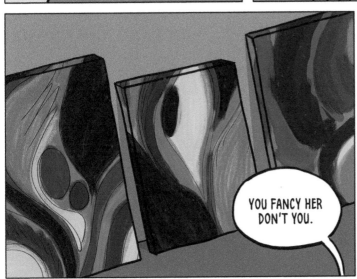

YOU FANCY HER
DON'T YOU.

WHAT!?
I DO *NOT!*

...I MEAN...
WHO ARE YOU
TALKING ABOUT?

HAHAHA!

SHUT UP!

GOD!
I DON'T KNOW WHY
YOU HAD TO BE SUCH
A NIGHTMARE AT THE
GALLERY! YOU NEARLY
RUINED THIS FOR
ME!

PIZZA PALACE   PIZZA PALACE

I WAS ONLY
BEING HONEST.

YOU WERE BEING
RUDE! YOU KNOW
THEY'RE TWO
DIFFERENT THINGS,
RIGHT?

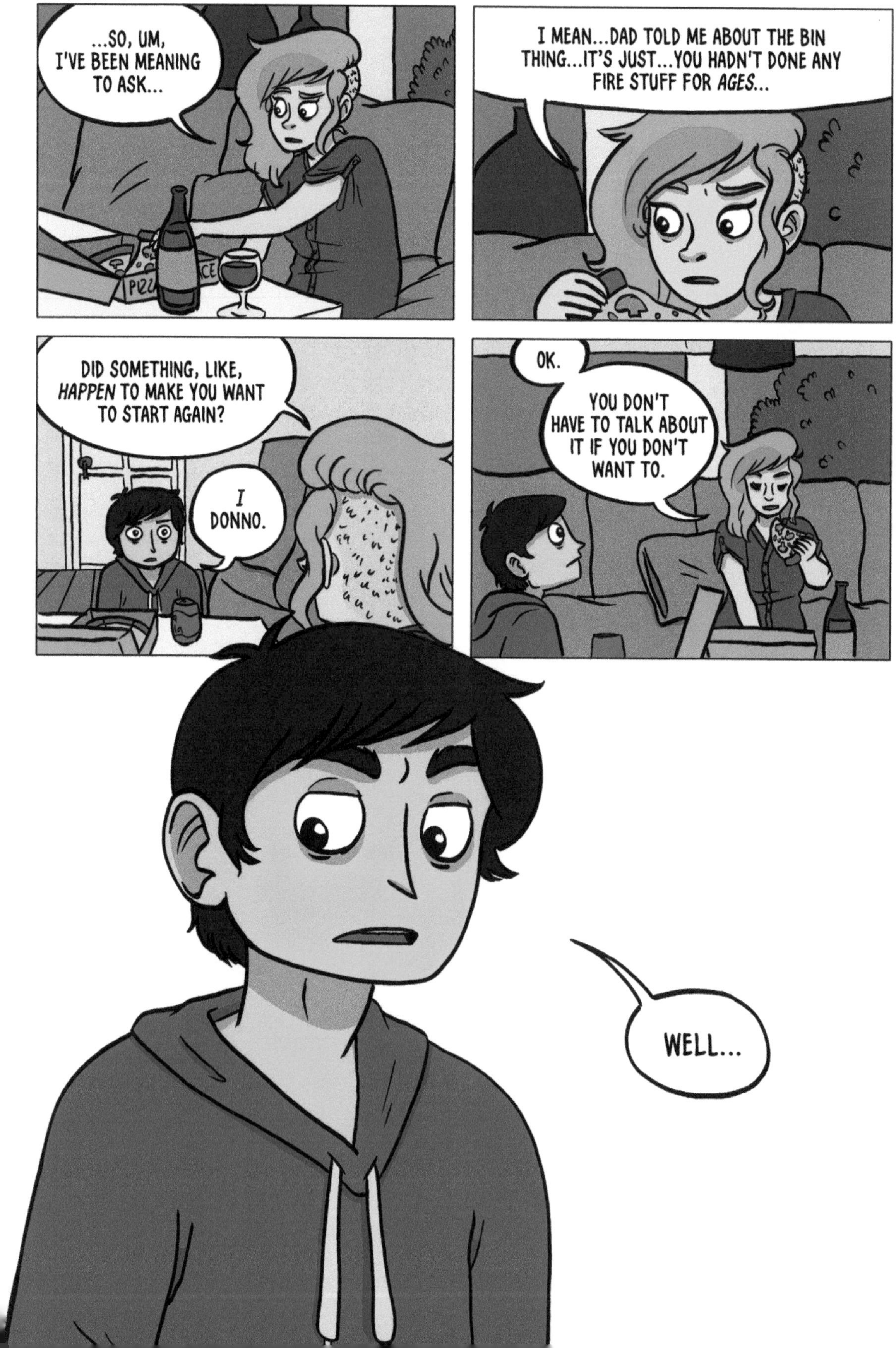
...SO, UM, I'VE BEEN MEANING TO ASK...
PIZZ
I MEAN...DAD TOLD ME ABOUT THE BIN THING...IT'S JUST...YOU HADN'T DONE ANY FIRE STUFF FOR *AGES*...
DID SOMETHING, LIKE, *HAPPEN* TO MAKE YOU WANT TO START AGAIN?
I DONNO.
OK.
YOU DON'T HAVE TO TALK ABOUT IT IF YOU DON'T WANT TO.
WELL...

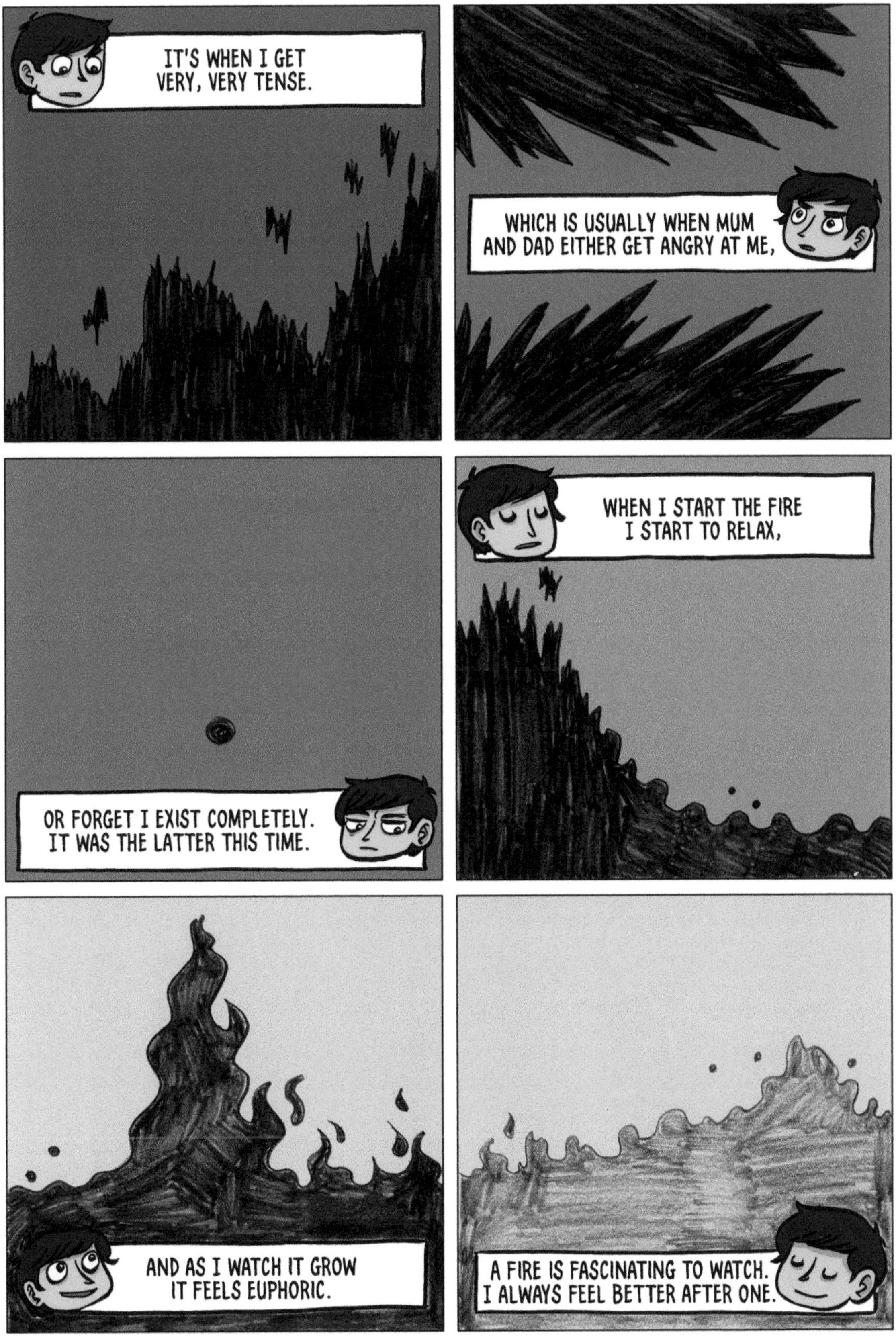
IT'S WHEN I GET VERY, VERY TENSE.
WHICH IS USUALLY WHEN MUM AND DAD EITHER GET ANGRY AT ME,
OR FORGET I EXIST COMPLETELY. IT WAS THE LATTER THIS TIME.
WHEN I START THE FIRE I START TO RELAX,
AND AS I WATCH IT GROW IT FEELS EUPHORIC.
A FIRE IS FASCINATING TO WATCH. I ALWAYS FEEL BETTER AFTER ONE.

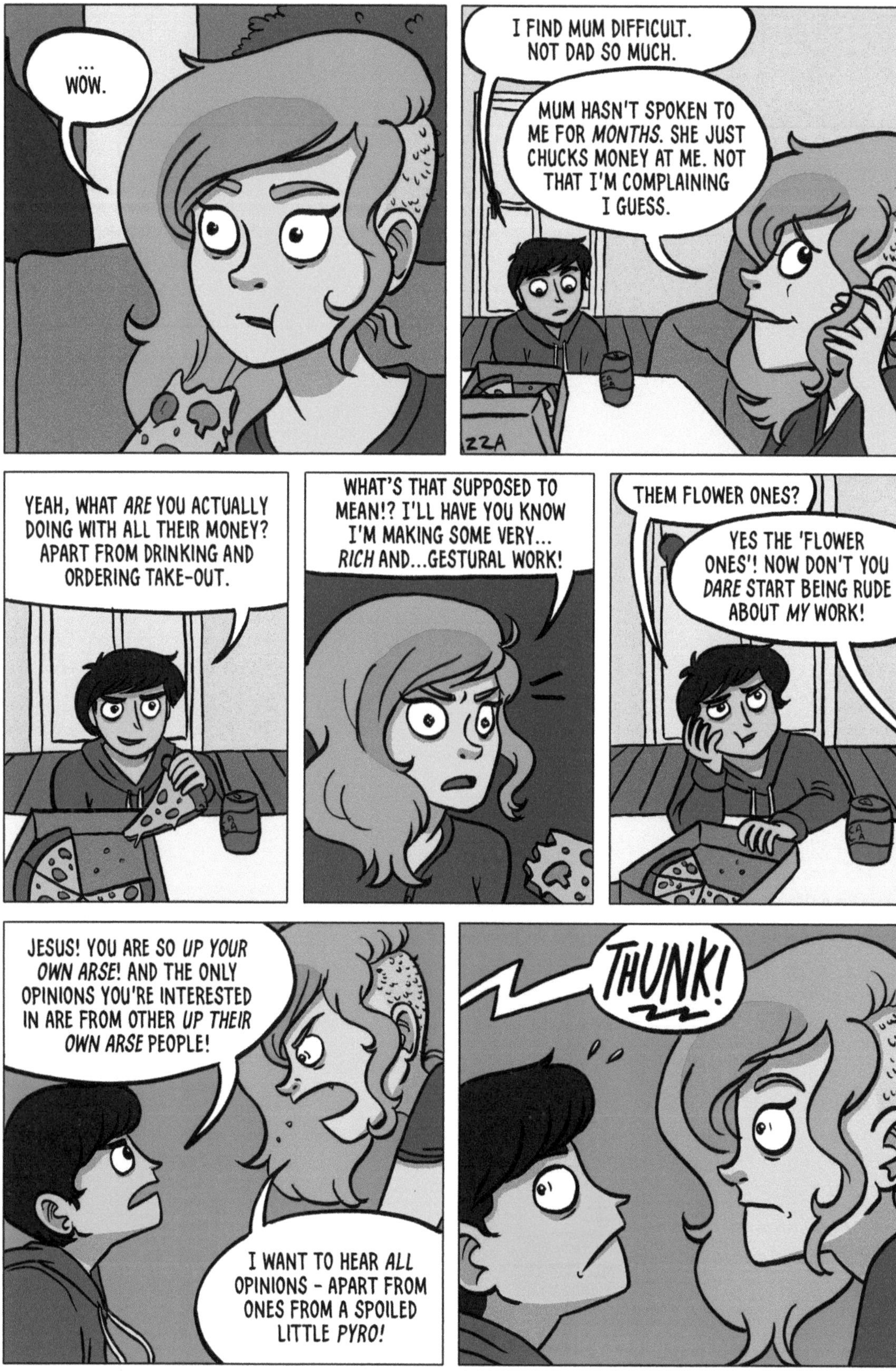

... WOW.
I FIND MUM DIFFICULT. NOT DAD SO MUCH.
MUM HASN'T SPOKEN TO ME FOR *MONTHS*. SHE JUST CHUCKS MONEY AT ME. NOT THAT I'M COMPLAINING I GUESS.
ZZA
YEAH, WHAT *ARE* YOU ACTUALLY DOING WITH ALL THEIR MONEY? APART FROM DRINKING AND ORDERING TAKE-OUT.
WHAT'S THAT SUPPOSED TO MEAN!? I'LL HAVE YOU KNOW I'M MAKING SOME VERY... *RICH* AND...GESTURAL WORK!
THEM FLOWER ONES?
YES THE 'FLOWER ONES'! NOW DON'T YOU *DARE* START BEING RUDE ABOUT *MY* WORK!
JESUS! YOU ARE SO *UP YOUR OWN ARSE*! AND THE ONLY OPINIONS YOU'RE INTERESTED IN ARE FROM OTHER *UP THEIR OWN ARSE* PEOPLE!
I WANT TO HEAR *ALL* OPINIONS - APART FROM ONES FROM A SPOILED LITTLE *PYRO!*
THUNK!

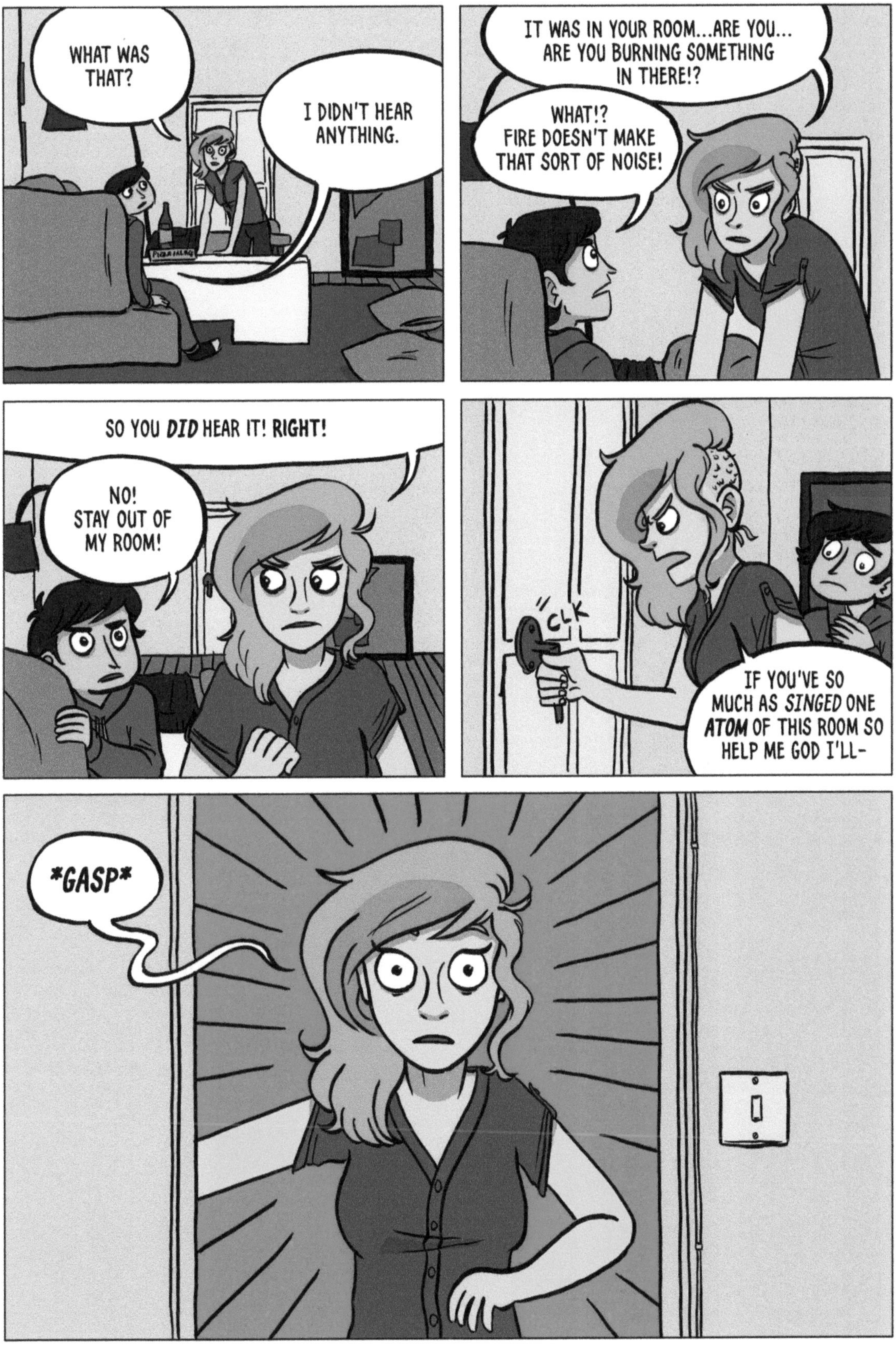
WHAT WAS THAT?
I DIDN'T HEAR ANYTHING.
IT WAS IN YOUR ROOM...ARE YOU... ARE YOU BURNING SOMETHING IN THERE!?
WHAT!? FIRE DOESN'T MAKE THAT SORT OF NOISE!
SO YOU *DID* HEAR IT! **RIGHT!**
NO! STAY OUT OF MY ROOM!
CLK
IF YOU'VE SO MUCH AS *SINGED* ONE ***ATOM*** OF THIS ROOM SO HELP ME GOD I'LL-
GASP

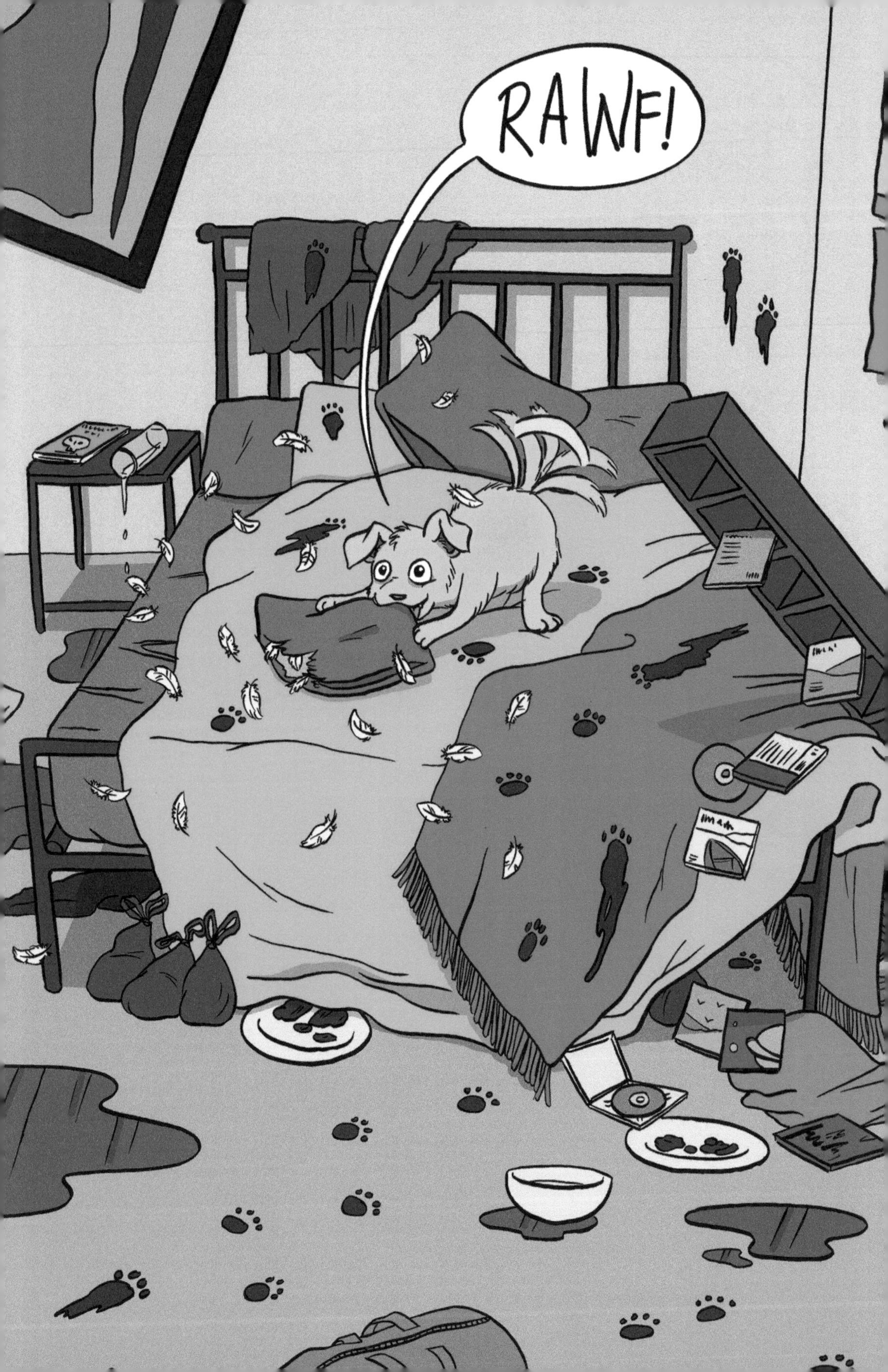
RAWF!

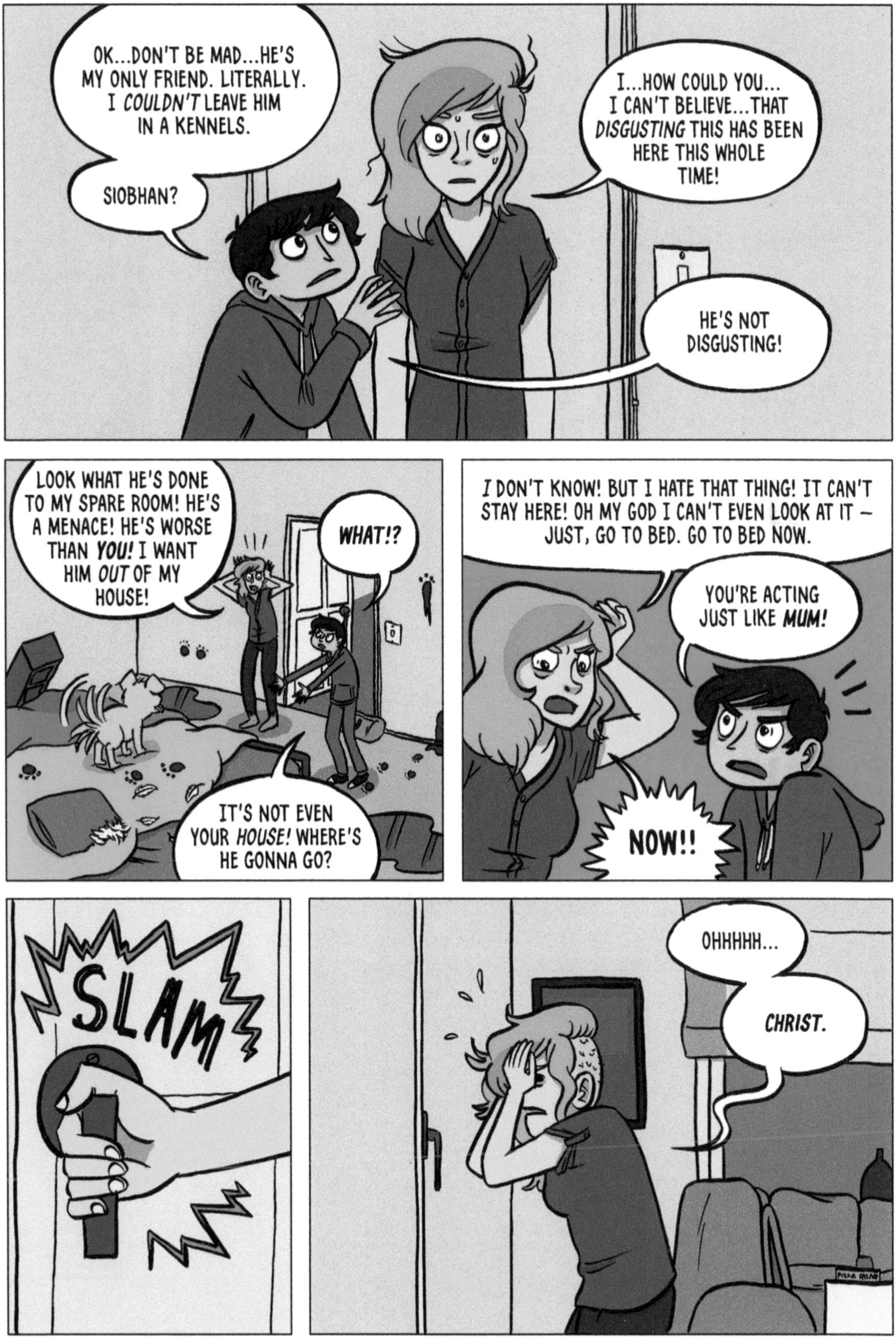
OK...DON'T BE MAD...HE'S MY ONLY FRIEND. LITERALLY. I *COULDN'T* LEAVE HIM IN A KENNELS.
SIOBHAN?
I...HOW COULD YOU... I CAN'T BELIEVE...THAT *DISGUSTING* THIS HAS BEEN HERE THIS WHOLE TIME!
HE'S NOT DISGUSTING!
LOOK WHAT HE'S DONE TO MY SPARE ROOM! HE'S A MENACE! HE'S WORSE THAN *YOU!* I WANT HIM *OUT* OF MY HOUSE!
WHAT!?
IT'S NOT EVEN YOUR *HOUSE!* WHERE'S HE GONNA GO?
I DON'T KNOW! BUT I HATE THAT THING! IT CAN'T STAY HERE! OH MY GOD I CAN'T EVEN LOOK AT IT – JUST, GO TO BED. GO TO BED NOW.
YOU'RE ACTING JUST LIKE *MUM!*
NOW!!
SLAM
OHHHHH...
CHRIST.

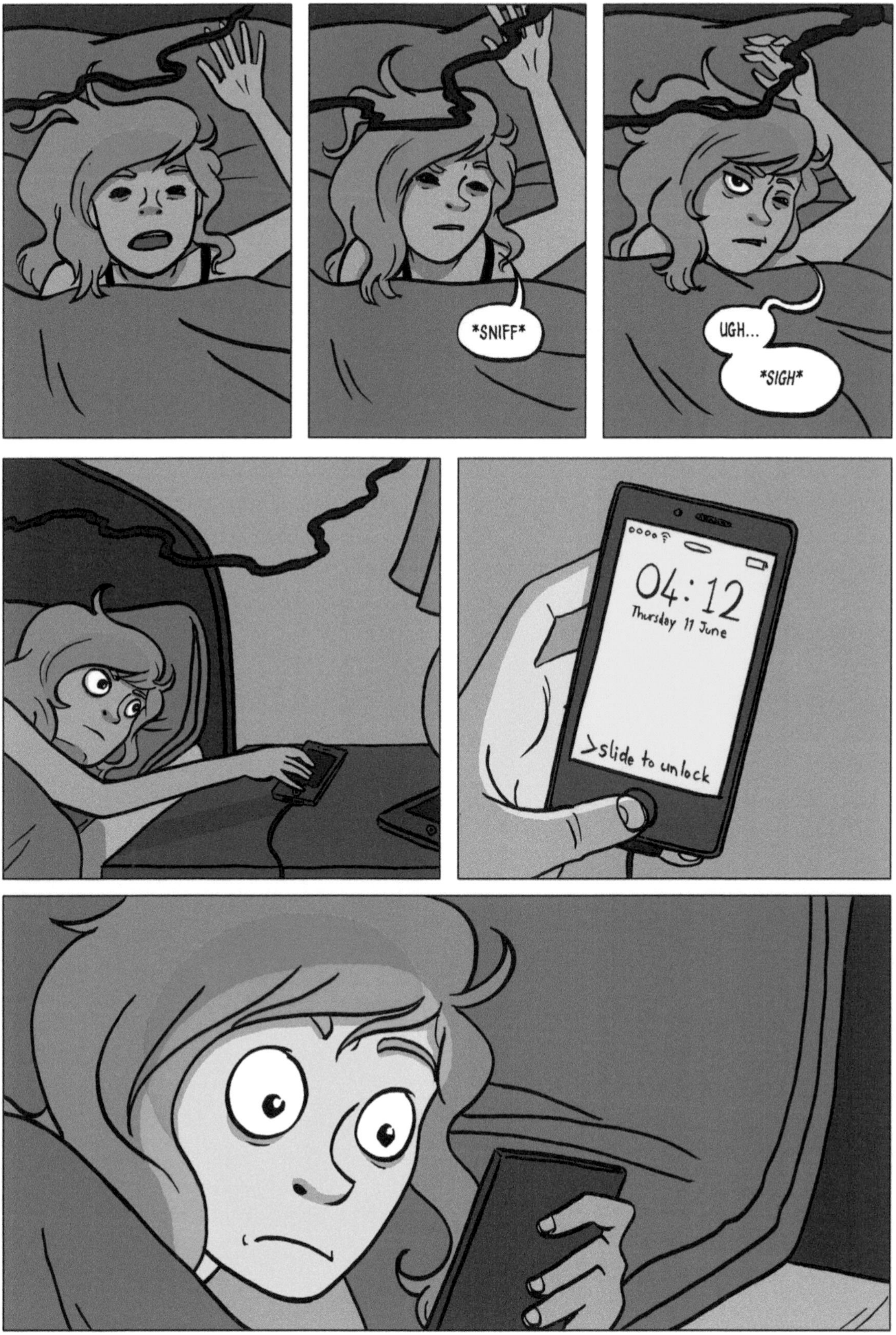
SNIFF
UGH...
SIGH
04:12
Thursday 11 June
>slide to unlock

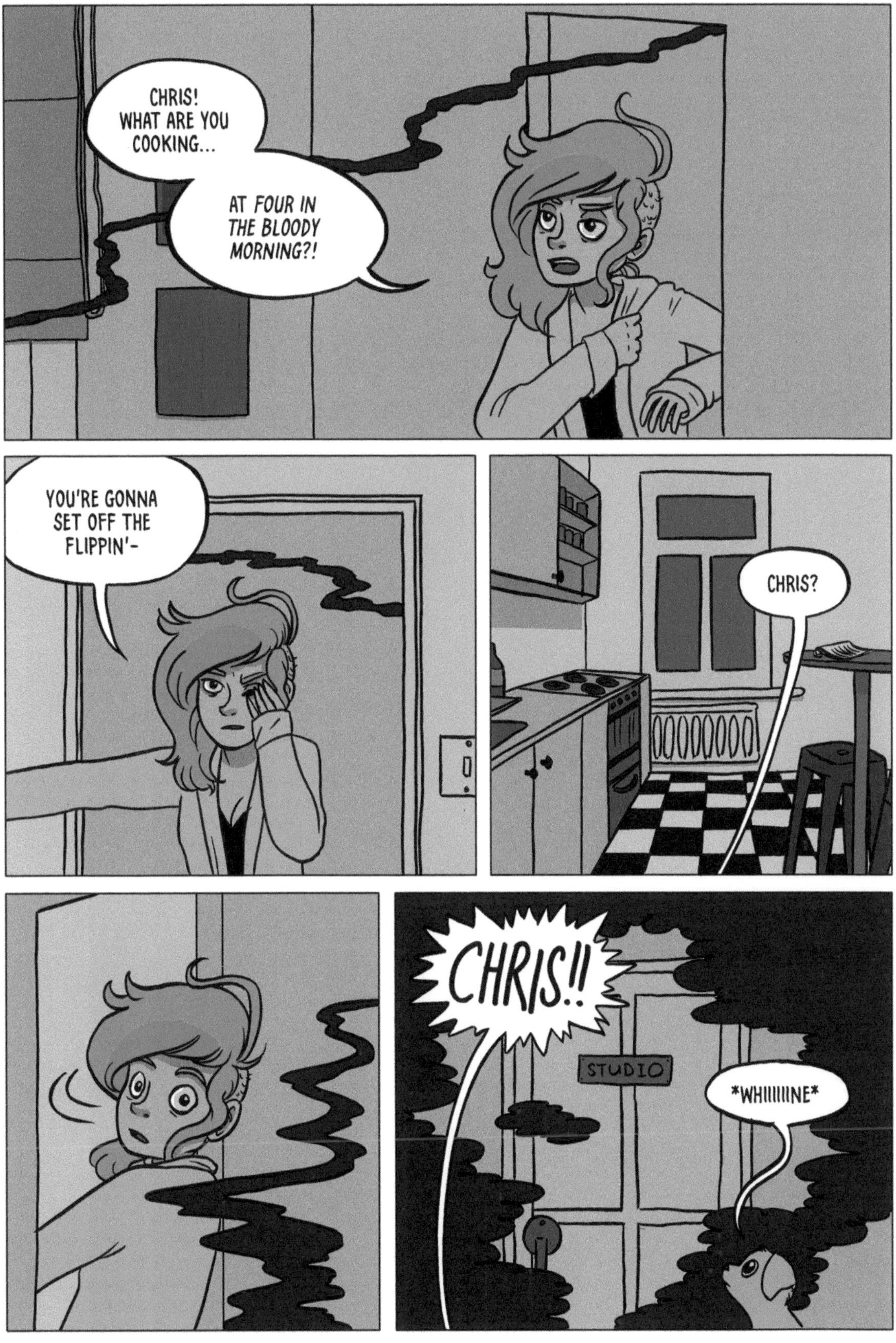
CHRIS!
WHAT ARE YOU
COOKING...
AT FOUR IN
THE BLOODY
MORNING?!
YOU'RE GONNA
SET OFF THE
FLIPPIN'-
CHRIS?
CHRIS!!
STUDIO
WHIIIIIINE

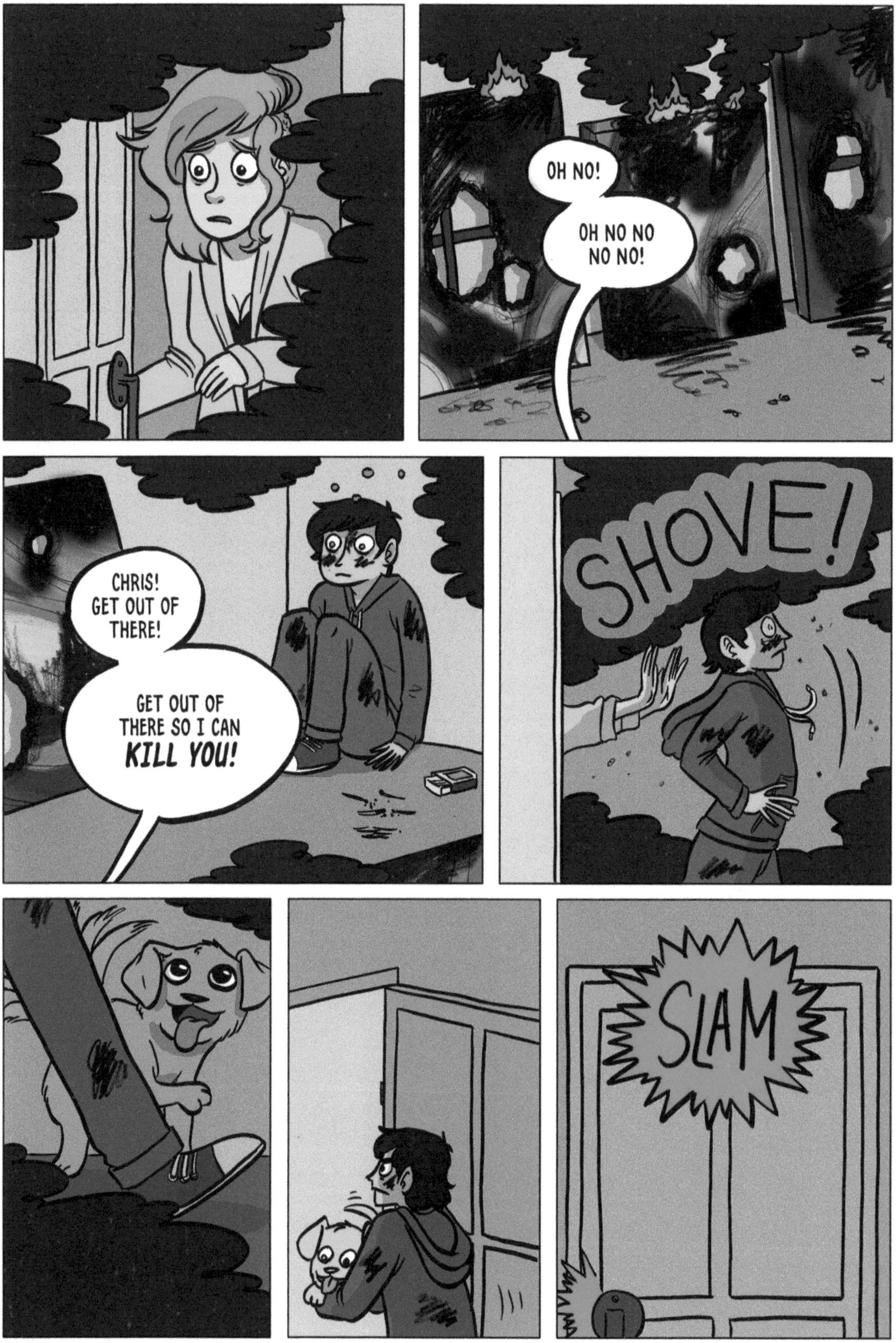
OH NO!
OH NO NO NO NO!
CHRIS! GET OUT OF THERE!
GET OUT OF THERE SO I CAN KILL YOU!
SHOVE!
SLAM

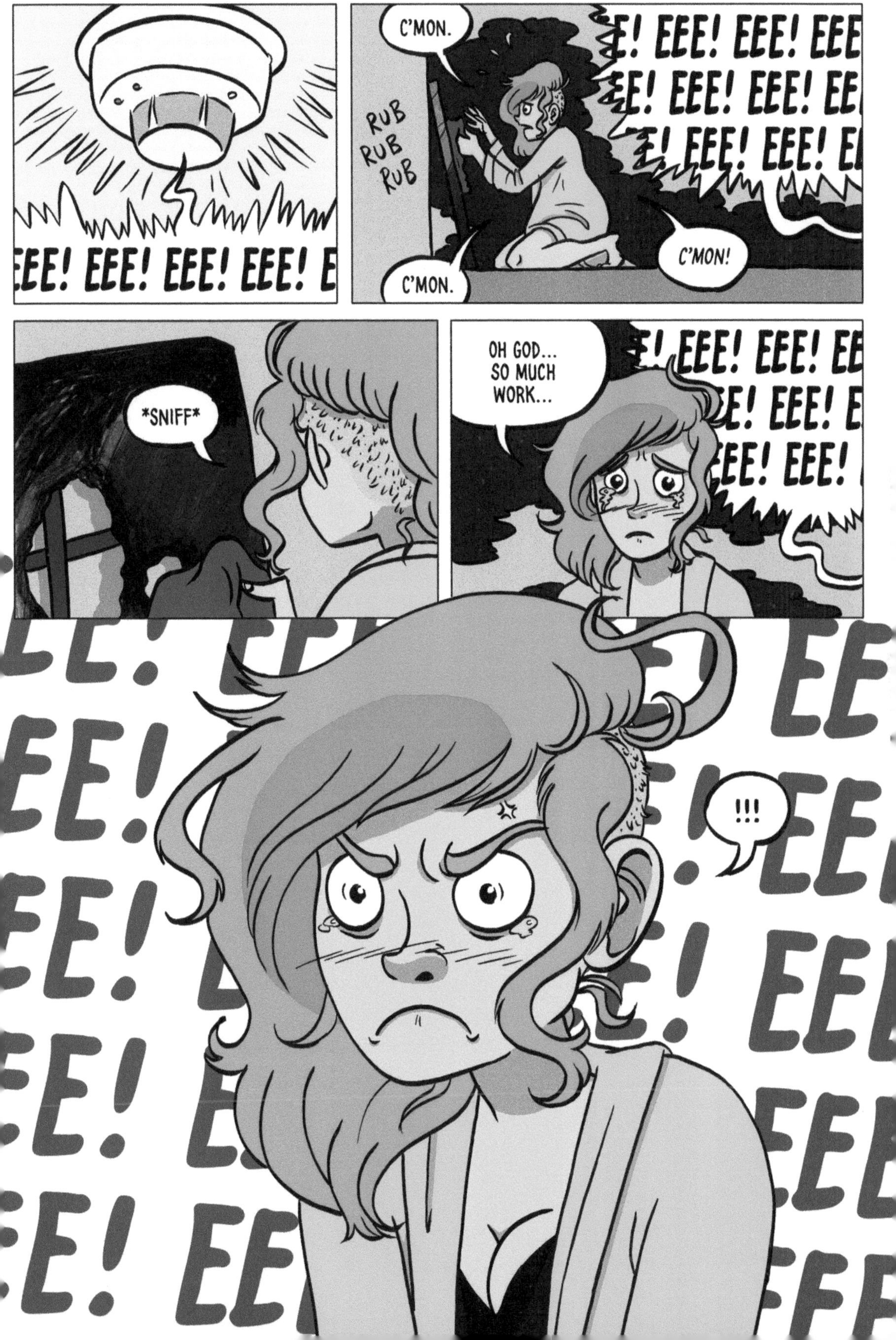
EEE! EEE! EEE! EEE! E
C'MON.
RUB RUB RUB
E! EEE! EEE! EEE
EE! EEE! EEE! EE
E! EEE! EEE! E
C'MON.
C'MON!
SNIFF
OH GOD... SO MUCH WORK...
E! EEE! EEE! EE
E! EEE! E
EEE! EEE!
!!!

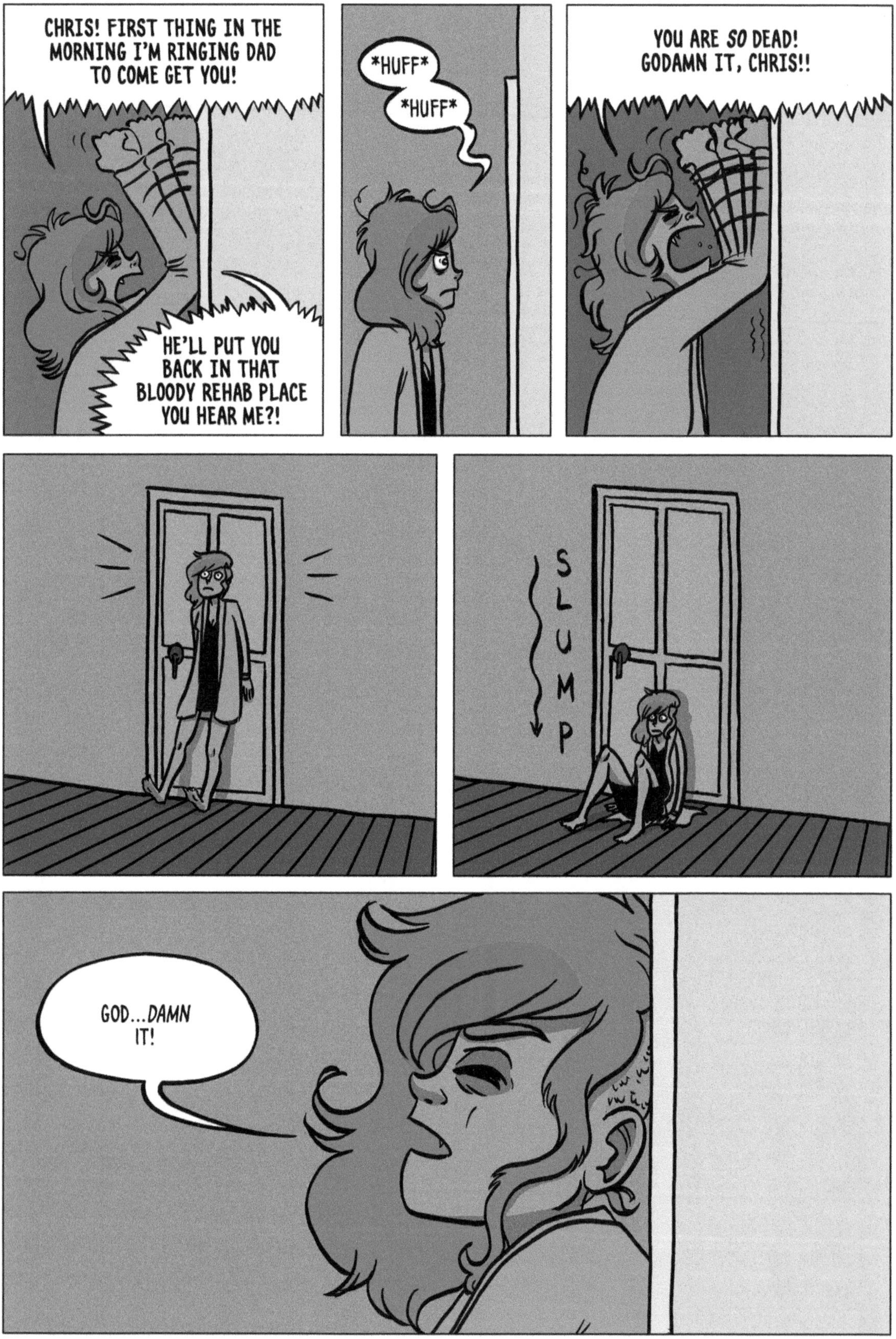
CHRIS! FIRST THING IN THE MORNING I'M RINGING DAD TO COME GET YOU!
HE'LL PUT YOU BACK IN THAT BLOODY REHAB PLACE YOU HEAR ME?!
HUFF
HUFF
YOU ARE *SO* DEAD! GODAMN IT, CHRIS!!
SLUMP
GOD...*DAMN* IT!

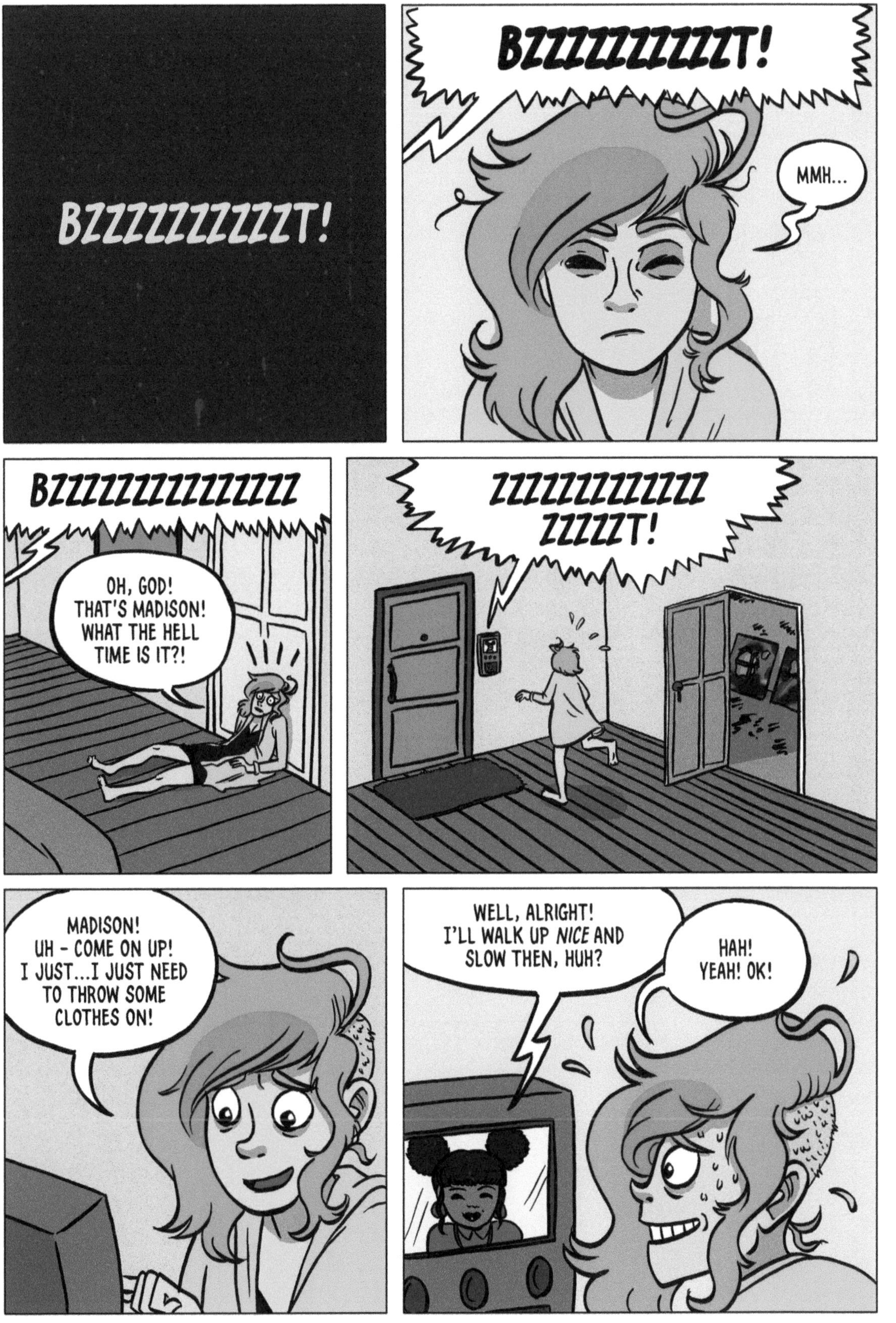
BZZZZZZZZZZZT!
BZZZZZZZZZZZT!
MMH...
BZZZZZZZZZZZZZZZZ
OH, GOD! THAT'S MADISON! WHAT THE HELL TIME IS IT?!
ZZZZZZZZZZZZZZ ZZZZZT!
MADISON! UH - COME ON UP! I JUST...I JUST NEED TO THROW SOME CLOTHES ON!
WELL, ALRIGHT! I'LL WALK UP *NICE* AND SLOW THEN, HUH?
HAH! YEAH! OK!

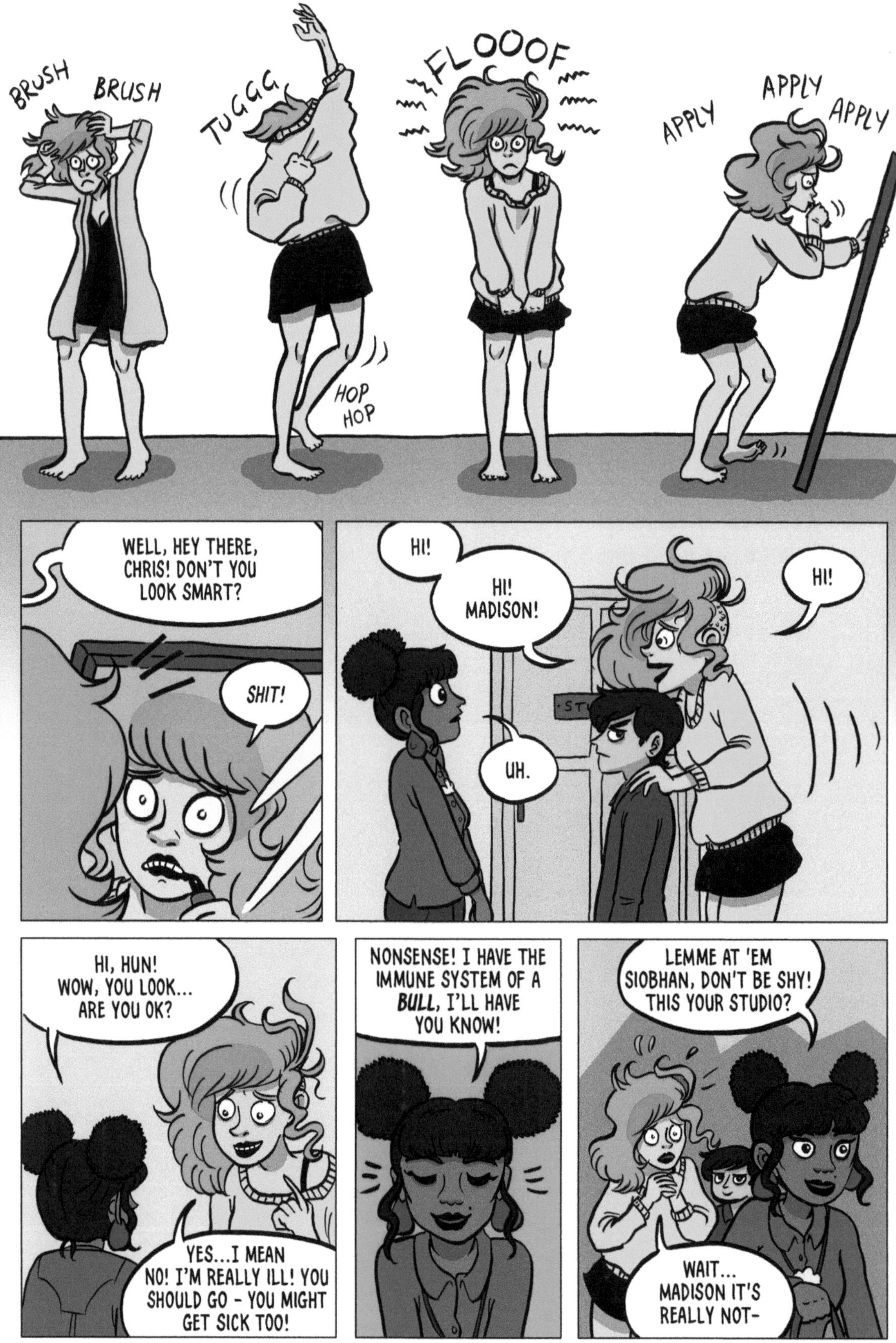

BRUSH
BRUSH
TUGGG
HOP HOP
FLOOOF
APPLY
APPLY
APPLY
WELL, HEY THERE, CHRIS! DON'T YOU LOOK SMART?
SHIT!
HI!
HI! MADISON!
HI!
UH.
HI, HUN! WOW, YOU LOOK... ARE YOU OK?
YES...I MEAN NO! I'M REALLY ILL! YOU SHOULD GO - YOU MIGHT GET SICK TOO!
NONSENSE! I HAVE THE IMMUNE SYSTEM OF A **BULL**, I'LL HAVE YOU KNOW!
LEMME AT 'EM SIOBHAN, DON'T BE SHY! THIS YOUR STUDIO?
WAIT... MADISON IT'S REALLY NOT-

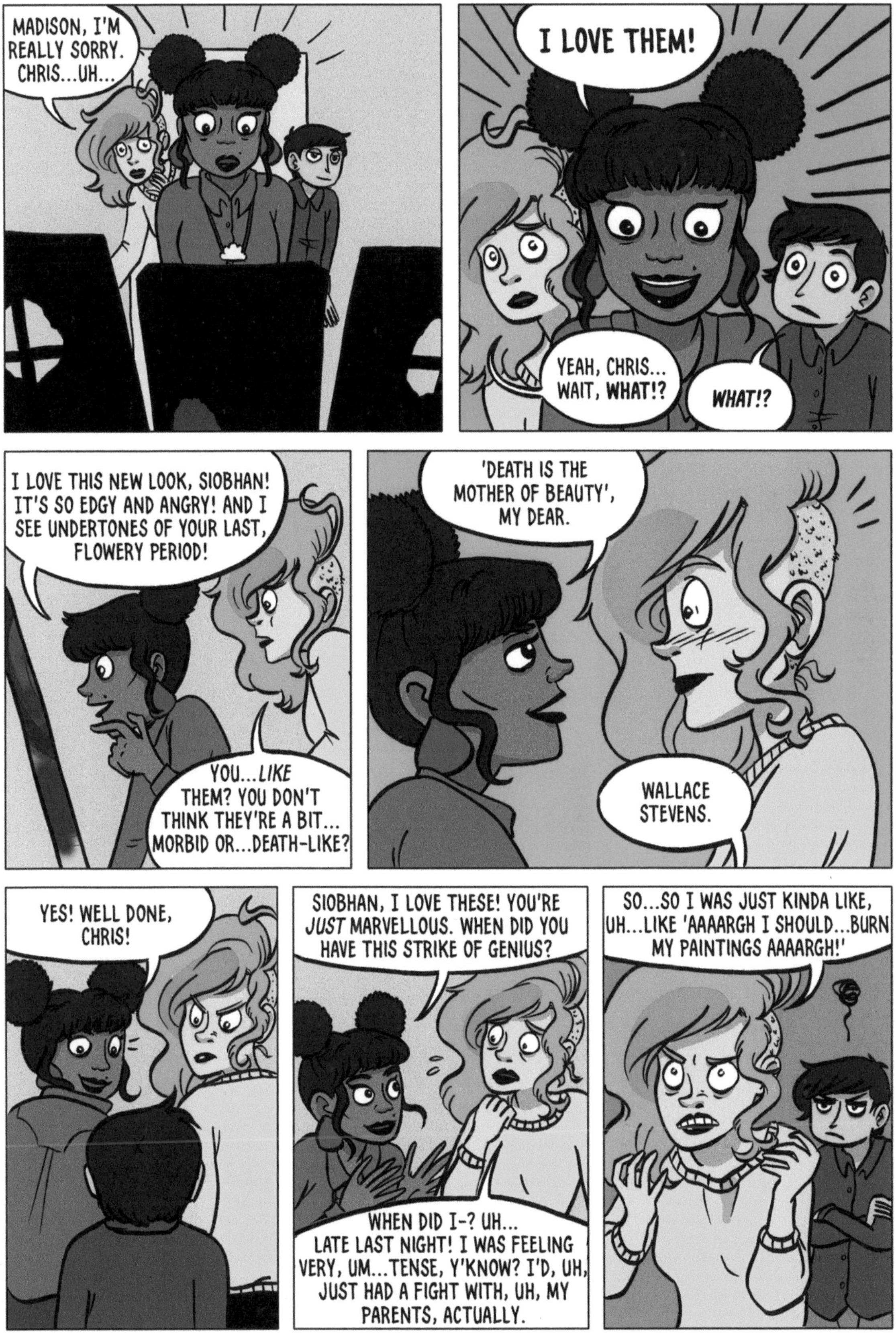
MADISON, I'M REALLY SORRY. CHRIS...UH...
I LOVE THEM!
YEAH, CHRIS... WAIT, WHAT!?
WHAT!?
I LOVE THIS NEW LOOK, SIOBHAN! IT'S SO EDGY AND ANGRY! AND I SEE UNDERTONES OF YOUR LAST, FLOWERY PERIOD!
YOU...LIKE THEM? YOU DON'T THINK THEY'RE A BIT... MORBID OR...DEATH-LIKE?
'DEATH IS THE MOTHER OF BEAUTY', MY DEAR.
WALLACE STEVENS.
YES! WELL DONE, CHRIS!
SIOBHAN, I LOVE THESE! YOU'RE JUST MARVELLOUS. WHEN DID YOU HAVE THIS STRIKE OF GENIUS?
WHEN DID I-? UH... LATE LAST NIGHT! I WAS FEELING VERY, UM...TENSE, Y'KNOW? I'D, UH, JUST HAD A FIGHT WITH, UH, MY PARENTS, ACTUALLY.
SO...SO I WAS JUST KINDA LIKE, UH...LIKE 'AAAARGH I SHOULD...BURN MY PAINTINGS AAAARGH!'

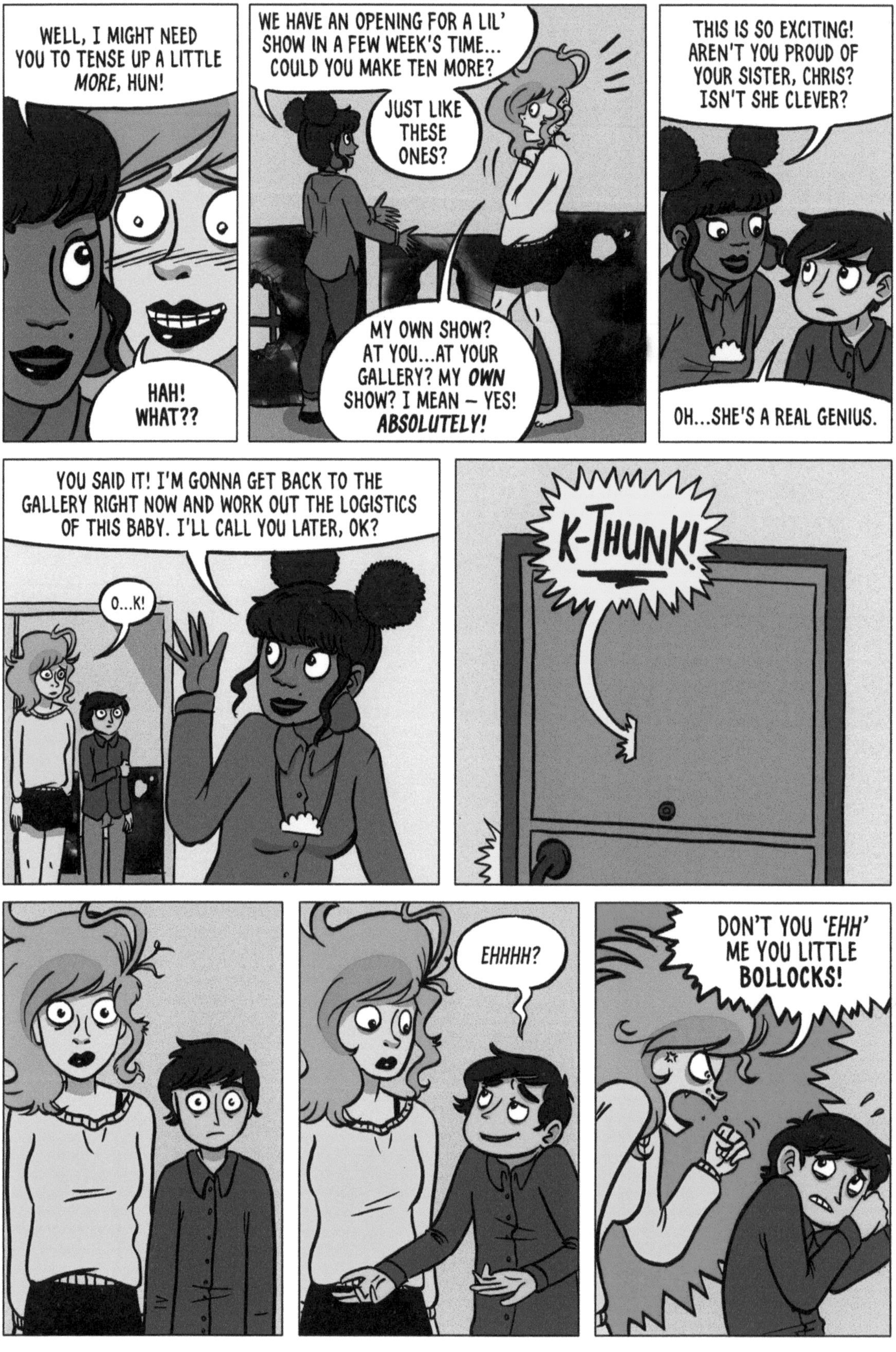
WELL, I MIGHT NEED YOU TO TENSE UP A LITTLE *MORE*, HUN!
HAH! WHAT??
WE HAVE AN OPENING FOR A LIL' SHOW IN A FEW WEEK'S TIME... COULD YOU MAKE TEN MORE?
JUST LIKE THESE ONES?
MY OWN SHOW? AT YOU...AT YOUR GALLERY? MY ***OWN*** SHOW? I MEAN – YES! ***ABSOLUTELY!***
THIS IS SO EXCITING! AREN'T YOU PROUD OF YOUR SISTER, CHRIS? ISN'T SHE CLEVER?
OH...SHE'S A REAL GENIUS.
YOU SAID IT! I'M GONNA GET BACK TO THE GALLERY RIGHT NOW AND WORK OUT THE LOGISTICS OF THIS BABY. I'LL CALL YOU LATER, OK?
O...K!
K-THUNK!
EHHHH?
DON'T YOU *'EHH'* ME YOU LITTLE **BOLLOCKS!**

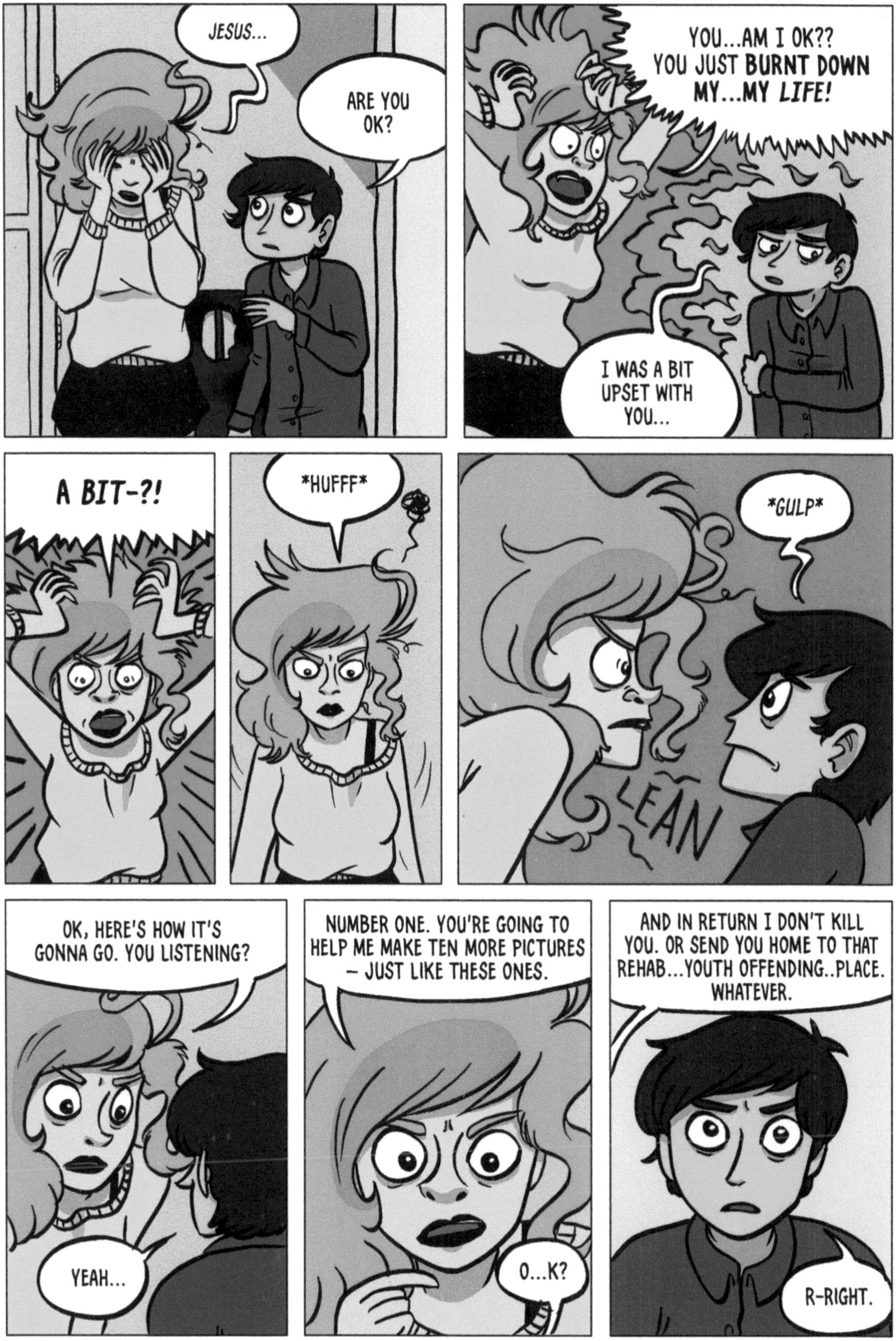
JESUS...
ARE YOU OK?
YOU...AM I OK?? YOU JUST BURNT DOWN MY...MY LIFE!
I WAS A BIT UPSET WITH YOU...
A BIT-?!
HUFFF
GULP
LEAN
OK, HERE'S HOW IT'S GONNA GO. YOU LISTENING?
YEAH...
NUMBER ONE. YOU'RE GOING TO HELP ME MAKE TEN MORE PICTURES – JUST LIKE THESE ONES.
O...K?
AND IN RETURN I DON'T KILL YOU. OR SEND YOU HOME TO THAT REHAB...YOUTH OFFENDING..PLACE. WHATEVER.
R-RIGHT.

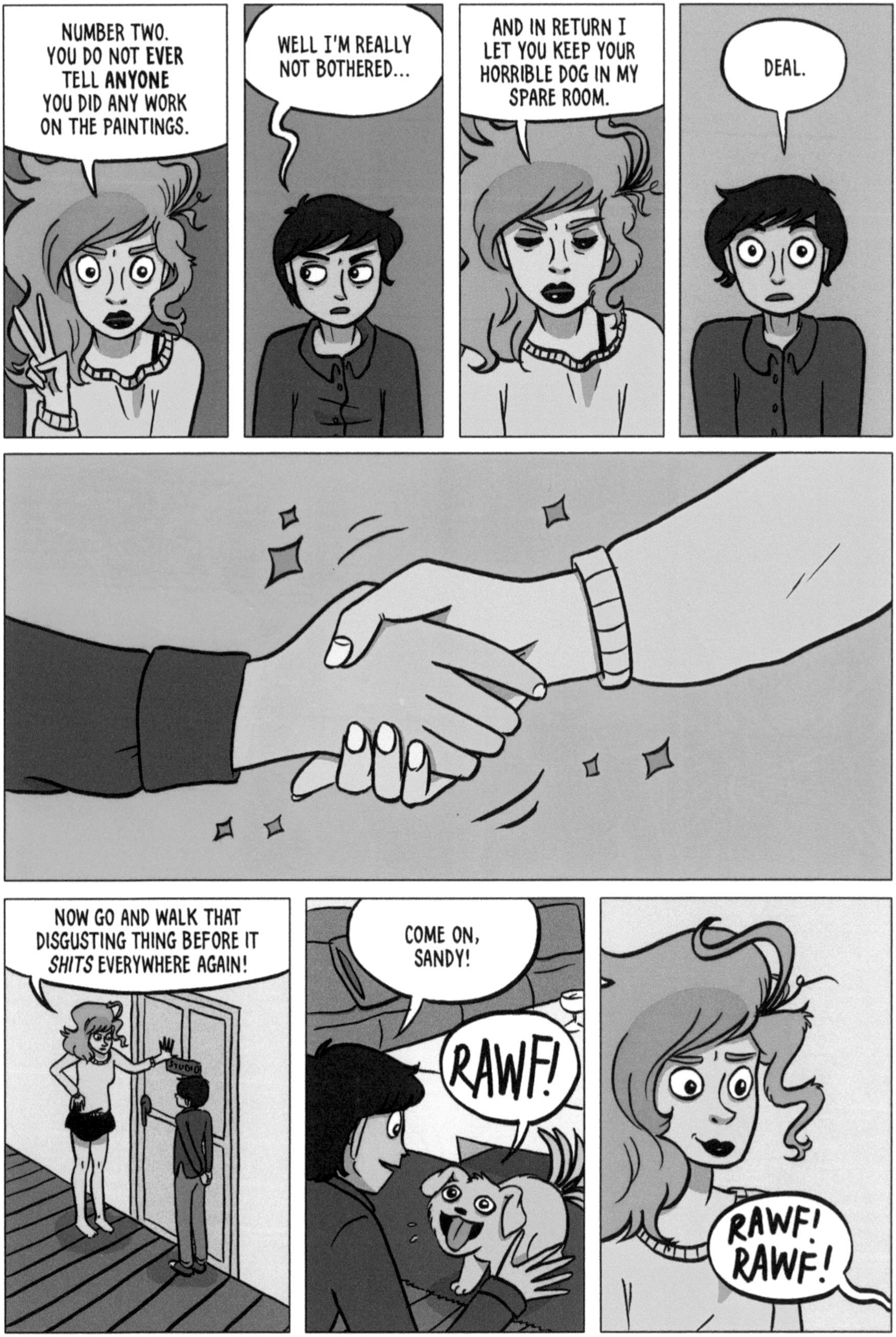
NUMBER TWO. YOU DO NOT EVER TELL **ANYONE** YOU DID ANY WORK ON THE PAINTINGS.
WELL I'M REALLY NOT BOTHERED...
AND IN RETURN I LET YOU KEEP YOUR HORRIBLE DOG IN MY SPARE ROOM.
DEAL.
NOW GO AND WALK THAT DISGUSTING THING BEFORE IT *SHITS* EVERYWHERE AGAIN!
STUDIO
COME ON, SANDY!
RAWF!
RAWF! RAWF!

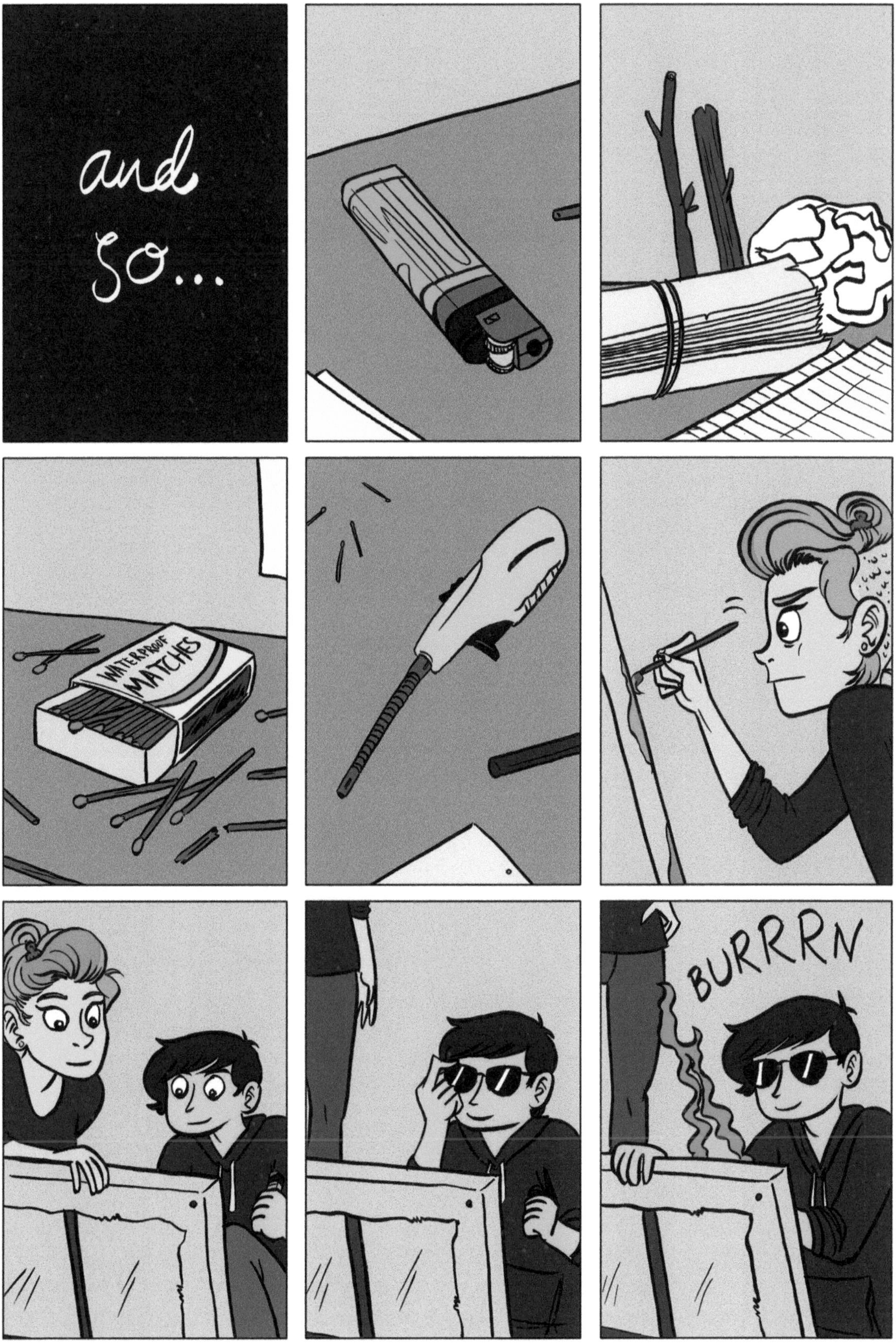
and so...
WATERPROOF MATCHES
BURRRN

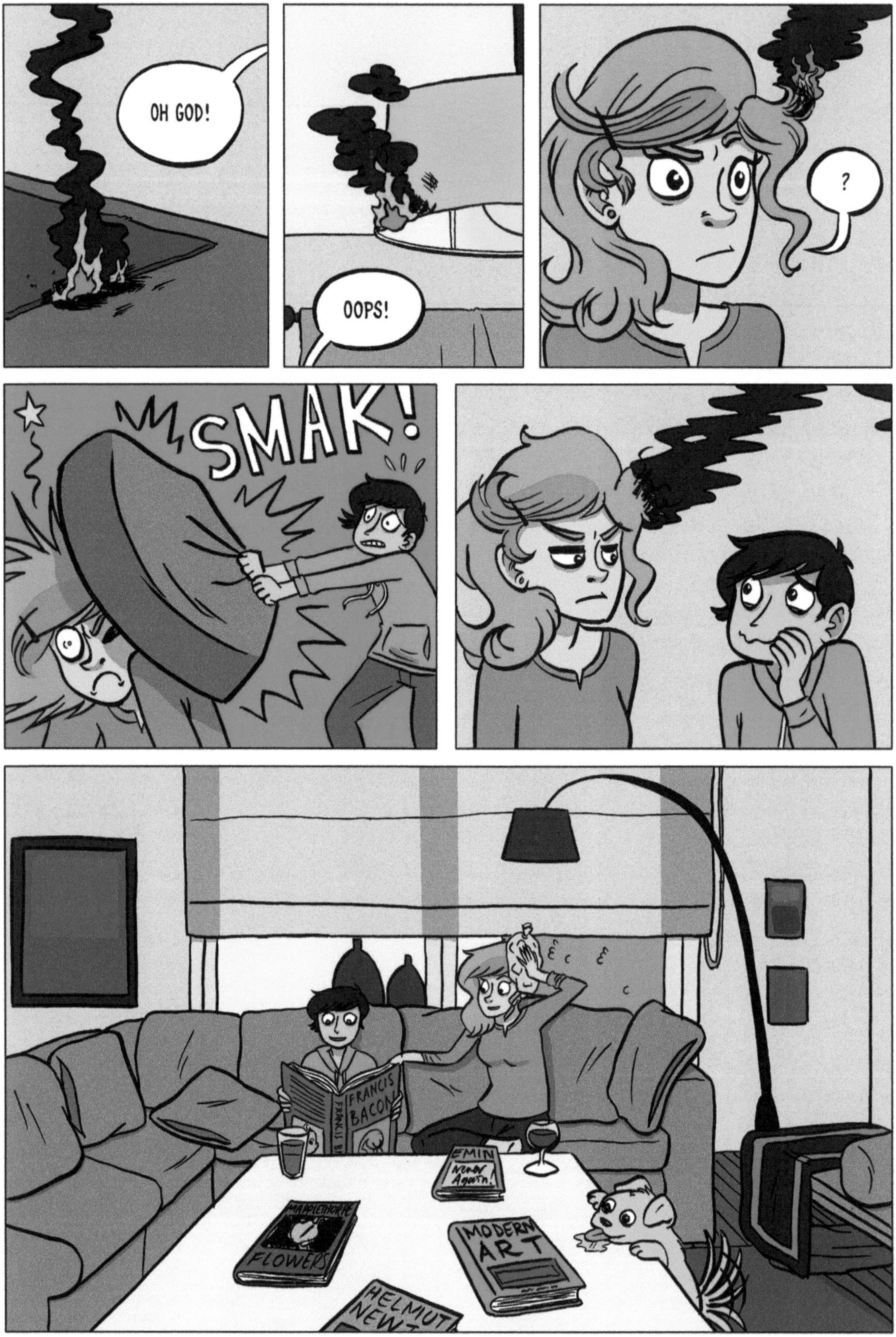
OH GOD!
OOPS!
?
SMAK!
FRANCIS BACON
EMIN
Never Again!
MAPPLETHORPE
FLOWERS
MODERN ART
HELMUT

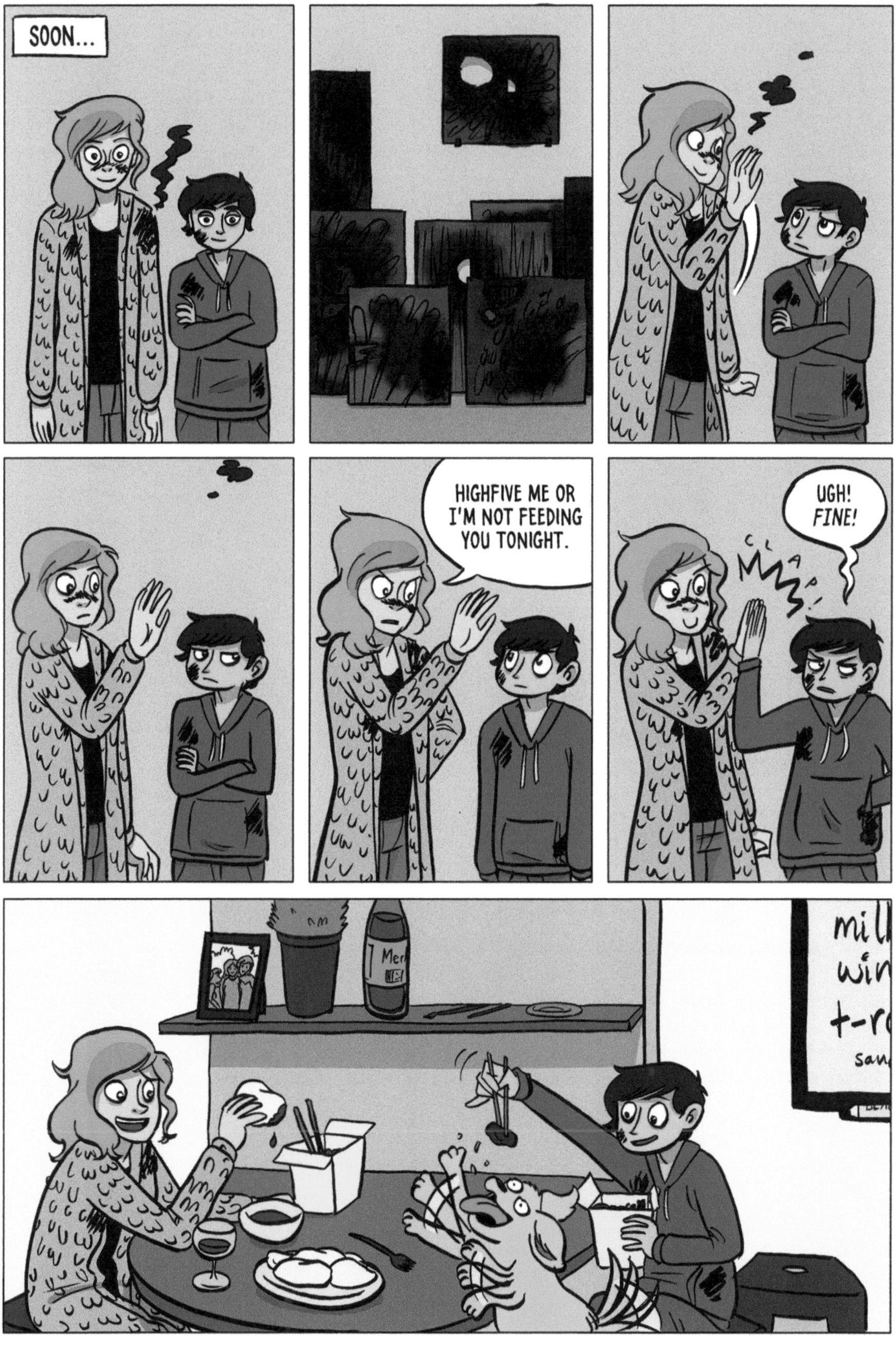
SOON...
HIGHFIVE ME OR I'M NOT FEEDING YOU TONIGHT.
CLAP!
UGH! FINE!

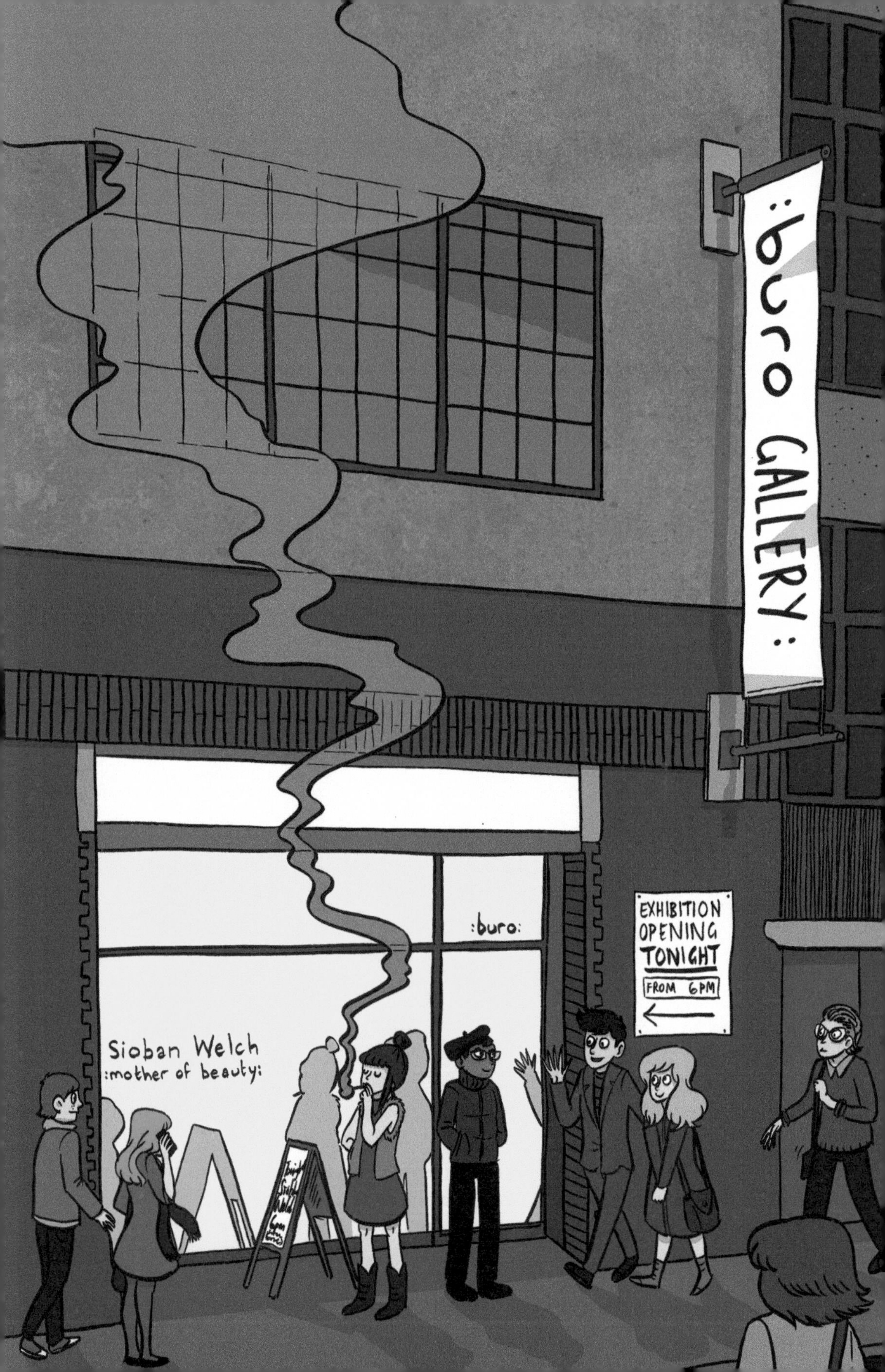
:buro GALLERY:
:buro:
Sioban Welch
:mother of beauty:
EXHIBITION OPENING TONIGHT
FROM 6PM

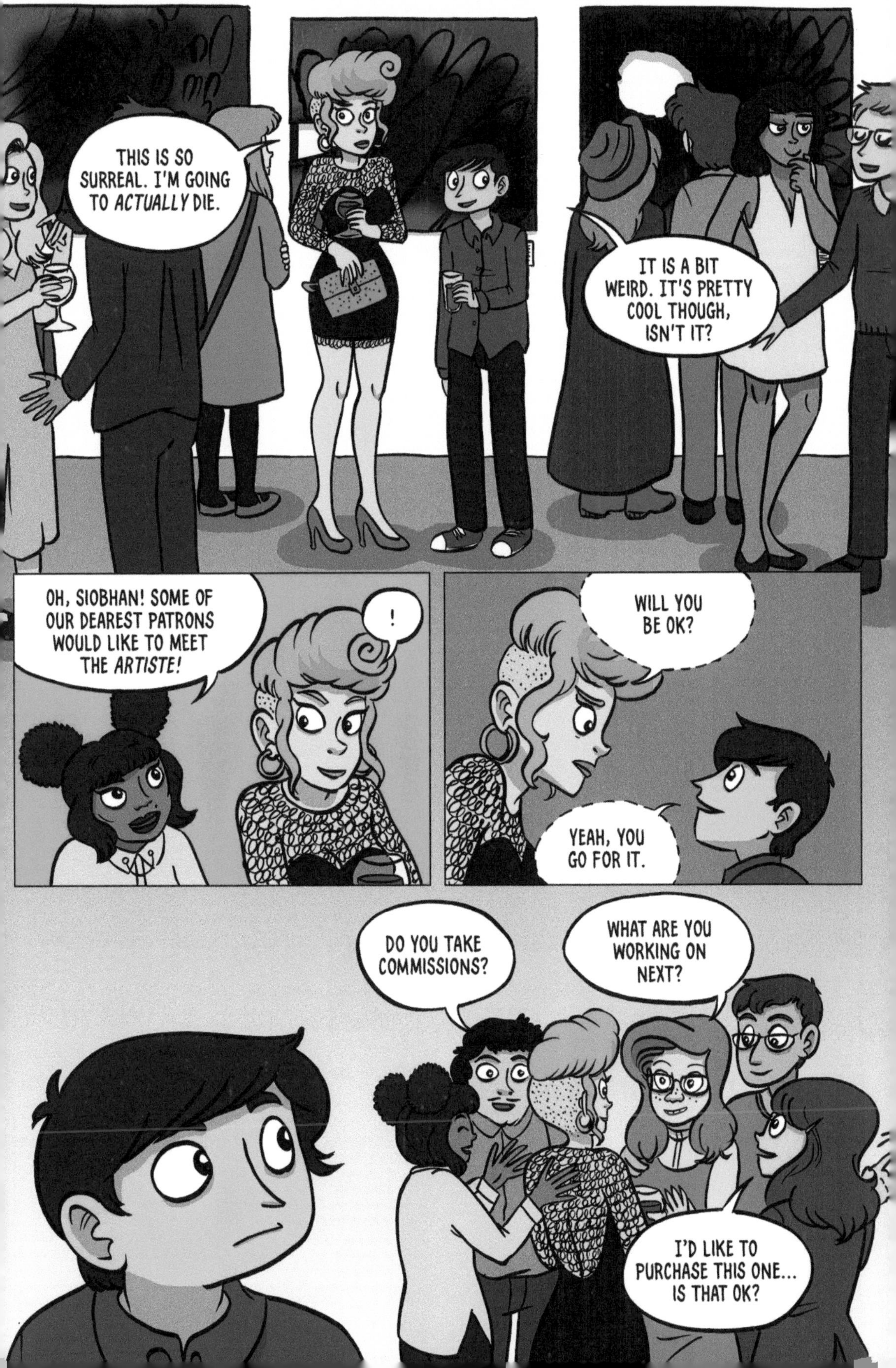

THIS IS SO SURREAL. I'M GOING TO *ACTUALLY* DIE.
IT IS A BIT WEIRD. IT'S PRETTY COOL THOUGH, ISN'T IT?
OH, SIOBHAN! SOME OF OUR DEAREST PATRONS WOULD LIKE TO MEET THE *ARTISTE!*
!
WILL YOU BE OK?
YEAH, YOU GO FOR IT.
DO YOU TAKE COMMISSIONS?
WHAT ARE YOU WORKING ON NEXT?
I'D LIKE TO PURCHASE THIS ONE... IS THAT OK?

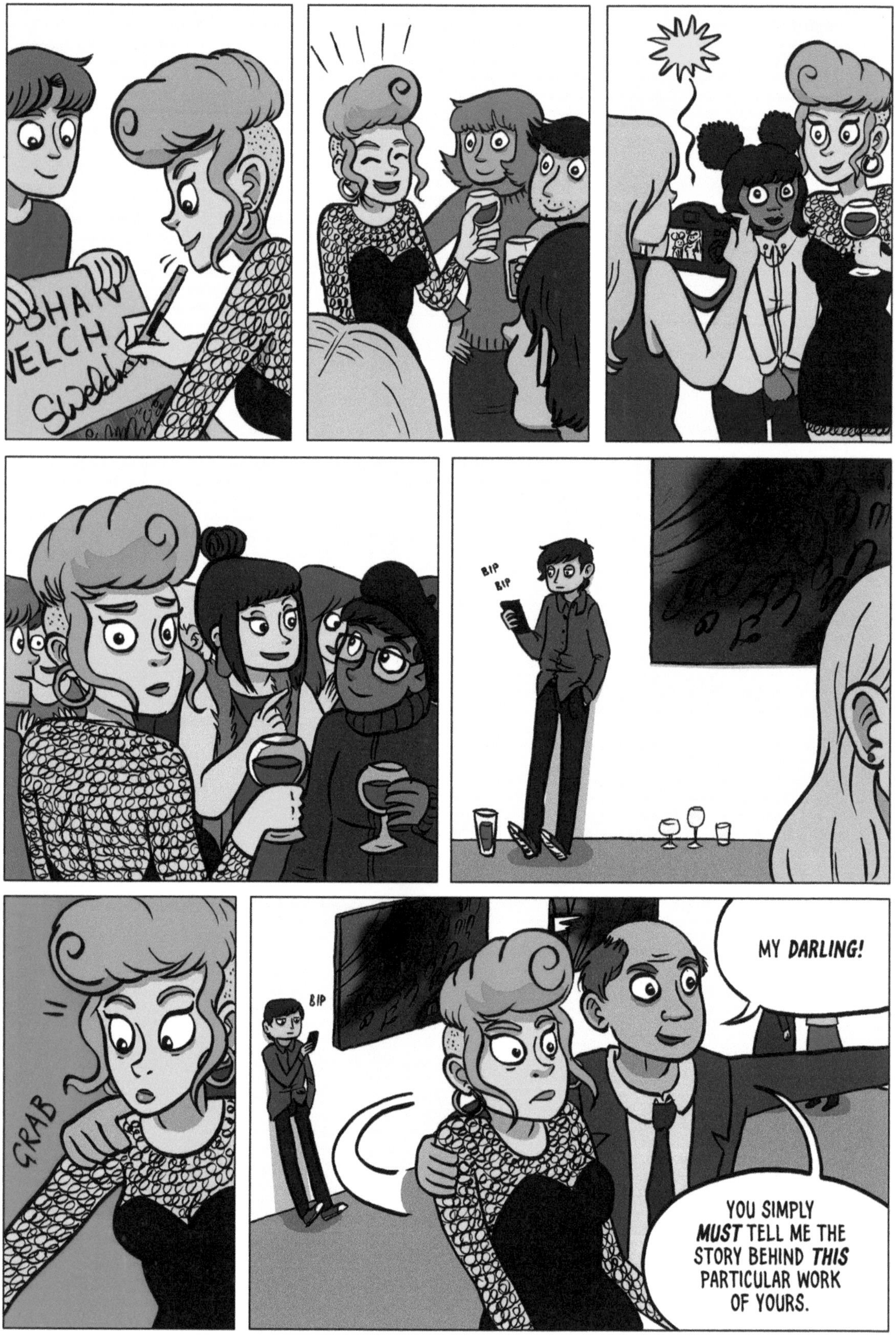
BHAN
VELCH
BIP
BIP
GRAB
BIP
MY **DARLING!**
YOU SIMPLY **MUST** TELL ME THE STORY BEHIND **THIS** PARTICULAR WORK OF YOURS.

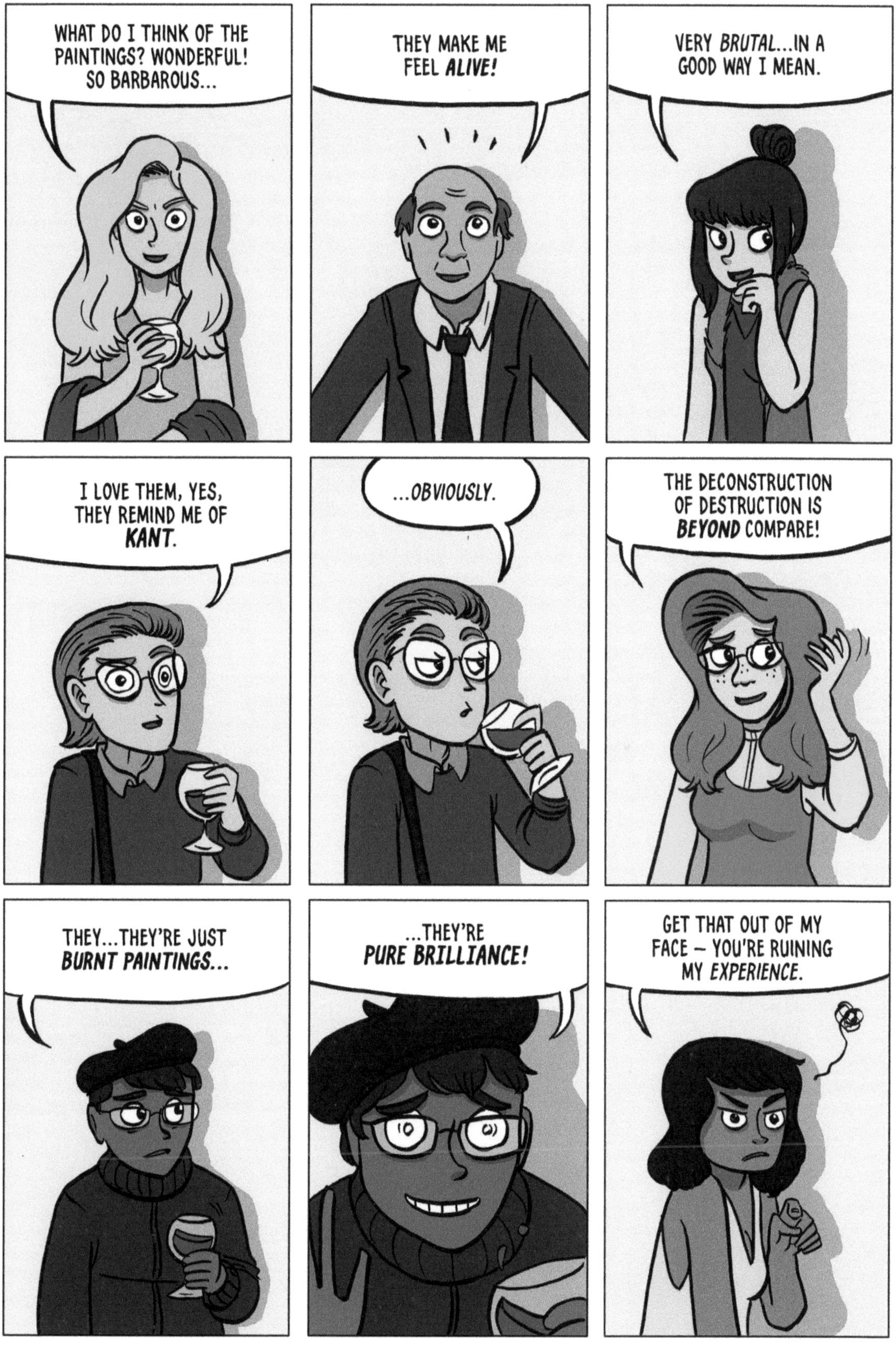
WHAT DO I THINK OF THE PAINTINGS? WONDERFUL! SO BARBAROUS...
THEY MAKE ME FEEL *ALIVE!*
VERY *BRUTAL*...IN A GOOD WAY I MEAN.
I LOVE THEM, YES, THEY REMIND ME OF ***KANT***.
...*OBVIOUSLY*.
THE DECONSTRUCTION OF DESTRUCTION IS ***BEYOND*** COMPARE!
THEY...THEY'RE JUST ***BURNT PAINTINGS...***
...THEY'RE ***PURE BRILLIANCE!***
GET THAT OUT OF MY FACE – YOU'RE RUINING MY *EXPERIENCE*.

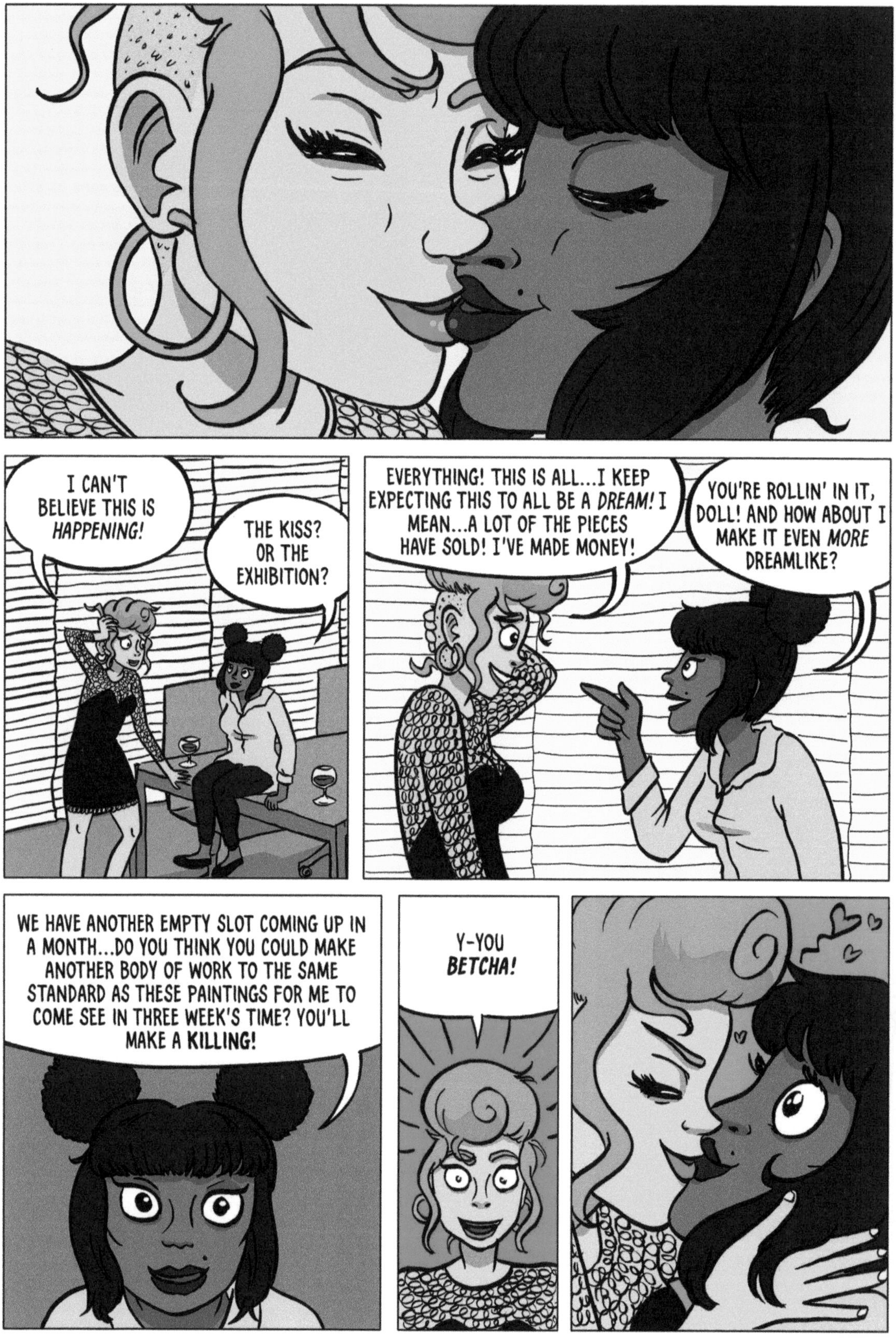
I CAN'T BELIEVE THIS IS *HAPPENING!*
THE KISS? OR THE EXHIBITION?
EVERYTHING! THIS IS ALL...I KEEP EXPECTING THIS TO ALL BE A *DREAM!* I MEAN...A LOT OF THE PIECES HAVE SOLD! I'VE MADE MONEY!
YOU'RE ROLLIN' IN IT, DOLL! AND HOW ABOUT I MAKE IT EVEN *MORE* DREAMLIKE?
WE HAVE ANOTHER EMPTY SLOT COMING UP IN A MONTH...DO YOU THINK YOU COULD MAKE ANOTHER BODY OF WORK TO THE SAME STANDARD AS THESE PAINTINGS FOR ME TO COME SEE IN THREE WEEK'S TIME? YOU'LL MAKE A **KILLING!**
Y-YOU ***BETCHA!***

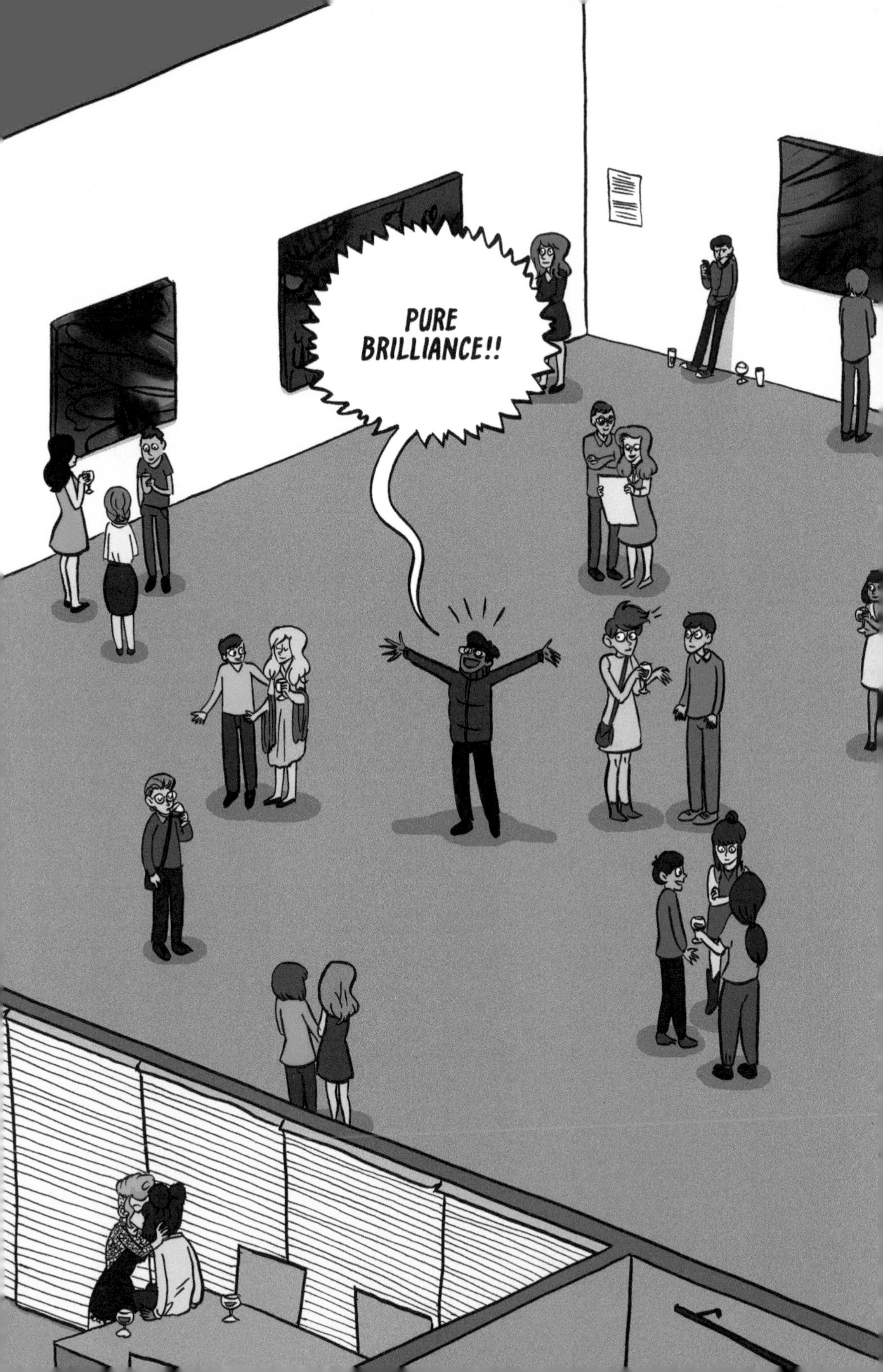
PURE BRILLIANCE!!

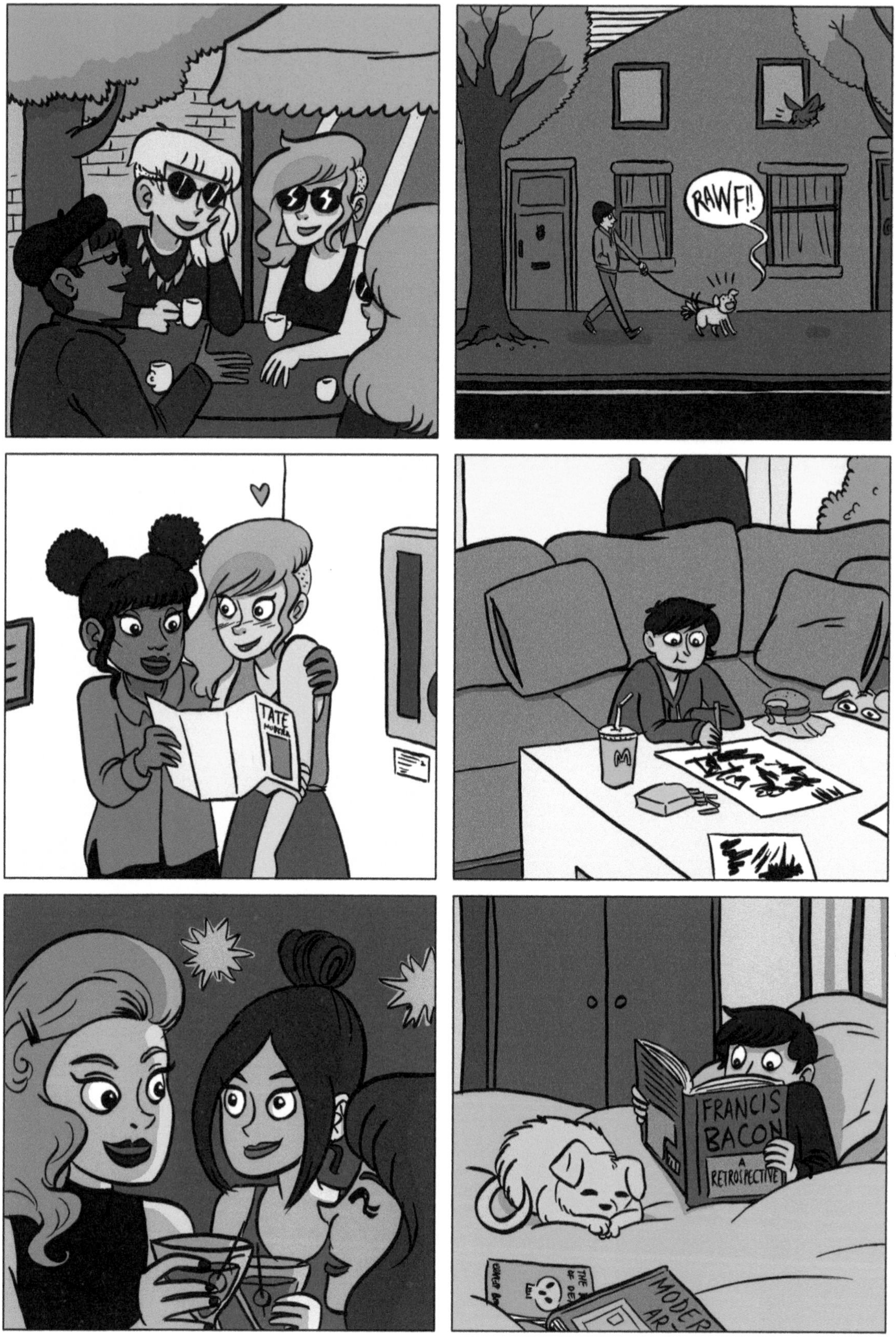
RAWF!!
TATE
FRANCIS BACON
A RETROSPECTIVE

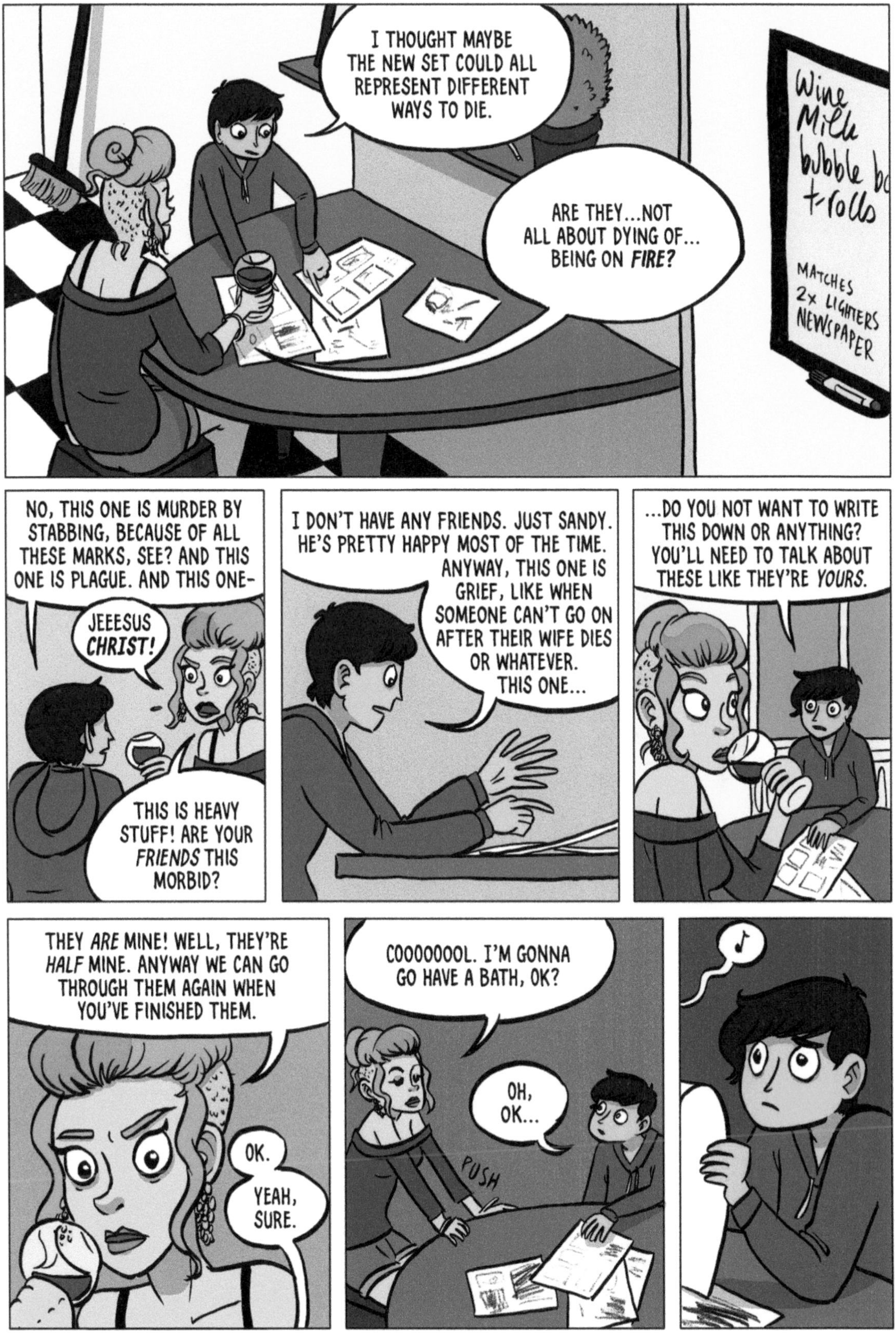

I THOUGHT MAYBE THE NEW SET COULD ALL REPRESENT DIFFERENT WAYS TO DIE.
ARE THEY...NOT ALL ABOUT DYING OF... BEING ON *FIRE?*
Wine
Milk
bubble b
+ rolls
MATCHES
2x LIGHTERS
NEWSPAPER
NO, THIS ONE IS MURDER BY STABBING, BECAUSE OF ALL THESE MARKS, SEE? AND THIS ONE IS PLAGUE. AND THIS ONE-
JEEESUS *CHRIST!*
THIS IS HEAVY STUFF! ARE YOUR *FRIENDS* THIS MORBID?
I DON'T HAVE ANY FRIENDS. JUST SANDY. HE'S PRETTY HAPPY MOST OF THE TIME.
ANYWAY, THIS ONE IS GRIEF, LIKE WHEN SOMEONE CAN'T GO ON AFTER THEIR WIFE DIES OR WHATEVER. THIS ONE...
...DO YOU NOT WANT TO WRITE THIS DOWN OR ANYTHING? YOU'LL NEED TO TALK ABOUT THESE LIKE THEY'RE *YOURS.*
THEY *ARE* MINE! WELL, THEY'RE *HALF* MINE. ANYWAY WE CAN GO THROUGH THEM AGAIN WHEN YOU'VE FINISHED THEM.
OK.
YEAH, SURE.
COOOOOOOL. I'M GONNA GO HAVE A BATH, OK?
OH, OK...
PUSH
♪

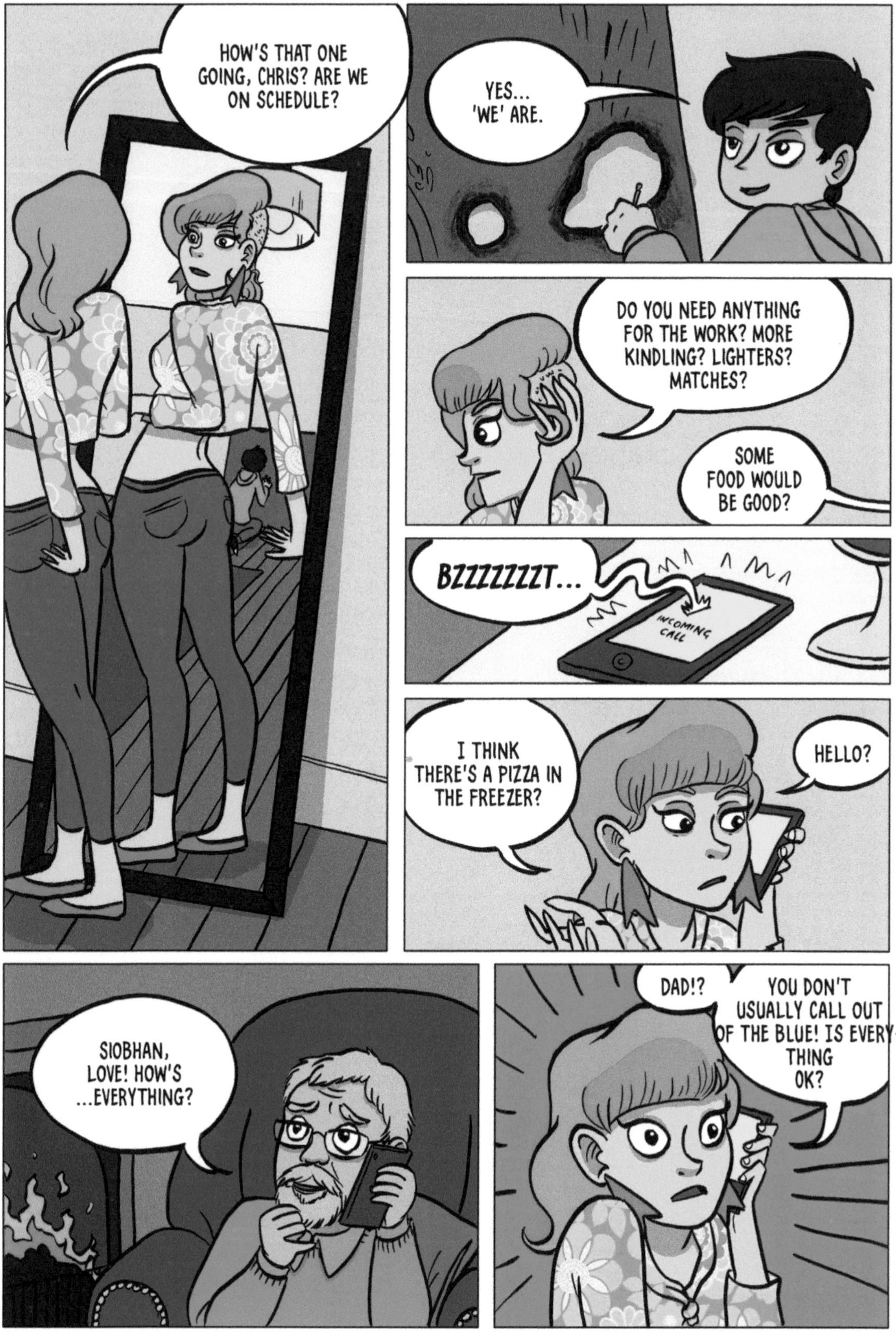
HOW'S THAT ONE GOING, CHRIS? ARE WE ON SCHEDULE?
YES... 'WE' ARE.
DO YOU NEED ANYTHING FOR THE WORK? MORE KINDLING? LIGHTERS? MATCHES?
SOME FOOD WOULD BE GOOD?
BZZZZZZZT...
INCOMING CALL
I THINK THERE'S A PIZZA IN THE FREEZER?
HELLO?
SIOBHAN, LOVE! HOW'S ...EVERYTHING?
DAD!?
YOU DON'T USUALLY CALL OUT OF THE BLUE! IS EVERY-THING OK?

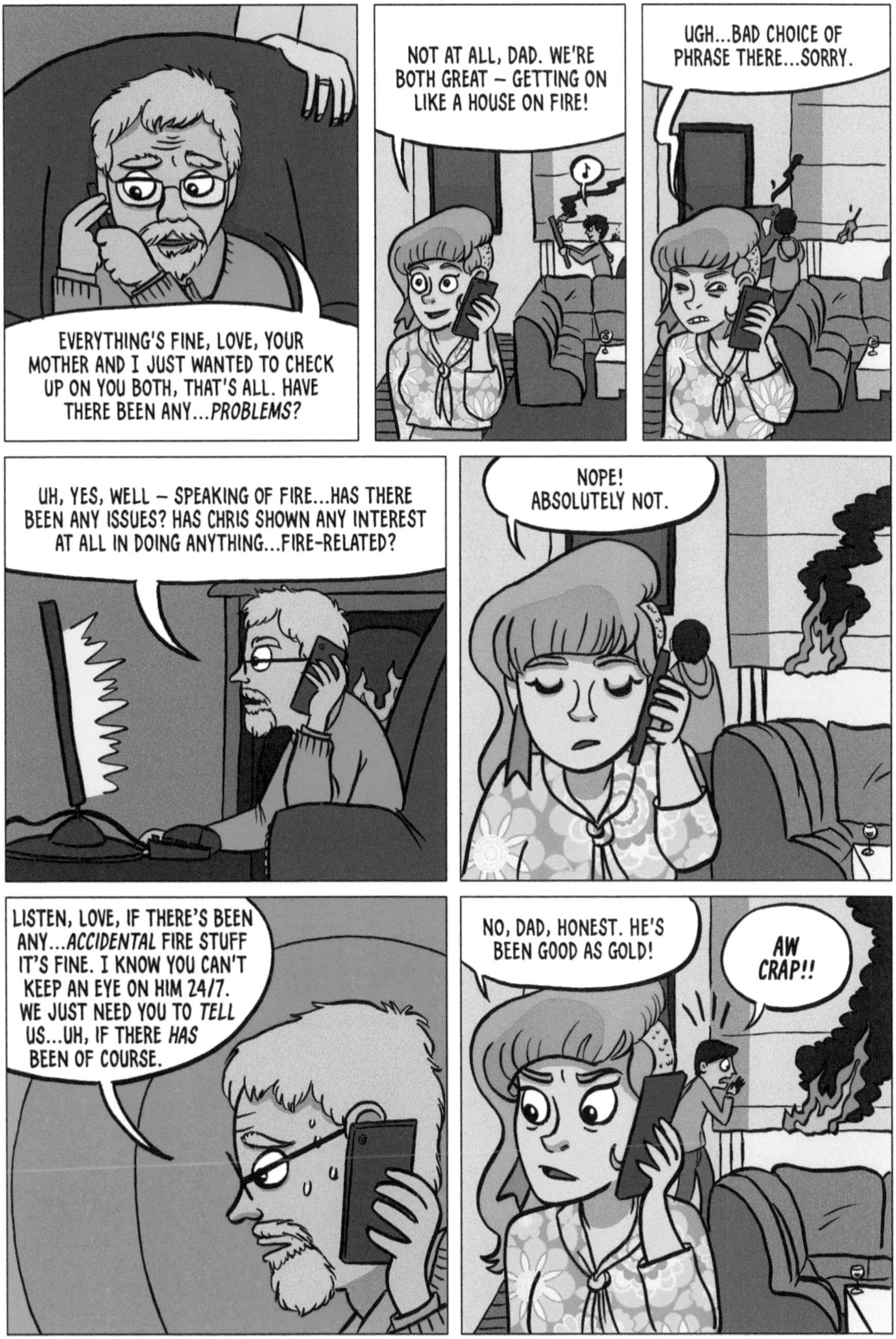
EVERYTHING'S FINE, LOVE, YOUR MOTHER AND I JUST WANTED TO CHECK UP ON YOU BOTH, THAT'S ALL. HAVE THERE BEEN ANY...*PROBLEMS?*
NOT AT ALL, DAD. WE'RE BOTH GREAT – GETTING ON LIKE A HOUSE ON FIRE!
♪
UGH...BAD CHOICE OF PHRASE THERE...SORRY.
UH, YES, WELL – SPEAKING OF FIRE...HAS THERE BEEN ANY ISSUES? HAS CHRIS SHOWN ANY INTEREST AT ALL IN DOING ANYTHING...FIRE-RELATED?
NOPE! ABSOLUTELY NOT.
LISTEN, LOVE, IF THERE'S BEEN ANY...*ACCIDENTAL* FIRE STUFF IT'S FINE. I KNOW YOU CAN'T KEEP AN EYE ON HIM 24/7. WE JUST NEED YOU TO *TELL* US...UH, IF THERE *HAS* BEEN OF COURSE.
NO, DAD, HONEST. HE'S BEEN GOOD AS GOLD!
AW CRAP!!

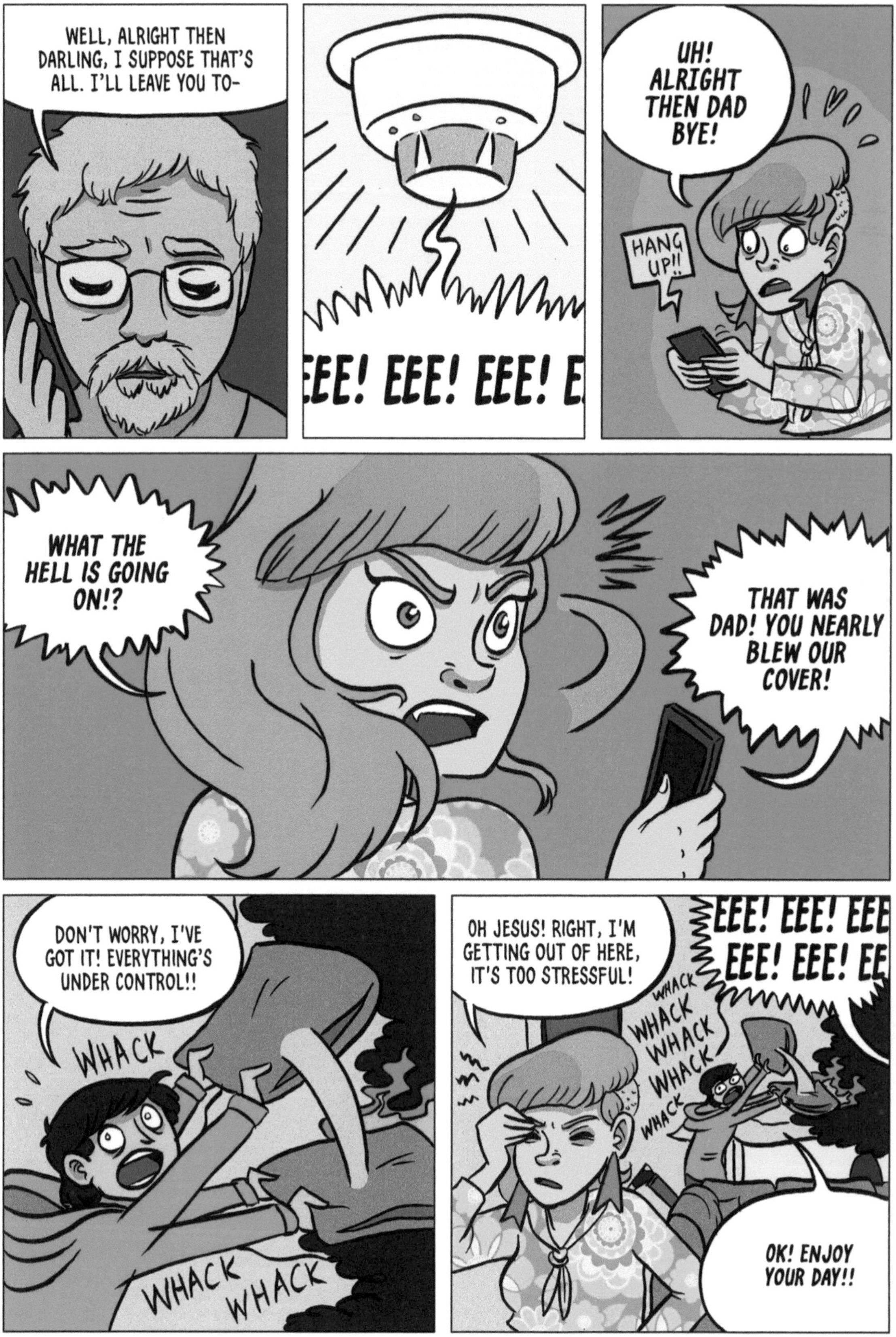
WELL, ALRIGHT THEN DARLING, I SUPPOSE THAT'S ALL. I'LL LEAVE YOU TO-
EEE! EEE! EEE!
UH! ALRIGHT THEN DAD BYE!
HANG UP!!
WHAT THE HELL IS GOING ON!?
THAT WAS DAD! YOU NEARLY BLEW OUR COVER!
DON'T WORRY, I'VE GOT IT! EVERYTHING'S UNDER CONTROL!!
WHACK
WHACK WHACK
OH JESUS! RIGHT, I'M GETTING OUT OF HERE, IT'S TOO STRESSFUL!
EEE! EEE! EEE! EEE! EEE!
WHACK WHACK WHACK WHACK WHACK
OK! ENJOY YOUR DAY!!

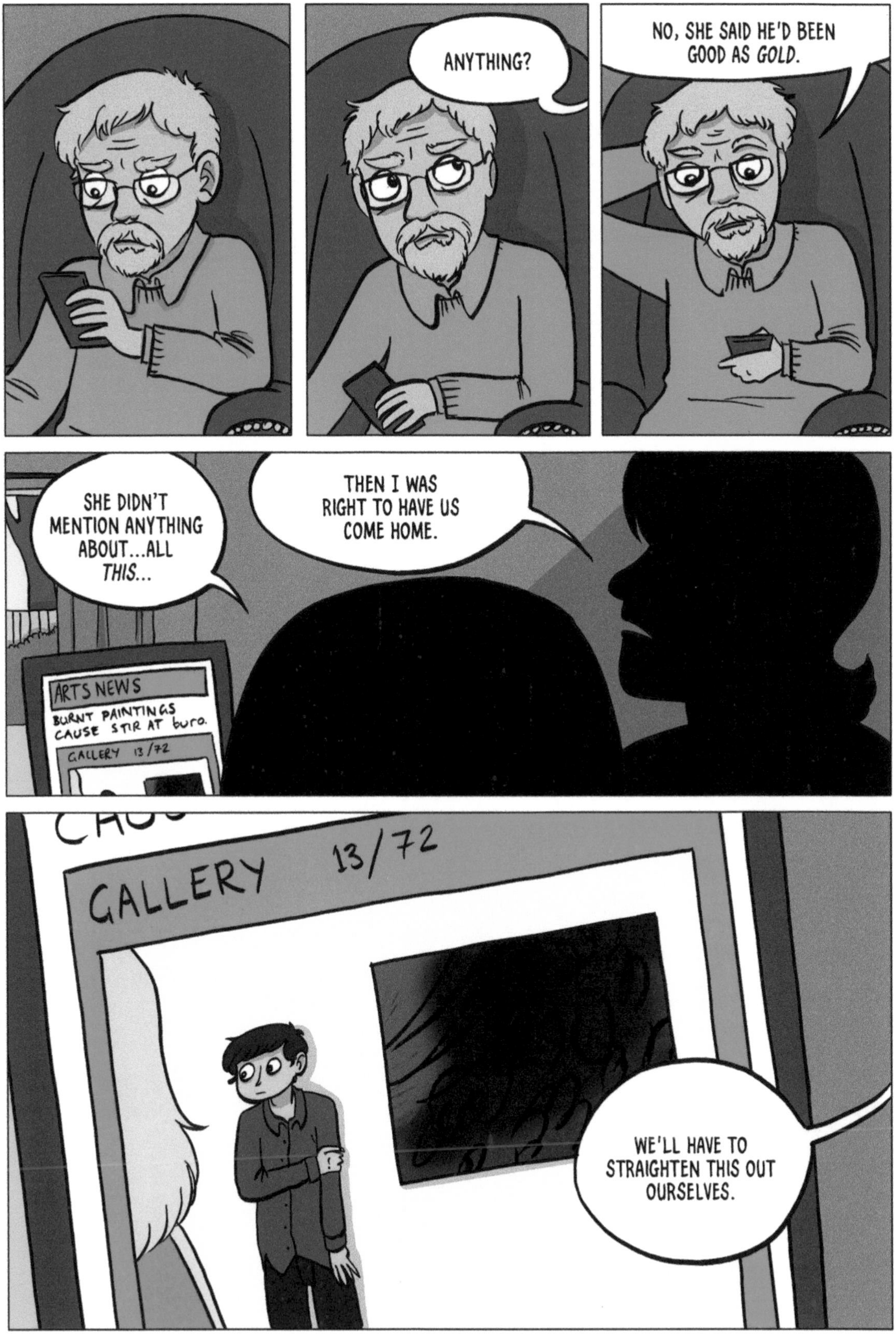
ANYTHING?
NO, SHE SAID HE'D BEEN GOOD AS *GOLD*.
SHE DIDN'T MENTION ANYTHING ABOUT...ALL *THIS*...
THEN I WAS RIGHT TO HAVE US COME HOME.
ARTS NEWS
BURNT PAINTINGS CAUSE STIR AT buro.
GALLERY 13/72
GALLERY 13/72
WE'LL HAVE TO STRAIGHTEN THIS OUT OURSELVES.

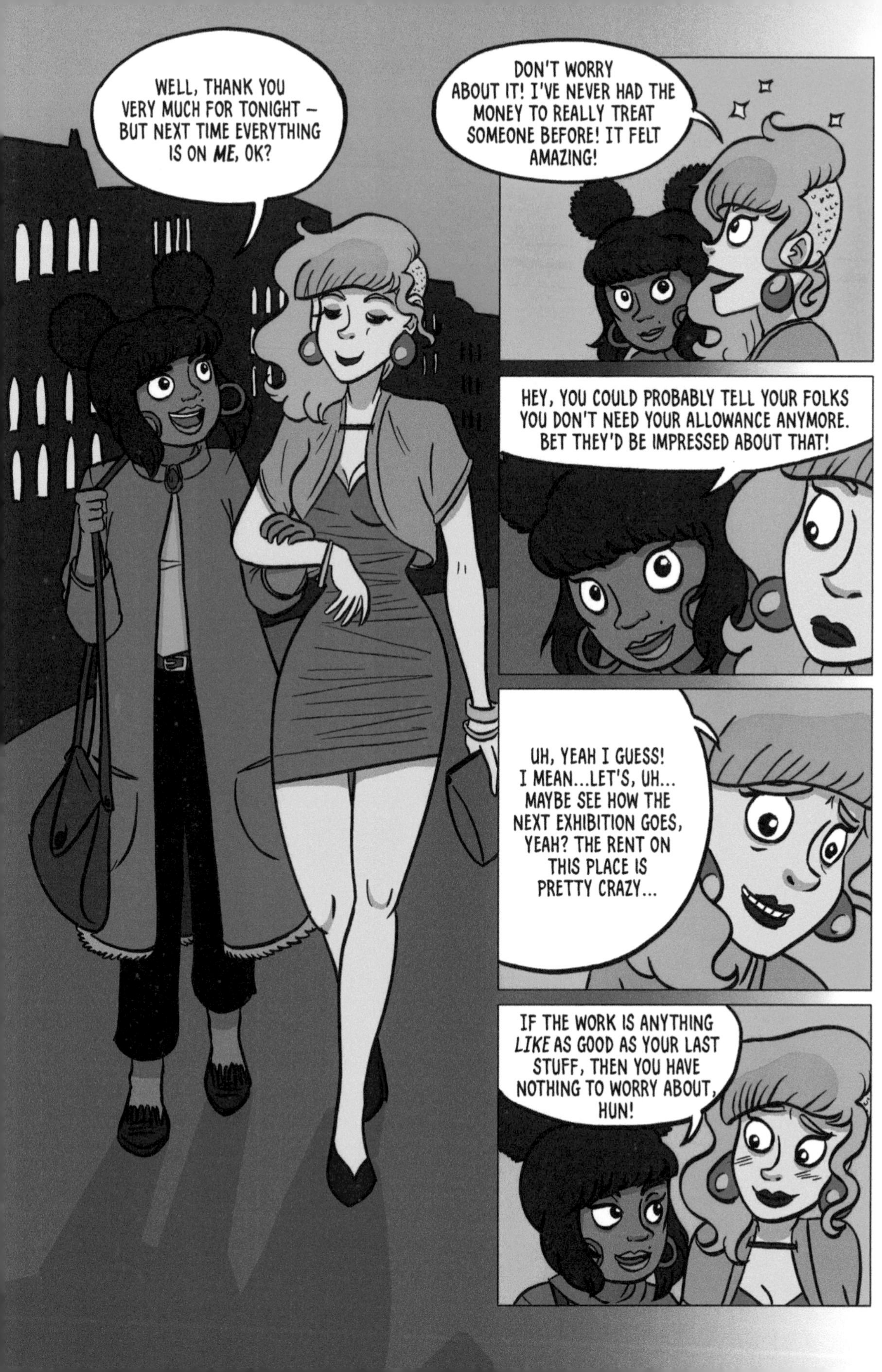
WELL, THANK YOU VERY MUCH FOR TONIGHT – BUT NEXT TIME EVERYTHING IS ON *ME*, OK?
DON'T WORRY ABOUT IT! I'VE NEVER HAD THE MONEY TO REALLY TREAT SOMEONE BEFORE! IT FELT AMAZING!
HEY, YOU COULD PROBABLY TELL YOUR FOLKS YOU DON'T NEED YOUR ALLOWANCE ANYMORE. BET THEY'D BE IMPRESSED ABOUT THAT!
UH, YEAH I GUESS! I MEAN...LET'S, UH... MAYBE SEE HOW THE NEXT EXHIBITION GOES, YEAH? THE RENT ON THIS PLACE IS PRETTY CRAZY...
IF THE WORK IS ANYTHING *LIKE* AS GOOD AS YOUR LAST STUFF, THEN YOU HAVE NOTHING TO WORRY ABOUT, HUN!

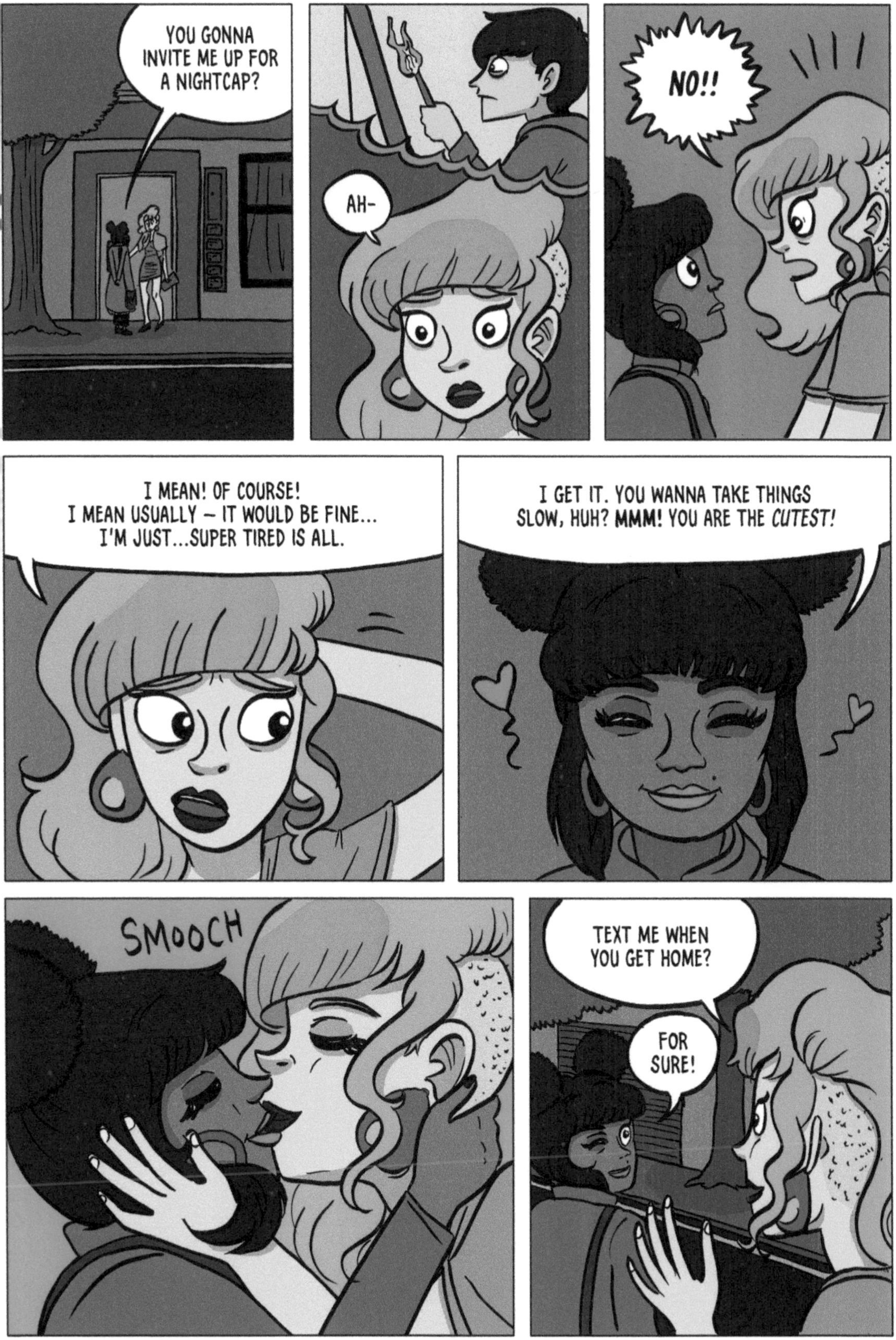
YOU GONNA INVITE ME UP FOR A NIGHTCAP?
AH-
NO!!
I MEAN! OF COURSE! I MEAN USUALLY – IT WOULD BE FINE... I'M JUST...SUPER TIRED IS ALL.
I GET IT. YOU WANNA TAKE THINGS SLOW, HUH? MMM! YOU ARE THE CUTEST!
SMOOCH
TEXT ME WHEN YOU GET HOME?
FOR SURE!

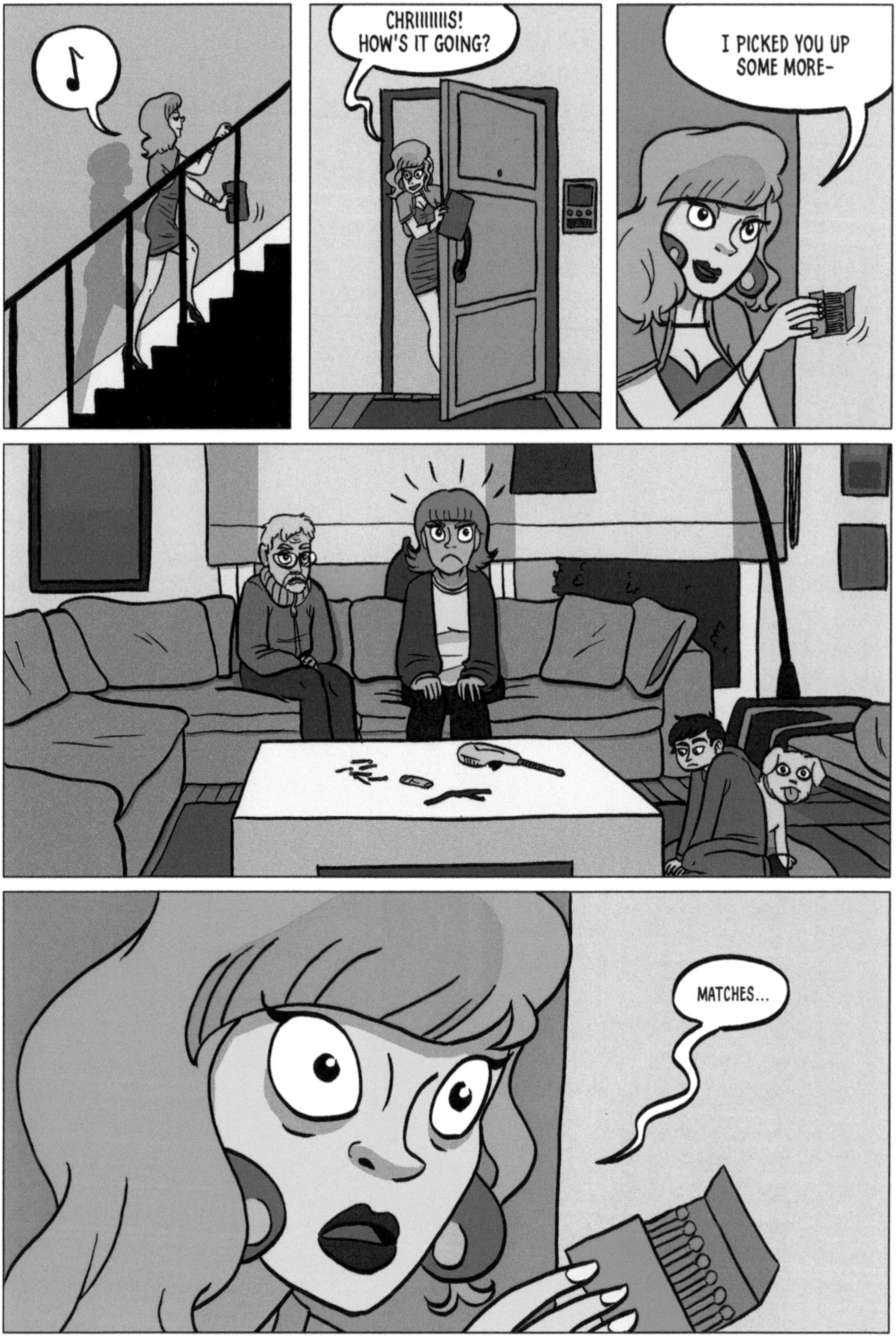
♪
CHRIIIIIIIS! HOW'S IT GOING?
I PICKED YOU UP SOME MORE-
MATCHES...

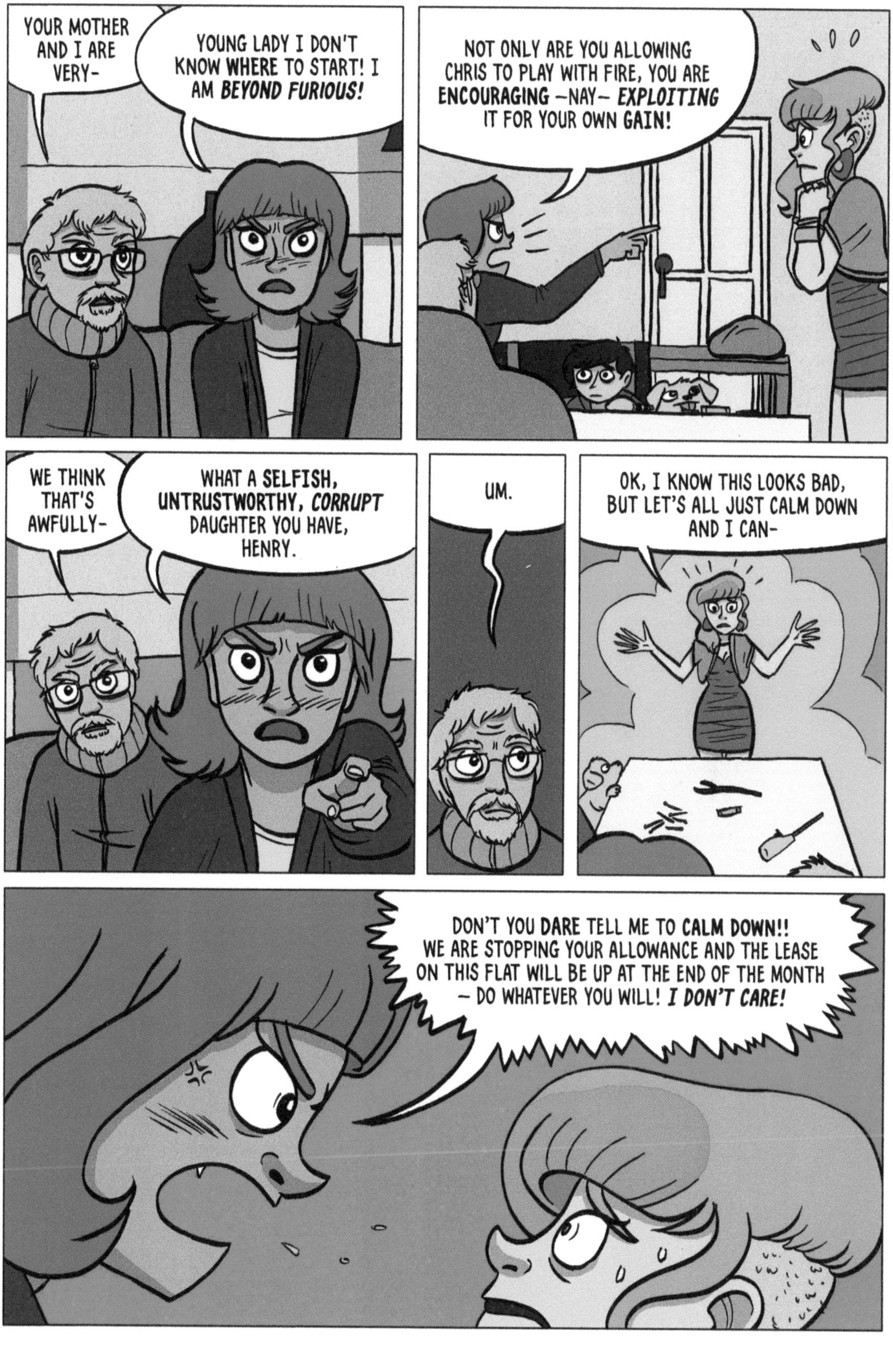
YOUR MOTHER AND I ARE VERY-
YOUNG LADY I DON'T KNOW **WHERE** TO START! I AM ***BEYOND FURIOUS!***
NOT ONLY ARE YOU ALLOWING CHRIS TO PLAY WITH FIRE, YOU ARE **ENCOURAGING** –NAY– ***EXPLOITING*** IT FOR YOUR OWN **GAIN!**
WE THINK THAT'S AWFULLY-
WHAT A **SELFISH, UNTRUSTWORTHY, *CORRUPT*** DAUGHTER YOU HAVE, HENRY.
UM.
OK, I KNOW THIS LOOKS BAD, BUT LET'S ALL JUST CALM DOWN AND I CAN-
DON'T YOU **DARE** TELL ME TO **CALM DOWN!!** WE ARE STOPPING YOUR ALLOWANCE AND THE LEASE ON THIS FLAT WILL BE UP AT THE END OF THE MONTH – DO WHATEVER YOU WILL! ***I DON'T CARE!***

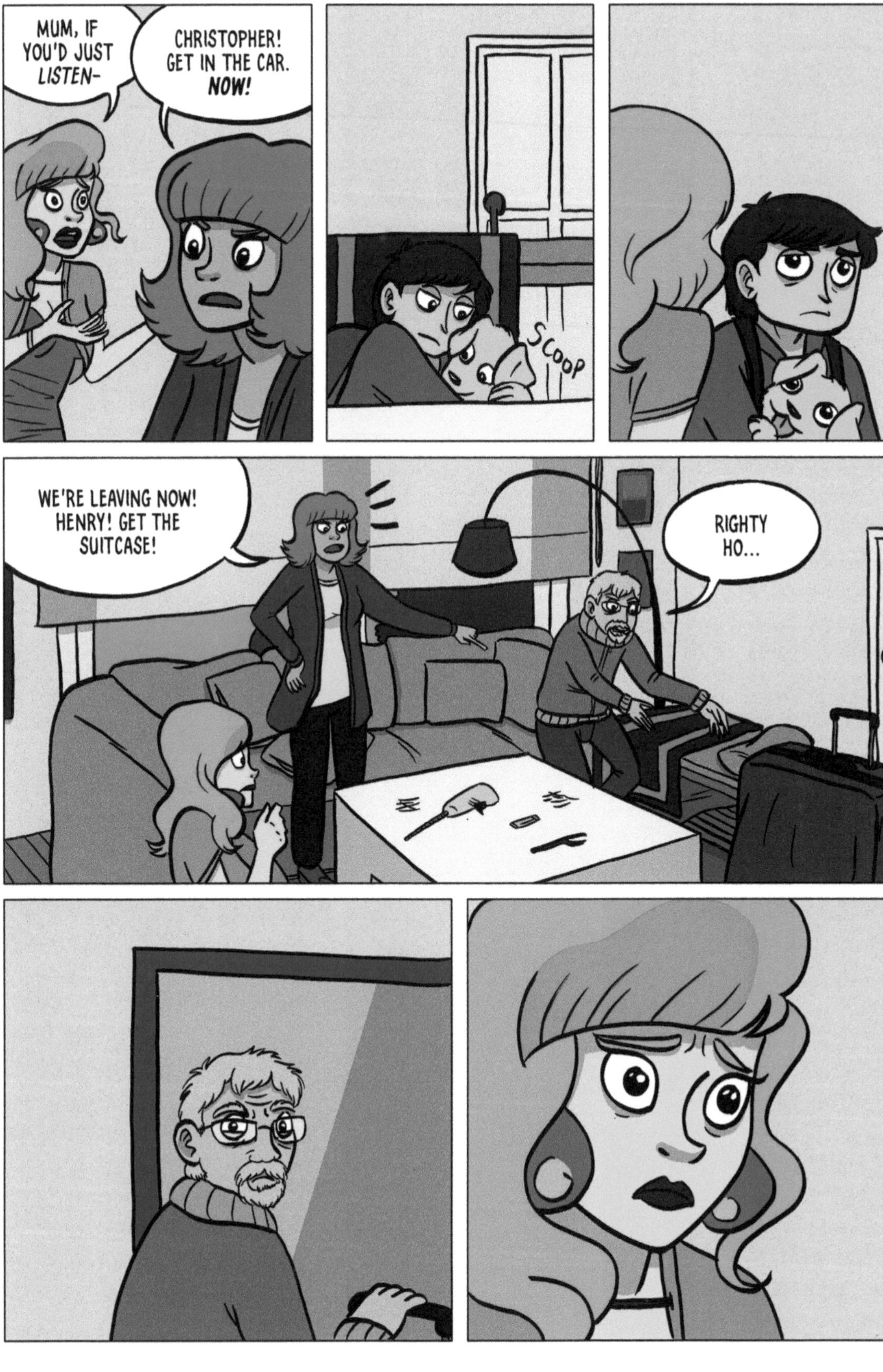

MUM, IF YOU'D JUST *LISTEN*-
CHRISTOPHER! GET IN THE CAR. ***NOW!***
SCOOP
WE'RE LEAVING NOW! HENRY! GET THE SUITCASE!
RIGHTY HO...

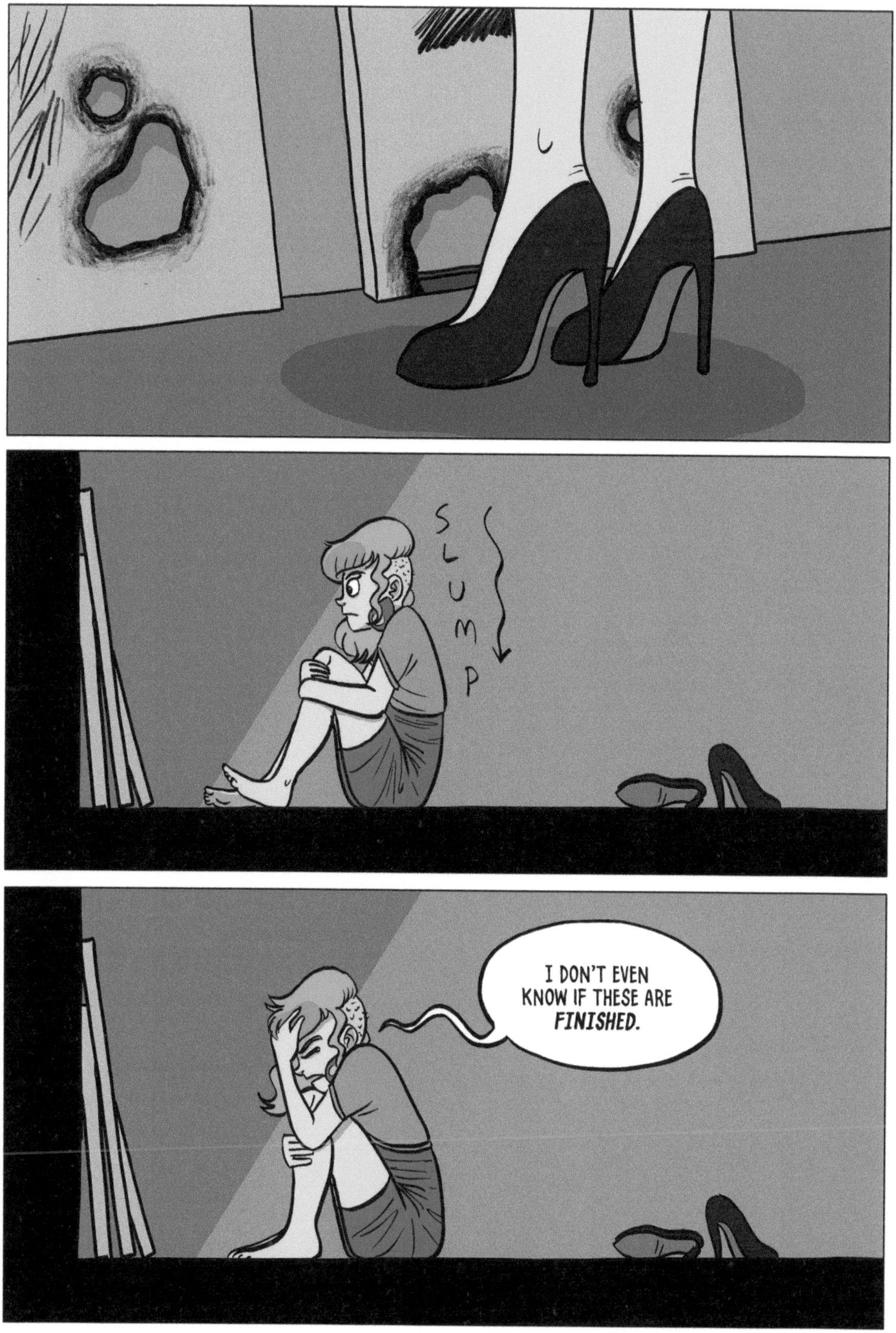
SLUMP
I DON'T EVEN KNOW IF THESE ARE *FINISHED.*

THREE WEEKS LATER.

I'VE BEEN UP ALMOST EVERY NIGHT WORKING ON THESE, MADDIE! IT'S BEEN TOUGH BUT I REALLY THINK THEY'RE SOMETHING SPECIAL!

I'M EXCITED TO SEE 'EM, HUN!

TA-DAH!

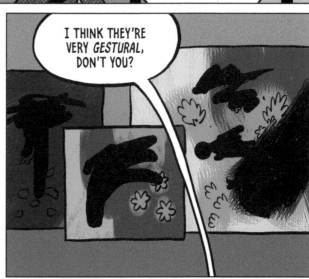

I THINK THEY'RE VERY *GESTURAL*, DON'T YOU?

LIKE, UH, LIKE WHAT YOU FIRST LIKED ABOUT MY EARLY WORK...BUT THESE ARE KIND OF... BOTH SORTS OF WORK PUT *TOGETHER*...LIKE A DECONSTRUCTION OF THEM, YEAH? AND VERY *ANGRY*. I HAD A LOT OF...**ANGER** WHEN I MADE THESE.

UHH, GOLLY, SIOBHAN...

I'M NOT GETTING *ANGER* FROM THESE...MORE LIKE... *DESPERATION*? THIS ISN'T THE SAME STANDARD OF MARK-MAKING YOU DEMONSTRATED WITH YOUR LAST BODY OF WORK.

BUT THEY'RE STILL *GOOD* THOUGH ...RIGHT?

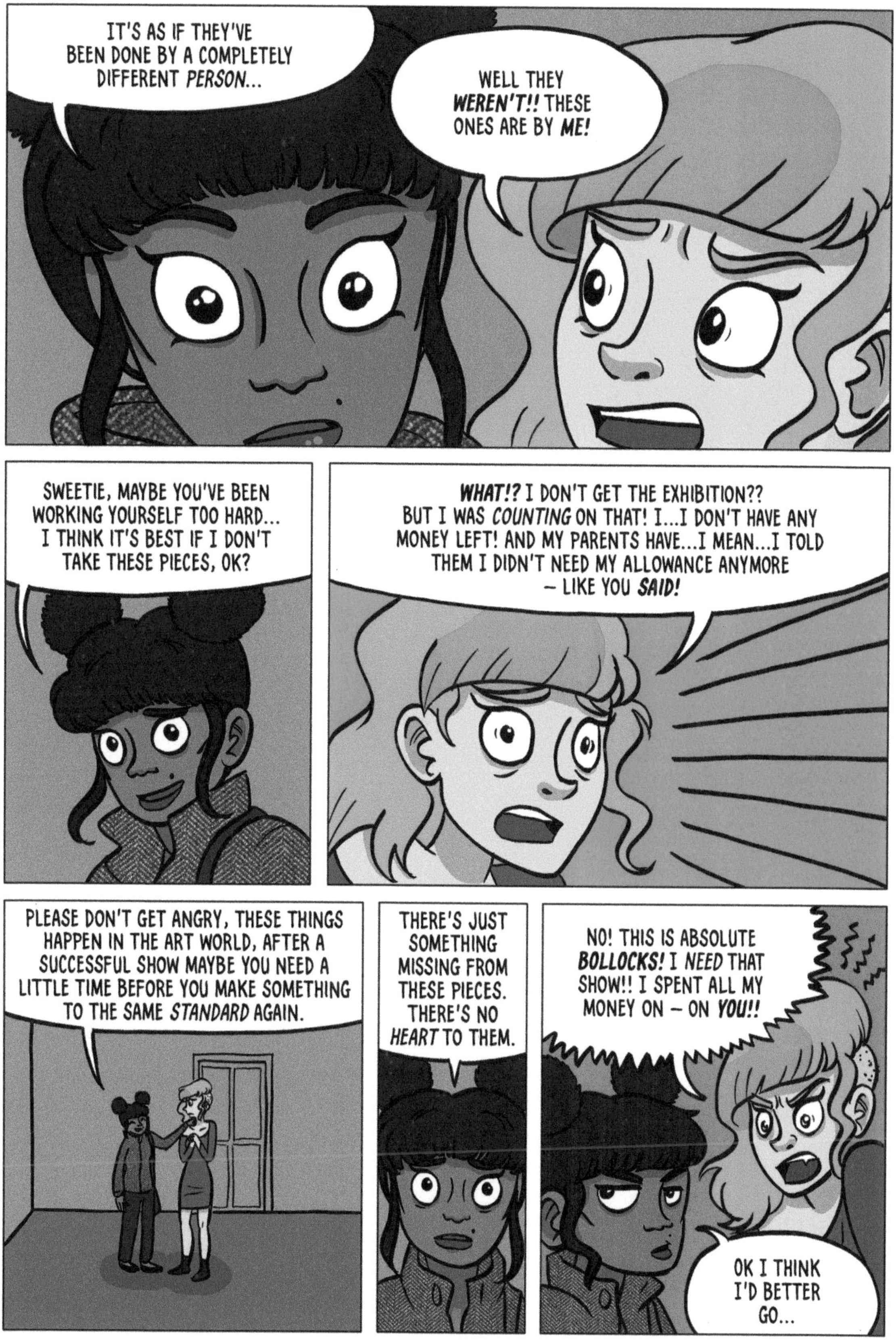
IT'S AS IF THEY'VE BEEN DONE BY A COMPLETELY DIFFERENT *PERSON*...
WELL THEY ***WEREN'T!!*** THESE ONES ARE BY ***ME!***
SWEETIE, MAYBE YOU'VE BEEN WORKING YOURSELF TOO HARD... I THINK IT'S BEST IF I DON'T TAKE THESE PIECES, OK?
WHAT!? I DON'T GET THE EXHIBITION?? BUT I WAS *COUNTING* ON THAT! I...I DON'T HAVE ANY MONEY LEFT! AND MY PARENTS HAVE...I MEAN...I TOLD THEM I DIDN'T NEED MY ALLOWANCE ANYMORE – LIKE YOU ***SAID!***
PLEASE DON'T GET ANGRY, THESE THINGS HAPPEN IN THE ART WORLD, AFTER A SUCCESSFUL SHOW MAYBE YOU NEED A LITTLE TIME BEFORE YOU MAKE SOMETHING TO THE SAME *STANDARD* AGAIN.
THERE'S JUST SOMETHING MISSING FROM THESE PIECES. THERE'S NO *HEART* TO THEM.
NO! THIS IS ABSOLUTE ***BOLLOCKS!*** I *NEED* THAT SHOW!! I SPENT ALL MY MONEY ON – ON ***YOU!!***
OK I THINK I'D BETTER GO...

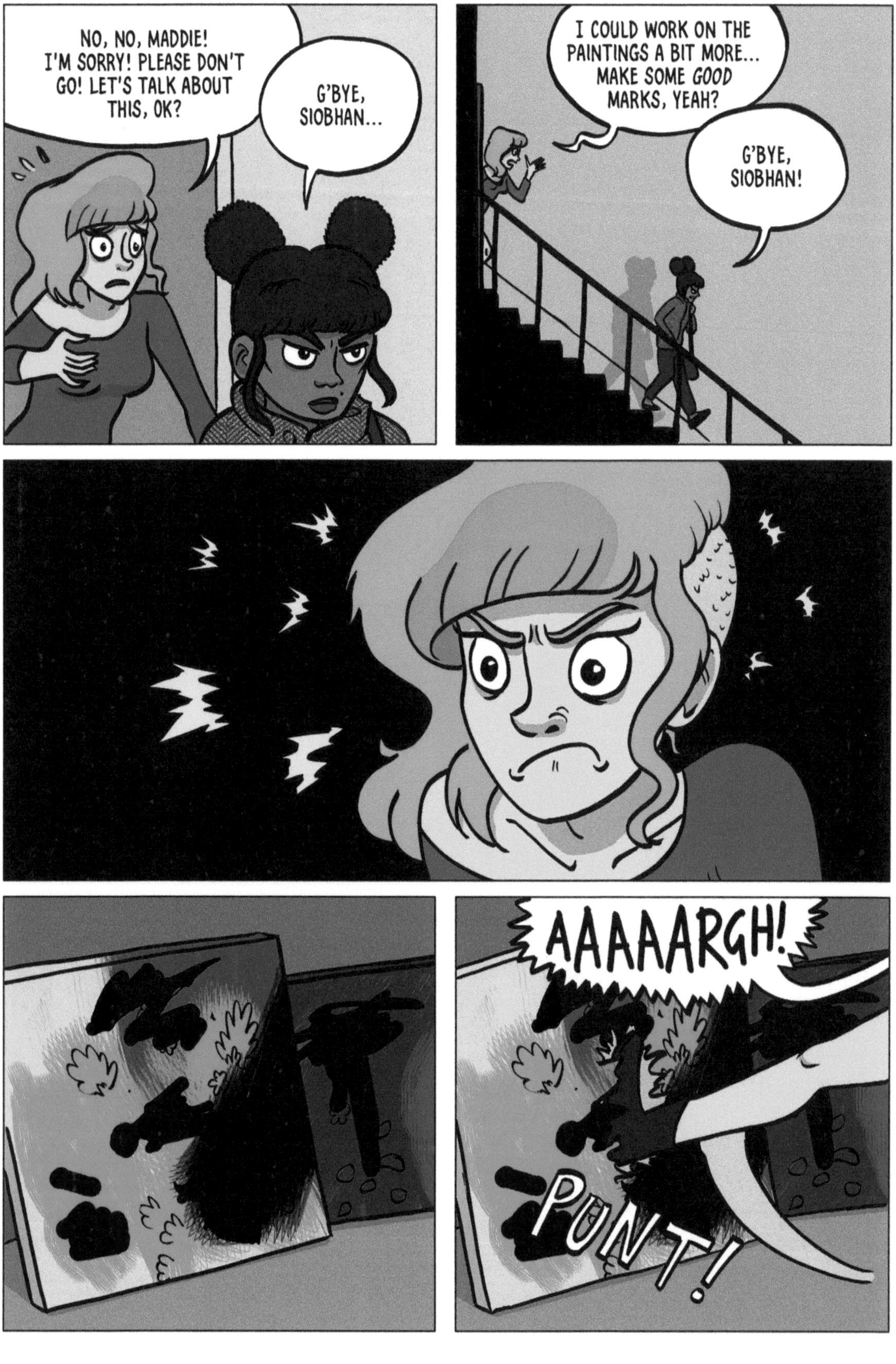
NO, NO, MADDIE! I'M SORRY! PLEASE DON'T GO! LET'S TALK ABOUT THIS, OK?
G'BYE, SIOBHAN...
I COULD WORK ON THE PAINTINGS A BIT MORE... MAKE SOME GOOD MARKS, YEAH?
G'BYE, SIOBHAN!
AAAAARGH!
PUNT!

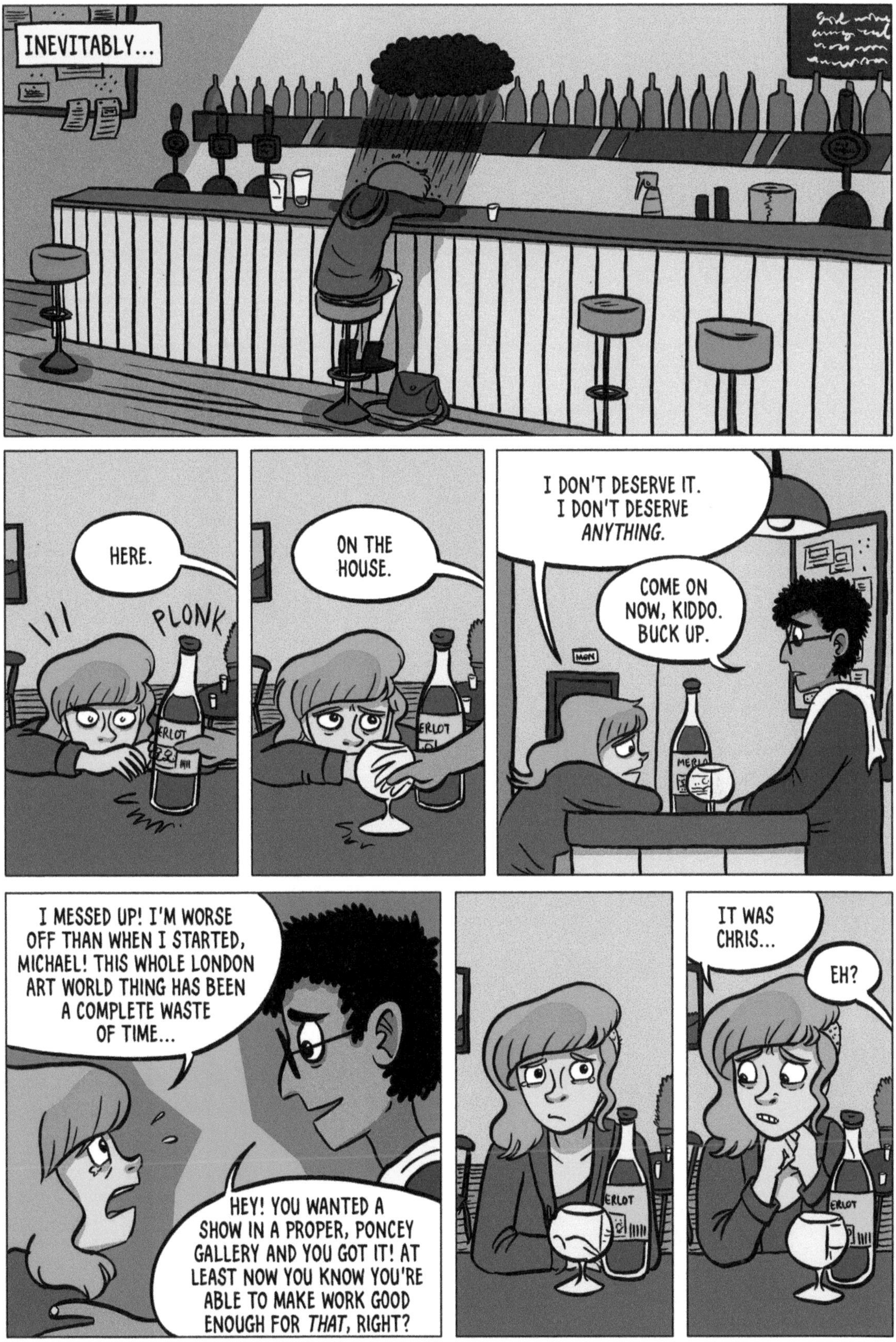

INEVITABLY...
HERE.
PLONK
ON THE HOUSE.
I DON'T DESERVE IT. I DON'T DESERVE *ANYTHING*.
COME ON NOW, KIDDO. BUCK UP.
I MESSED UP! I'M WORSE OFF THAN WHEN I STARTED, MICHAEL! THIS WHOLE LONDON ART WORLD THING HAS BEEN A COMPLETE WASTE OF TIME...
HEY! YOU WANTED A SHOW IN A PROPER, PONCEY GALLERY AND YOU GOT IT! AT LEAST NOW YOU KNOW YOU'RE ABLE TO MAKE WORK GOOD ENOUGH FOR *THAT*, RIGHT?
IT WAS CHRIS...
EH?

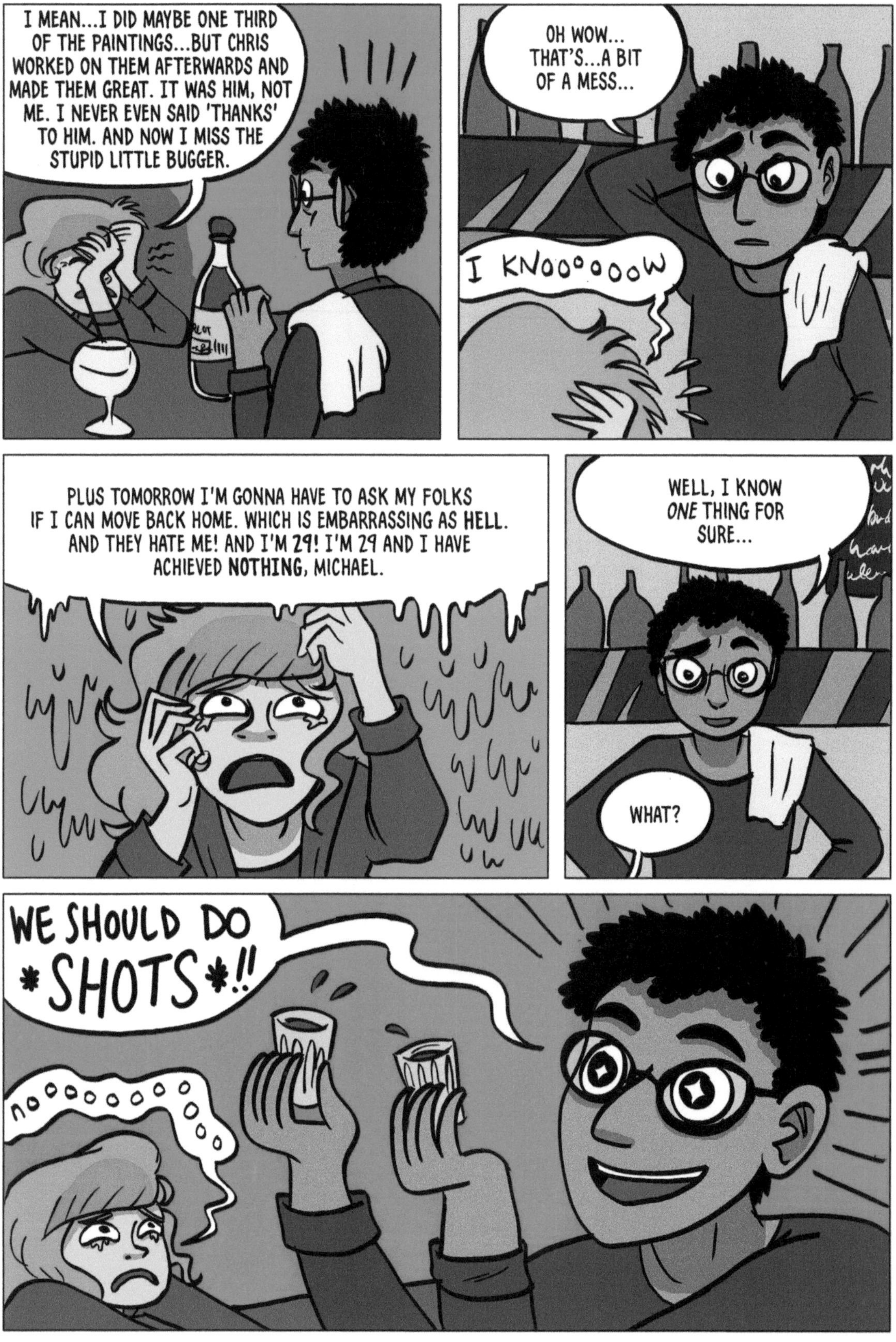
I MEAN...I DID MAYBE ONE THIRD OF THE PAINTINGS...BUT CHRIS WORKED ON THEM AFTERWARDS AND MADE THEM GREAT. IT WAS HIM, NOT ME. I NEVER EVEN SAID 'THANKS' TO HIM. AND NOW I MISS THE STUPID LITTLE BUGGER.
OH WOW... THAT'S...A BIT OF A MESS...
I KNOOOOOOW
PLUS TOMORROW I'M GONNA HAVE TO ASK MY FOLKS IF I CAN MOVE BACK HOME. WHICH IS EMBARRASSING AS HELL. AND THEY HATE ME! AND I'M 29! I'M 29 AND I HAVE ACHIEVED NOTHING, MICHAEL.
WELL, I KNOW ONE THING FOR SURE...
WHAT?
WE SHOULD DO *SHOTS*!!
noooooooooooo

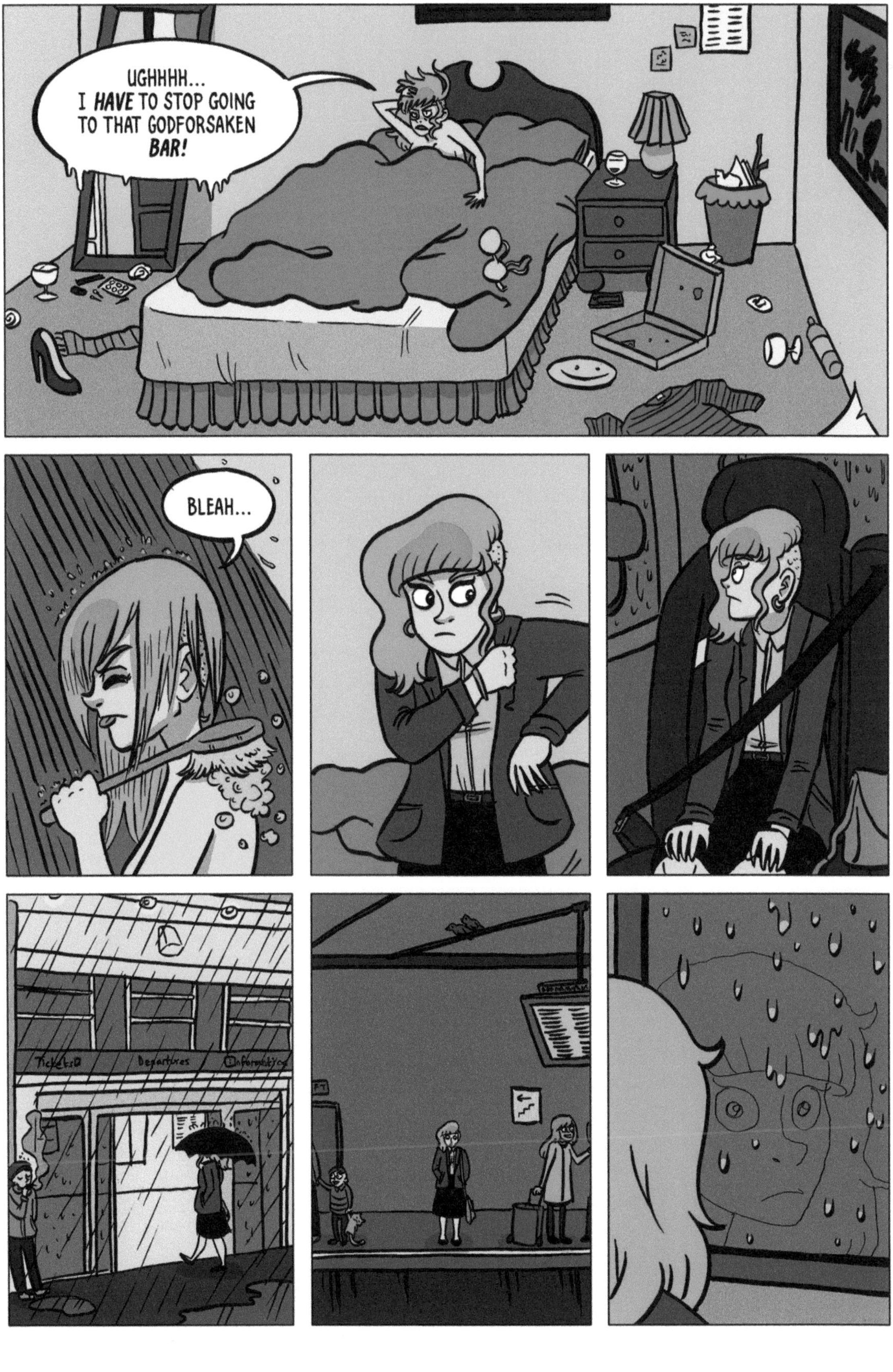
UGHHHH... I *HAVE* TO STOP GOING TO THAT GODFORSAKEN *BAR!*
BLEAH...
Departures

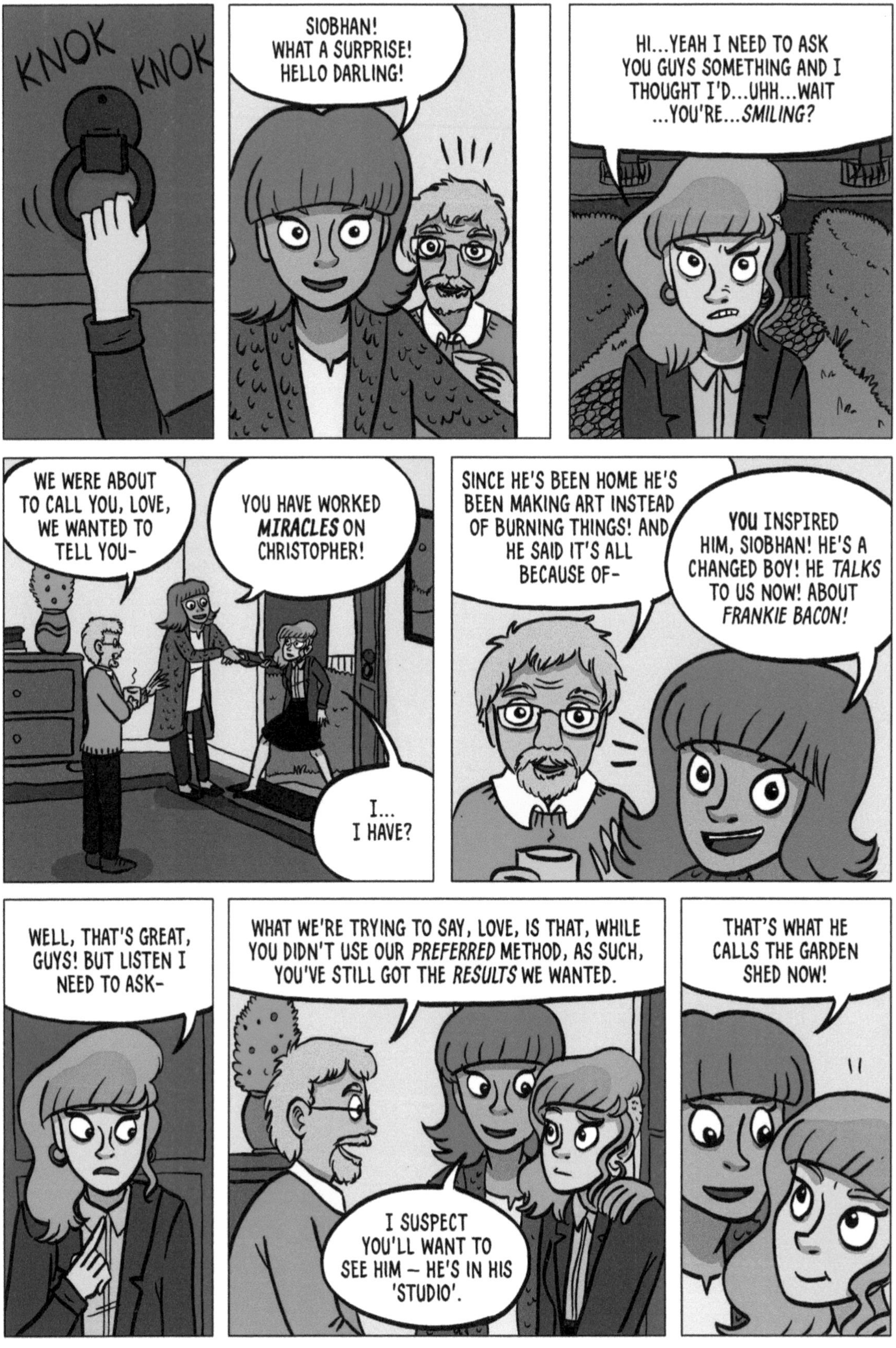
KNOK KNOK
SIOBHAN! WHAT A SURPRISE! HELLO DARLING!
HI...YEAH I NEED TO ASK YOU GUYS SOMETHING AND I THOUGHT I'D...UHH...WAIT ...YOU'RE...*SMILING*?
WE WERE ABOUT TO CALL YOU, LOVE, WE WANTED TO TELL YOU-
YOU HAVE WORKED ***MIRACLES*** ON CHRISTOPHER!
I... I HAVE?
SINCE HE'S BEEN HOME HE'S BEEN MAKING ART INSTEAD OF BURNING THINGS! AND HE SAID IT'S ALL BECAUSE OF-
YOU INSPIRED HIM, SIOBHAN! HE'S A CHANGED BOY! HE *TALKS* TO US NOW! ABOUT *FRANKIE BACON!*
WELL, THAT'S GREAT, GUYS! BUT LISTEN I NEED TO ASK-
WHAT WE'RE TRYING TO SAY, LOVE, IS THAT, WHILE YOU DIDN'T USE OUR *PREFERRED* METHOD, AS SUCH, YOU'VE STILL GOT THE *RESULTS* WE WANTED.
I SUSPECT YOU'LL WANT TO SEE HIM – HE'S IN HIS 'STUDIO'.
THAT'S WHAT HE CALLS THE GARDEN SHED NOW!

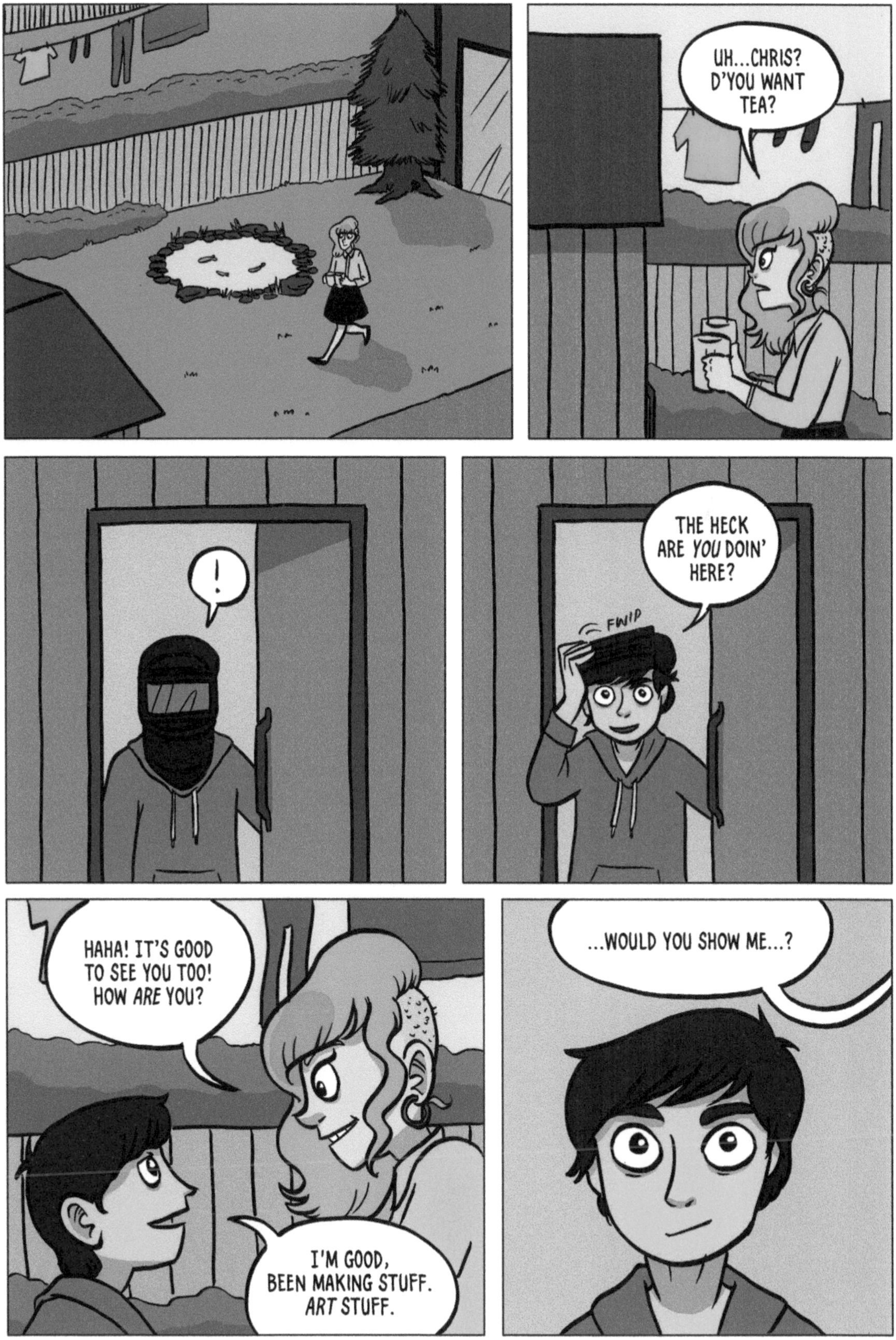
UH...CHRIS? D'YOU WANT TEA?
!
THE HECK ARE *YOU* DOIN' HERE?
FWIP
HAHA! IT'S GOOD TO SEE YOU TOO! HOW *ARE* YOU?
I'M GOOD, BEEN MAKING STUFF. *ART* STUFF.
...WOULD YOU SHOW ME...?

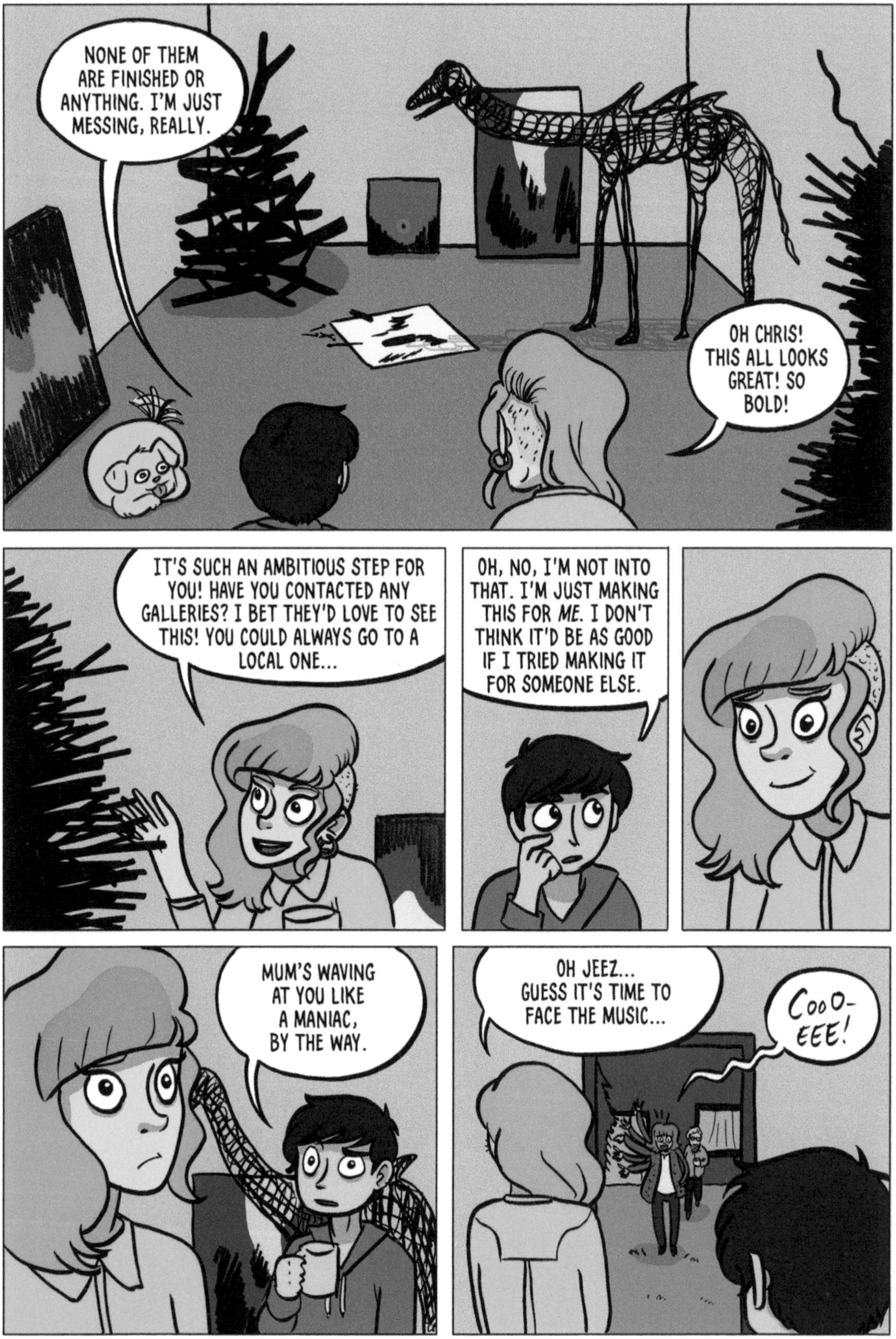
NONE OF THEM ARE FINISHED OR ANYTHING. I'M JUST MESSING, REALLY.
OH CHRIS! THIS ALL LOOKS GREAT! SO BOLD!
IT'S SUCH AN AMBITIOUS STEP FOR YOU! HAVE YOU CONTACTED ANY GALLERIES? I BET THEY'D LOVE TO SEE THIS! YOU COULD ALWAYS GO TO A LOCAL ONE...
OH, NO, I'M NOT INTO THAT. I'M JUST MAKING THIS FOR *ME*. I DON'T THINK IT'D BE AS GOOD IF I TRIED MAKING IT FOR SOMEONE ELSE.
MUM'S WAVING AT YOU LIKE A MANIAC, BY THE WAY.
OH JEEZ... GUESS IT'S TIME TO FACE THE MUSIC...
COOO-EEE!

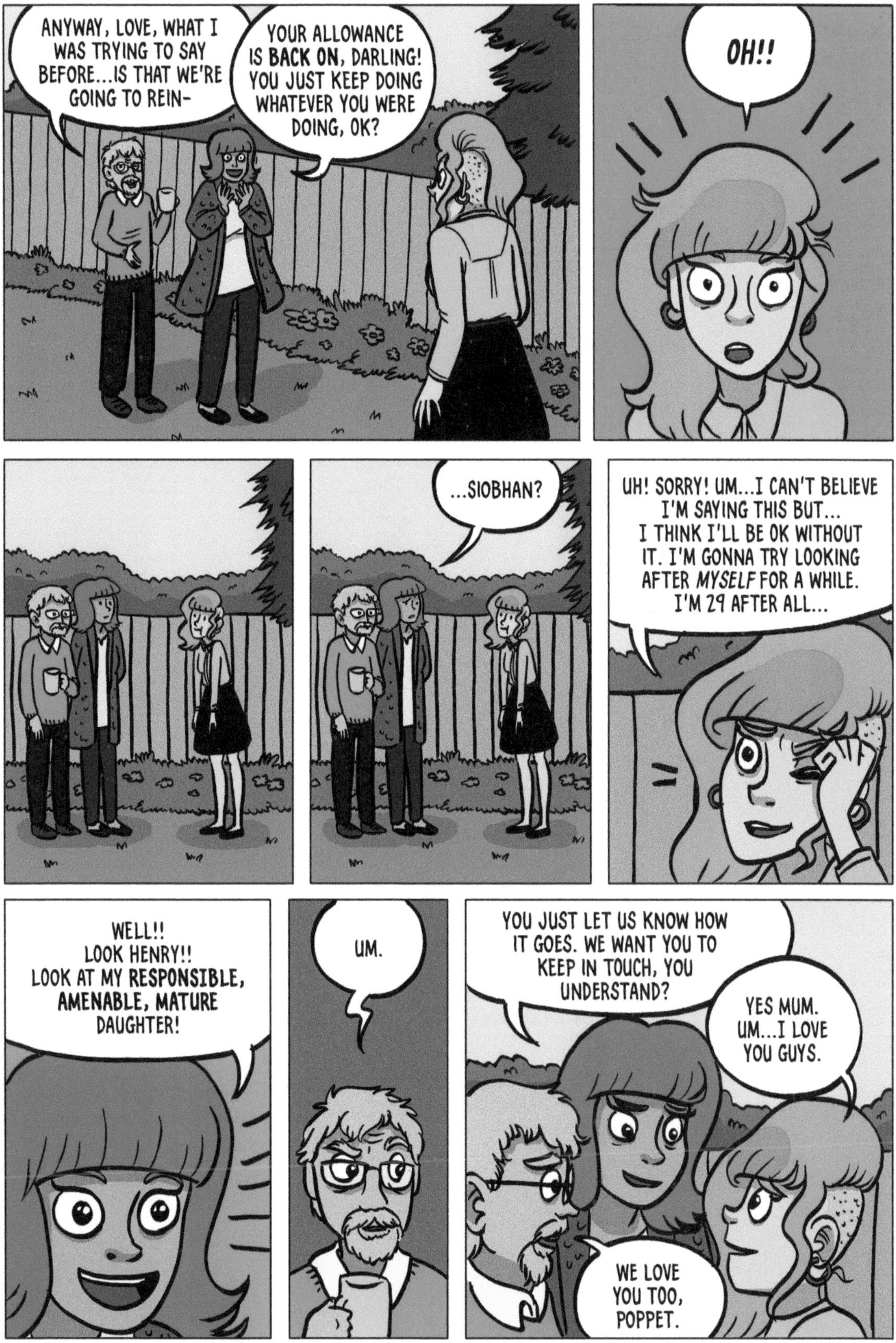
ANYWAY, LOVE, WHAT I WAS TRYING TO SAY BEFORE...IS THAT WE'RE GOING TO REIN-
YOUR ALLOWANCE IS **BACK ON**, DARLING! YOU JUST KEEP DOING WHATEVER YOU WERE DOING, OK?
OH!!
...SIOBHAN?
UH! SORRY! UM...I CAN'T BELIEVE I'M SAYING THIS BUT... I THINK I'LL BE OK WITHOUT IT. I'M GONNA TRY LOOKING AFTER *MYSELF* FOR A WHILE. I'M 29 AFTER ALL...
WELL!! LOOK HENRY!! LOOK AT MY **RESPONSIBLE, AMENABLE, MATURE** DAUGHTER!
UM.
YOU JUST LET US KNOW HOW IT GOES. WE WANT YOU TO KEEP IN TOUCH, YOU UNDERSTAND?
YES MUM. UM...I LOVE YOU GUYS.
WE LOVE YOU TOO, POPPET.

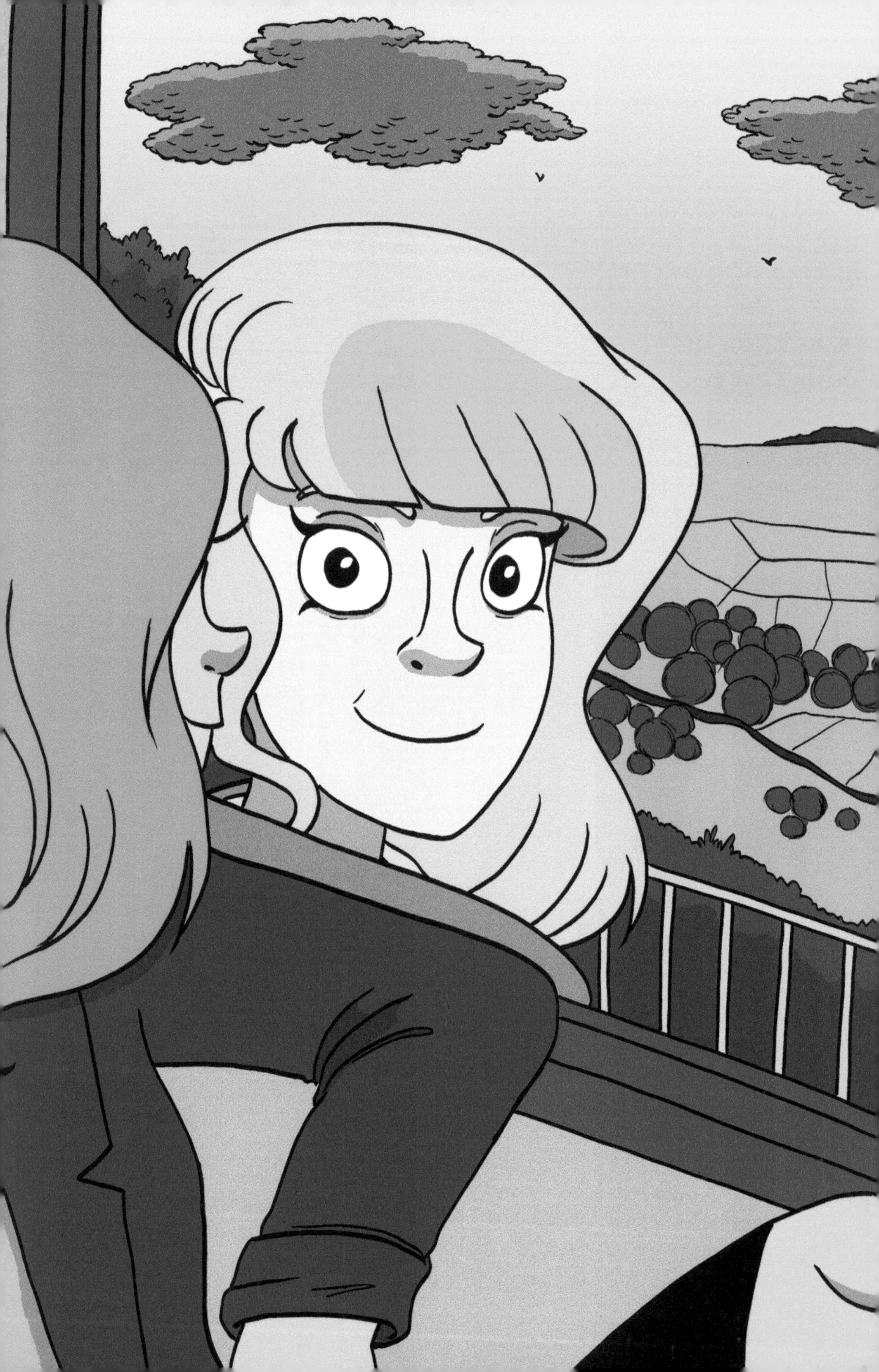

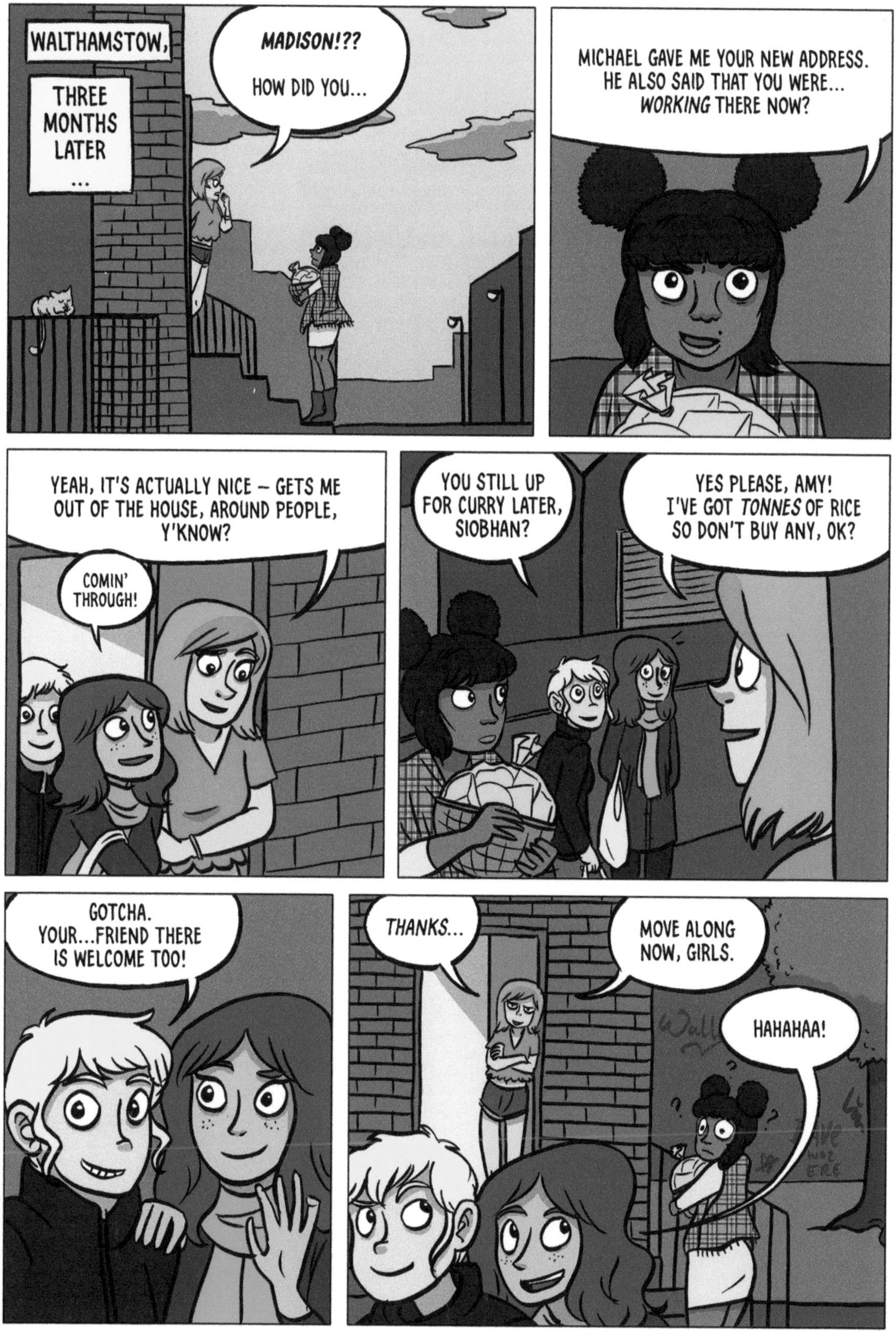
WALTHAMSTOW,
THREE MONTHS LATER ...
MADISON!?? HOW DID YOU...
MICHAEL GAVE ME YOUR NEW ADDRESS. HE ALSO SAID THAT YOU WERE... WORKING THERE NOW?
YEAH, IT'S ACTUALLY NICE – GETS ME OUT OF THE HOUSE, AROUND PEOPLE, Y'KNOW?
COMIN' THROUGH!
YOU STILL UP FOR CURRY LATER, SIOBHAN?
YES PLEASE, AMY! I'VE GOT TONNES OF RICE SO DON'T BUY ANY, OK?
GOTCHA. YOUR...FRIEND THERE IS WELCOME TOO!
THANKS...
MOVE ALONG NOW, GIRLS.
HAHAHAA!

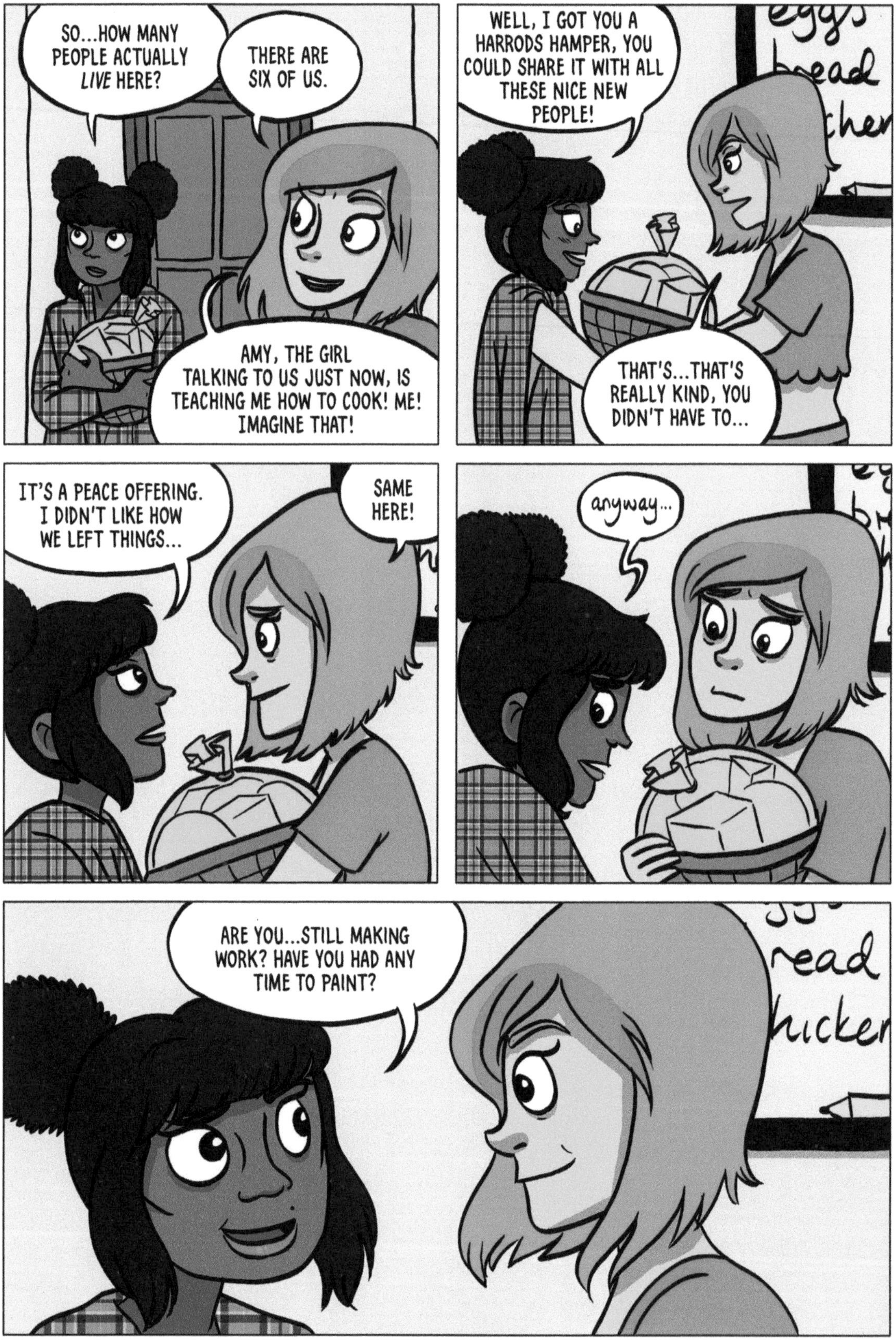
SO...HOW MANY PEOPLE ACTUALLY *LIVE* HERE?
THERE ARE SIX OF US.
AMY, THE GIRL TALKING TO US JUST NOW, IS TEACHING ME HOW TO COOK! ME! IMAGINE THAT!
WELL, I GOT YOU A HARRODS HAMPER, YOU COULD SHARE IT WITH ALL THESE NICE NEW PEOPLE!
THAT'S...THAT'S REALLY KIND, YOU DIDN'T HAVE TO...
IT'S A PEACE OFFERING. I DIDN'T LIKE HOW WE LEFT THINGS...
SAME HERE!
anyway...
ARE YOU...STILL MAKING WORK? HAVE YOU HAD ANY TIME TO PAINT?

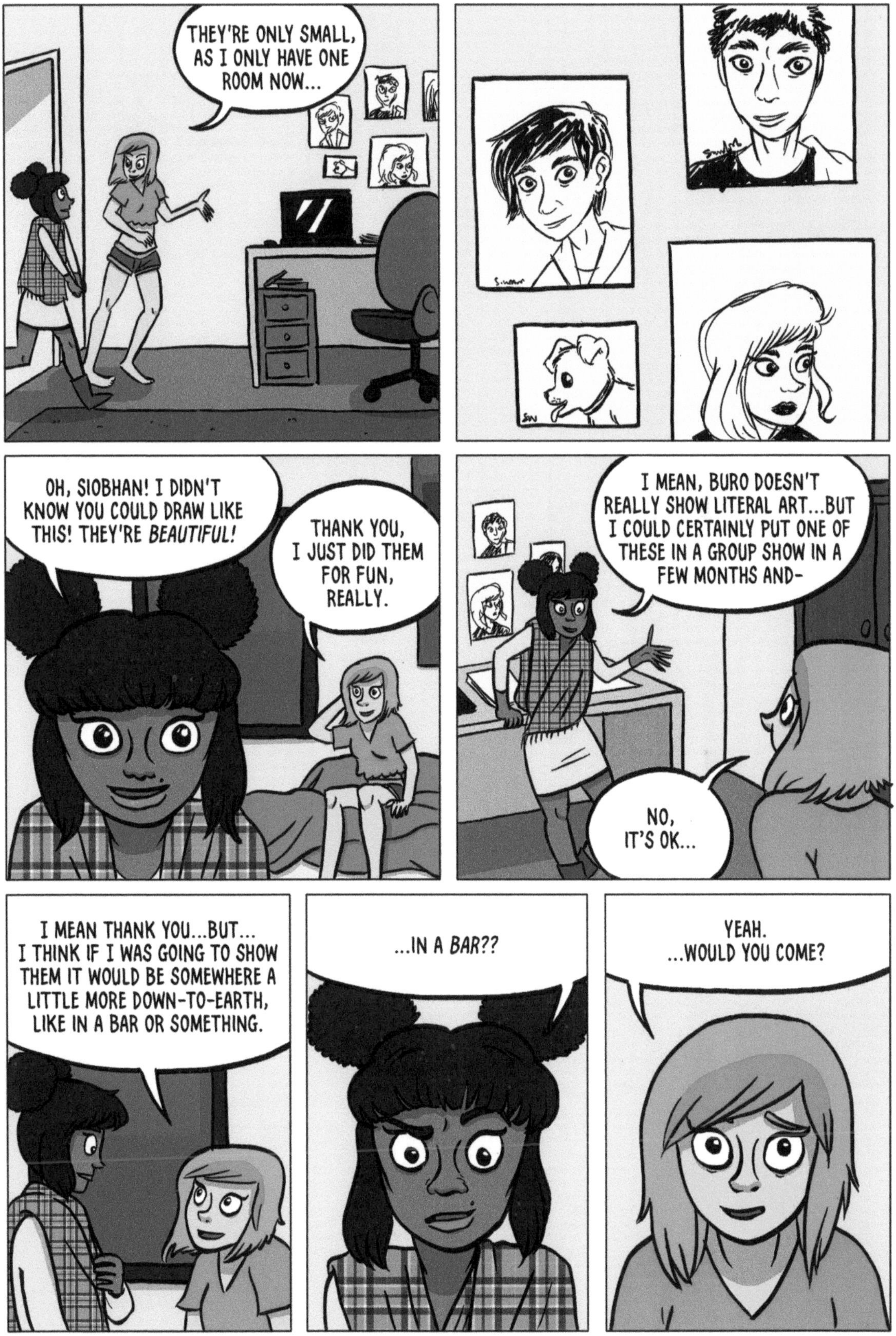
THEY'RE ONLY SMALL, AS I ONLY HAVE ONE ROOM NOW...
OH, SIOBHAN! I DIDN'T KNOW YOU COULD DRAW LIKE THIS! THEY'RE *BEAUTIFUL!*
THANK YOU, I JUST DID THEM FOR FUN, REALLY.
I MEAN, BURO DOESN'T REALLY SHOW LITERAL ART...BUT I COULD CERTAINLY PUT ONE OF THESE IN A GROUP SHOW IN A FEW MONTHS AND-
NO, IT'S OK...
I MEAN THANK YOU...BUT... I THINK IF I WAS GOING TO SHOW THEM IT WOULD BE SOMEWHERE A LITTLE MORE DOWN-TO-EARTH, LIKE IN A BAR OR SOMETHING.
...IN A *BAR??*
YEAH. ...WOULD YOU COME?

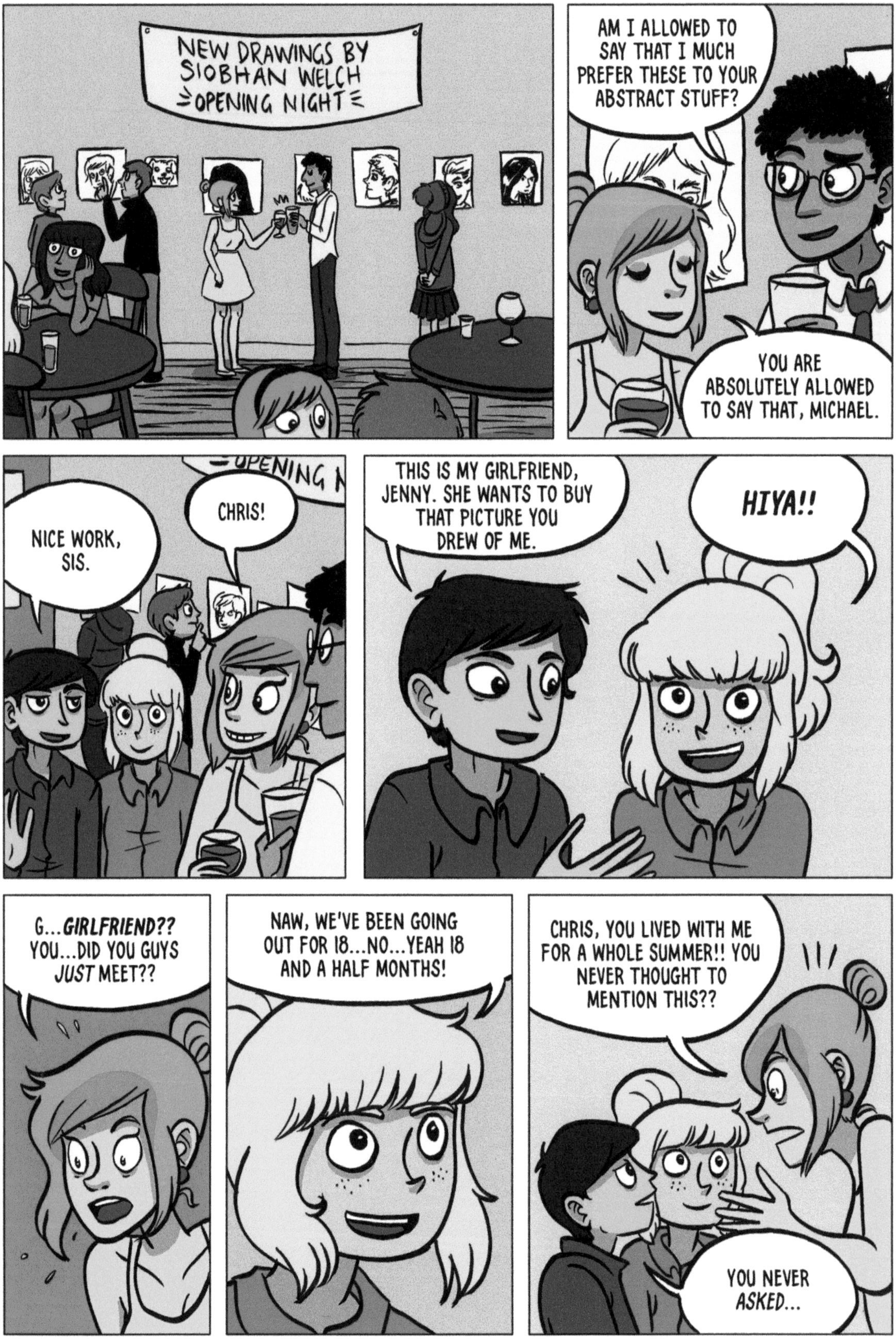
NEW DRAWINGS BY SIOBHAN WELCH
OPENING NIGHT
AM I ALLOWED TO SAY THAT I MUCH PREFER THESE TO YOUR ABSTRACT STUFF?
YOU ARE ABSOLUTELY ALLOWED TO SAY THAT, MICHAEL.
NICE WORK, SIS.
CHRIS!
THIS IS MY GIRLFRIEND, JENNY. SHE WANTS TO BUY THAT PICTURE YOU DREW OF ME.
HIYA!!
G...GIRLFRIEND?? YOU...DID YOU GUYS JUST MEET??
NAW, WE'VE BEEN GOING OUT FOR 18...NO...YEAH 18 AND A HALF MONTHS!
CHRIS, YOU LIVED WITH ME FOR A WHOLE SUMMER!! YOU NEVER THOUGHT TO MENTION THIS??
YOU NEVER ASKED...

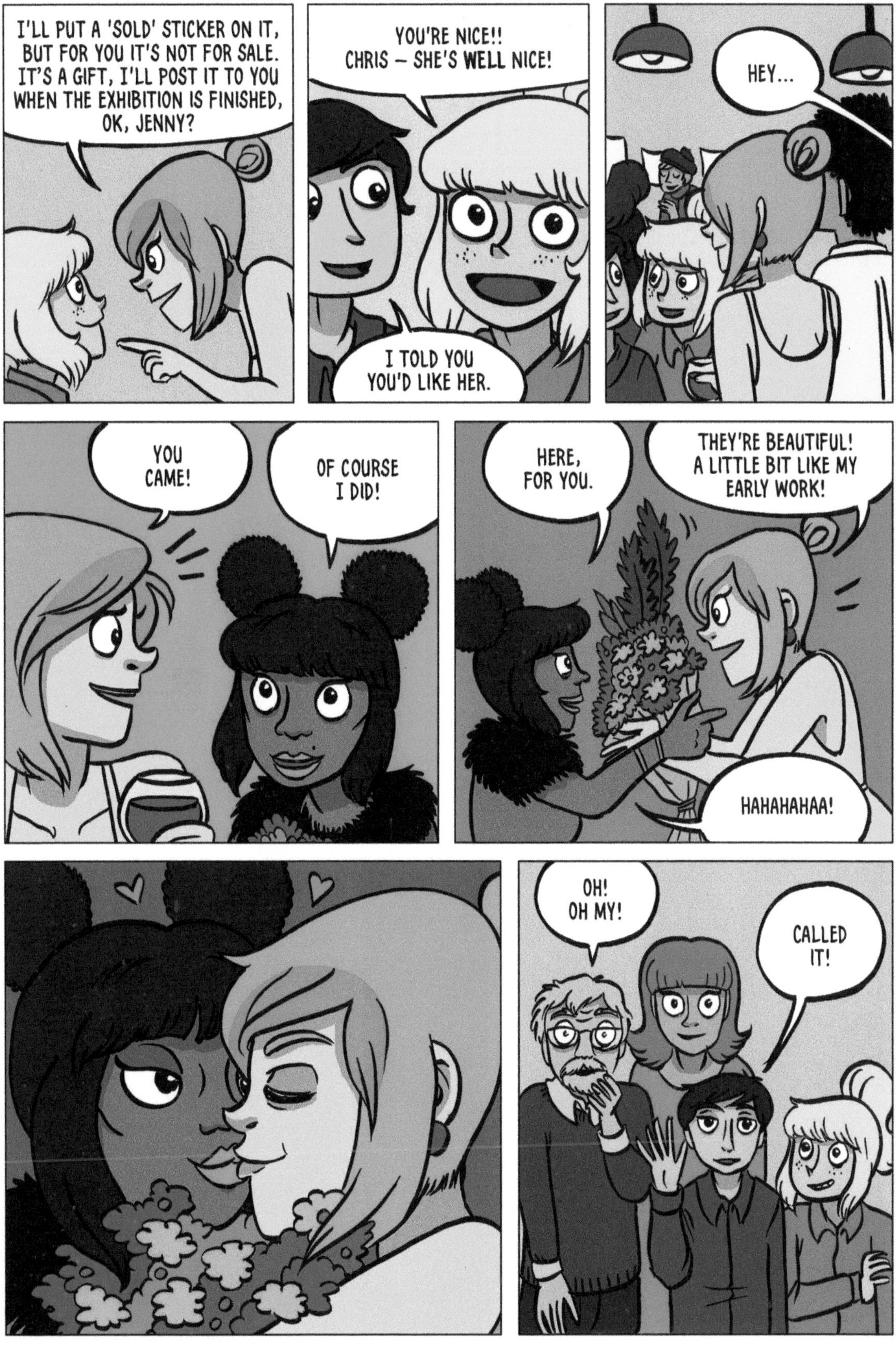
I'LL PUT A 'SOLD' STICKER ON IT, BUT FOR YOU IT'S NOT FOR SALE. IT'S A GIFT, I'LL POST IT TO YOU WHEN THE EXHIBITION IS FINISHED, OK, JENNY?
YOU'RE NICE!! CHRIS – SHE'S WELL NICE!
I TOLD YOU YOU'D LIKE HER.
HEY...
YOU CAME!
OF COURSE I DID!
HERE, FOR YOU.
THEY'RE BEAUTIFUL! A LITTLE BIT LIKE MY EARLY WORK!
HAHAHAHAA!
OH! OH MY!
CALLED IT!

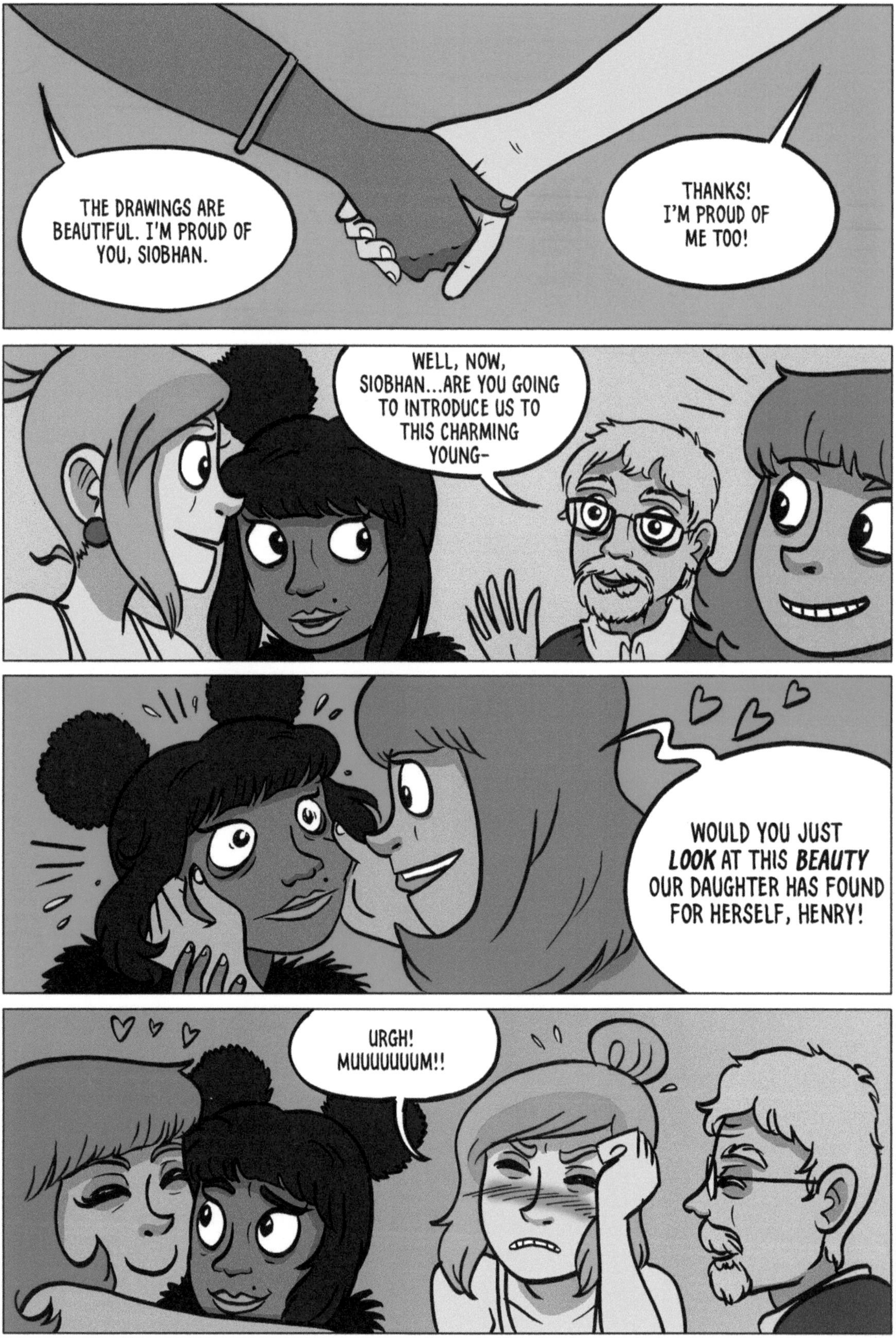
THE DRAWINGS ARE BEAUTIFUL. I'M PROUD OF YOU, SIOBHAN.
THANKS! I'M PROUD OF ME TOO!
WELL, NOW, SIOBHAN...ARE YOU GOING TO INTRODUCE US TO THIS CHARMING YOUNG-
WOULD YOU JUST ***LOOK*** AT THIS ***BEAUTY*** OUR DAUGHTER HAS FOUND FOR HERSELF, HENRY!
URGH! MUUUUUUUM!!

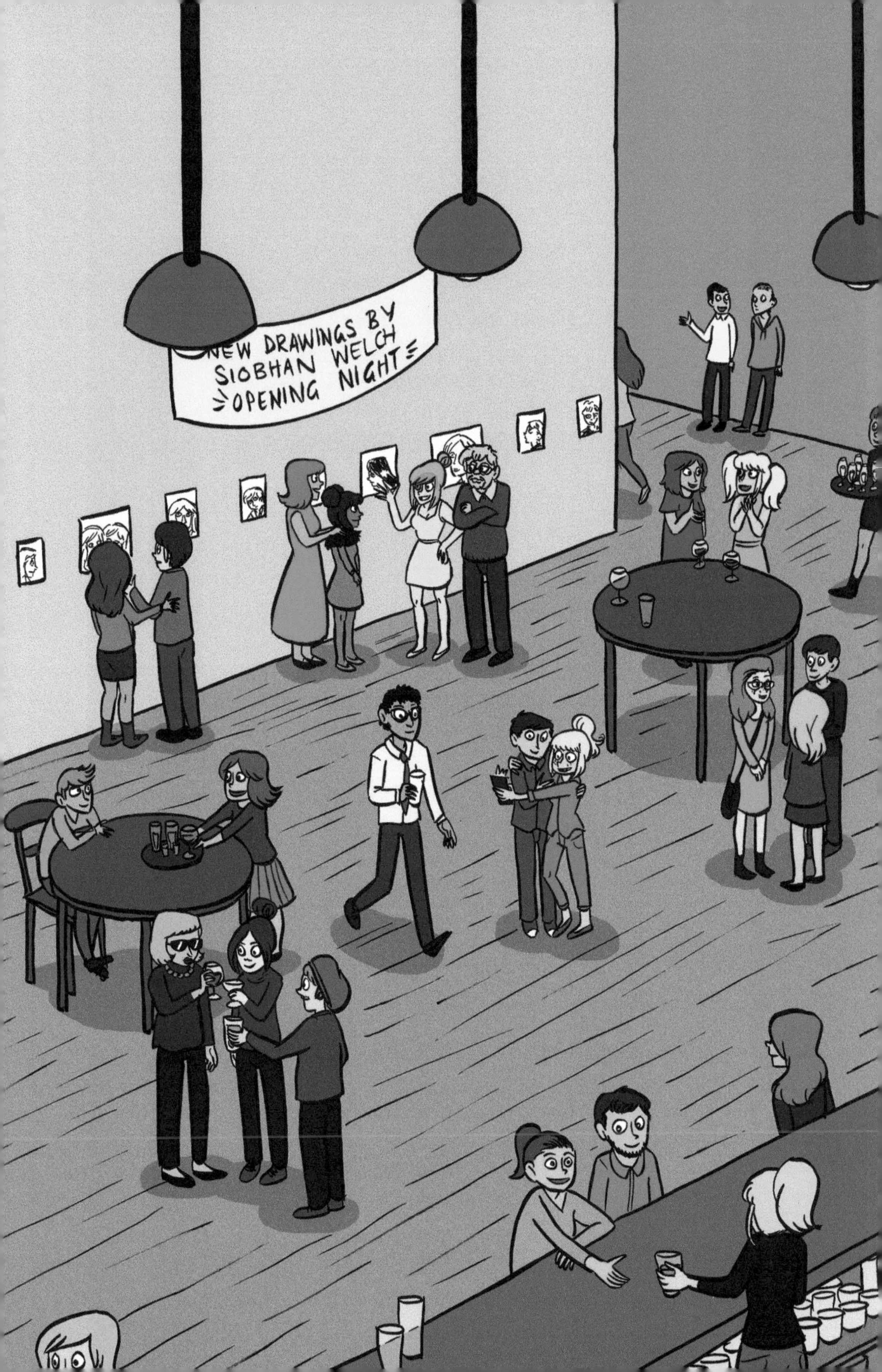

NEW DRAWINGS BY
SIOBHAN WELCH
OPENING NIGHT

RACHAEL SMITH IS A COMIC CREATOR
AND ILLUSTRATOR WHO LIVES IN
WEST YORKSHIRE, IN THE UK.

WWW.RACHAELSMITH.ORG